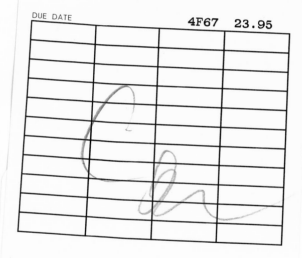

TRIPLETREE

TRIPLETREE

DEREK WILSON

Thomas Dunne Books
St. Martin's Minotaur ᛗ New York

THOMAS DUNNE BOOKS.
An imprint of St. Martin's Press.

TRIPLETREE. Copyright © 2003 by Derek Wilson. All rights reserved. Printed
in the United States of America. No part of this book may be used or repro-
duced in any manner whatsoever without written permission except in the
case of brief quotations embodied in critical articles or reviews. For information, address St. Martin's Press, 175 Fifth Avenue, New York, N.Y. 10010.

www.minotaurbooks.com

Library of Congress Cataloging-in-Publication Data

Wilson, Derek A.
     Tripletree / Derek Wilson.—1st U.S. ed.
          p. cm.
     ISBN 0-312-32874-5
     EAN 978-0312-32874-0
     1. Parapsychologists—Fiction. 2. Country homes—Fiction. 3. Parties—
Fiction. 4. Hanging—Fiction. 5. Witches—Fiction. 6. England—Fiction.
I. Title.

PR6073.I463T75   2004
823'.914—dc22   2004042823

First published in Great Britain by Constable,
an imprint of Constable & Robinson Ltd.

First U.S. Edition: June 2004

10 9 8 7 6 5 4 3 2 1

A Morning in September

The man was making a scene. The tall, solidly built, middle-aged man with the air of one unaccustomed to being thwarted stood in the arched entrance to Beaufort College, waving his arms and shouting.

'I'm not interested in your pettifogging rules! And I'm not one of your undergraduates to be bullied. Just give me the address!'

But the visitor had chosen the wrong adversary. George Bramley, senior porter, long accustomed to dealing with the wiles and tantrums of generations of Cambridge gentlemen and – latterly – ladies, stood his ground beside the notice which announced that the college was closed to sightseers. 'I'm sorry, sir.' He was the personification of polite officialdom. 'Rules are rules. Private addresses of senior members are just that – private. We aren't allowed to issue them to strangers.'

'Strangers!' The word acted like petrol on the fire of the caller's anger. 'Do I look like a debt collector or some other kind of working-class oik?'

Indeed he did not. Every inch of the man, from his MCC tie to his Lobb's handmade shoes, announced that here was someone who could afford – and would afford – only the best. 'The Vice Chancellor is a personal friend and if you don't stop your insolent obstruction I'll see that he hears about it.'

'That's your privilege, sir.'

The two protagonists glared at each other. Irresistible force and immovable object.

'Like I said, sir, if you care to leave your name and a contact number I'll see that Dr Gye gets it as soon as he comes into college.' Bramley offered an imperturbable smile.

'And when might that be?' The visitor grudgingly stood aside for a research student who wheeled her bicycle out on to Trumpington Street.

'He usually comes in two or three times a week during the long vac to collect his mail. More often if he has meetings.'

Suddenly the other man changed his approach. One hand went to an inside pocket of his immaculately cut jacket and emerged holding a slim wallet. 'Look, my business with Dr Gye is extremely urgent. I should be uncommonly grateful . . .' He opened the billfold and fingered a sheaf of banknotes.

The porter's eyes narrowed and his nose wrinkled as though a dead cat had been wafted beneath it. He turned abruptly towards the entrance to his lodge. 'Excuse me, sir, there goes my phone.' He disappeared within, leaving the caller straining his ears to detect the non-existent ringing of a telephone bell.

The visitor took a step forward as if to follow the college official into his sanctum, thought better of it and was just turning back towards the street when Bramley's head appeared round the door frame. 'And, if I were you, sir, I'd move that vehicle.' He nodded towards the gleaming blue BMW convertible parked directly in front of the college gateway. 'The traffic wardens round here tend to be clamp happy.'

Had Nathaniel Gye, lecturer in Paranormal Psychology at the University of Cambridge, been anywhere else in the city or had he arrived seconds later, the chain reaction of violence, misery and death of which he was the catalyst would not have happened. Sheldon Myles QC would have slipped behind the wheel of his elegant motor car and driven angrily back to London to seek some other solution to his problem. George Bramley would have regaled the junior porters with the story of how he had sent the 'toffee-nosed bastard off with a flea in his ear'. Dr Gye would have arrived, collected his messages and spent half an hour in his room sending off emails before walking to the University Library to collect some books. A criminal would have escaped justice and three people would still be alive.

But Nathaniel Gye was *not* elsewhere at the crucial moment. He emerged from Pembroke Street, cleaving a path through an ill-shepherded flock of Spanish tourists, dodged nimbly in front of an elderly cyclist, and with long, bouncing strides traced a diagonal path across the road towards Beaufort's fifteenth-century gate tower – the only portion of the original structure to survive a modernizing patron in the reign of Good King Charles.

The barrister had turned away from the college and was in the process of lowering himself into the driving seat of the BMW when he saw the tall figure in check shirt and shorts. 'Gye! So there you are,' he bellowed, in a tone that suggested that Nathaniel had been deliberately hiding from him.

'Why, it's Sheldon Myles, isn't it? What brings you to our traffic-choked town?' Gye held out a hand and had it perfunctorily shaken.

'Looking for you – a task not made easier by your bloody-minded college lackey.' Myles nodded towards the lodge.

Gye's silence was eloquent. He surveyed the other man with a slightly raised eyebrow, and expertly read the signs. He took in the lightweight Savile Row suit and the Jermyn Street shirt. They spoke of tradition, ample means, self-assurance, a secure establishment figure. Myles's face sent different signals. The dark eyes flickered, unable to hold a steady gaze. Between them lines furrowed into a deep V.

This, Gye thought, is a worried man – a very worried man.

Discomfited by the wordless scrutiny, the barrister mumbled a half-apology. 'Sorry, Gye, but officiousness riles me. I've got enough on my plate right now without . . . Look, Gye, what it is . . . I want to hire your services.'

'Hire?' Nathaniel was puzzled.

Myles hurried on. 'Not for myself, you understand.' He tapped his forehead. 'Still functioning OK in the top storey, thank God. No, it's my wife, June. She's terribly over-wrought. That awful business last month . . .' He stumbled for words. Embarrassing, Gye thought, for one of the country's most eloquent courtroom performers. 'She's getting some strange ideas . . . Needs sorting out.'

Gye nodded with sudden understanding. 'Oh. I see. You're looking for an analyst. I'm afraid I'm not your man. I'm a psychologist; a theoretician. I have no licence to practise. But I can put you on to someone first rate. He's –'

'No!' Myles shouted the word and a young woman manoeuvring a pushchair round them on the narrow pavement looked at him in alarm. 'No, it'll have to be you. June trusts you –'

'Your wife hardly knows me.'

The barrister ignored the interruption. 'And you can talk some sense into her. I'll make it worth your while, I promise you. You can name your fee.'

'That's beside the point.' Nathaniel glanced along the road in the direction of King's Parade. Some fifty yards away a figure in black and yellow was moving purposefully through the crowds of shoppers and tourists. 'Look, you'd better move this car if you don't want a ticket. Give me a lift as far as the University Library and you can tell me the problem. But I warn you, I can't do what you ask. I'm not qualified and, frankly, I don't have the time.'

Moments later, Gye was sinking into the soft cream leather upholstery as the BMW eased out into the traffic.

Once the need for eye contact was removed, Myles found it easier to talk coherently. The star performer of the Old Bailey who imposed his will on juries was not accustomed to begging favours. 'There are two reasons why you must not turn me down,' he explained. 'You were there. And if you don't get June to see straight, she'll go to the police and tell them she murdered that bloody woman.'

Five Weeks Before

The journey started badly and went downhill from there. First there was the weather. The August hot spell, instead of dissipating itself in electrical storms, went gaspingly on. People with short memories said it was unprecedented and blamed global warming. Seaside resorts had their best season for a decade. Suburban householders ignored the hosepipe ban and rigged garden showers for their fractious kids. In the Cambridgeshire commuter village of Great Maddisham the leaves of the plane trees ringing the green hung limp and dust-covered as the Gyes' five-year-old Mercedes passed them at a few minutes past four.

Then there was the timing. Kathryn Gye had got back from New York less than twenty-four hours before and was jet-lagged. She did not surface till noon and then moved sluggishly. But when Nathaniel suggested cancelling the trip and spending a quiet weekend at home with their two sons she would not hear of it. It was important to be at the Myleses' party. Lots of the 'right' people would be there and, besides that, she had arranged to do a feature on the Myleses and their home. By the time their sons, Edmund and Jeremy, had been delivered to a friend's house for their sleepover the sun was well past its zenith and Kathryn showed no sign of being ready.

Nat paced the ground floor of their open-plan, architect-designed house, his own case packed and standing by the front door. This was the Friday of the bank holiday weekend, he repeated. Had Kathryn totally failed to grasp the significance of that? The roads would be jam-packed. His wife, her long, dark hair hanging down loose over her white bathrobe, wandered barefoot from the kitchen area with a bowl of muesli in one hand and a spoon in the other. She shrugged. That was no problem; they would take a nook-and-cranny route. Nat groaned. In the five years that they had been living in England his Pittsburgh-born wife had not lost her fascination with the bucolic and picturesque. A 'nook-and-cranny' route meant a cross-country journey that was more byways than highways.

'That'll take us hours,' he protested. 'You're the one who's dead set on going to this pretentious, fancy dress affair. I assume you'd like us to get there before it's half over.' He flung his scrawny six foot one into an armchair. 'Or are we planning to make the grand entrance – "TV Celebrity Psychologist and International Journalist"? You know I hate that sort of thing.'

Kathryn leaned over and planted a kiss on top of his head. 'Do you know you're getting a bald patch? I've looked at the map. It's only a couple of hours to the Cotswolds.' She drifted back to the kitchen end and put her bowl in the dishwasher. 'I can be ready in a twink.' She crossed to the open staircase that swirled round one corner of the living space. 'Anyway, we'll need a bit of time. There's something I want to talk to you about.'

That 'something' was the third factor in Nat's ruined day. As they meandered through the unprepossessing brick villages of Bedfordshire, Kathryn announced in her usual direct way, 'Greg offered me the New York office.'

Nat braked sharply as he came round a bend and found himself suddenly behind a tractor and trailer. 'Why?' It was all he could think of to say.

'Presumably because the board think I'm the best person for the job.'

'You've only been running the London end for a couple of years.'

Kathryn Gye was the British editor of an upmarket

transatlantic magazine. *Panache*, as its masthead brazenly announced, was written 'for people there or getting there'. Founded in the Reagan-Thatcher era, it teetered on the fence between celebration of upper-crust life and gentle satire and had immediately caught the mood of yuppies, fat cats and other worshippers at the shrine of Mammon. By the time the policy of sanctified greed had plunged the Western world into recession the magazine had become something of a cult publication with a steadily growing circulation. Kathryn's rapid rise to the top London job had meant that she could work partly from the Mayfair office and partly from home, with occasional flits across the ocean to confer with her American superiors. It fitted in well with Nat's university activities and their lives had fallen into a workable routine.

'It seems I've impressed them.'

Nat glared at the wisps of straw that were blowing out of the trailer on to the car windscreen. 'How long has he given you to think it over?' he asked.

Kathryn stared out of the side window at the untidy, dusty farmyard into which the tractor was now turning. She took a deep breath. 'I have thought it over, Nat, and given him my answer.'

'The hell you have!' Nat shouted, turning to glare at his wife. 'Don't I count for anything in the decision-making process?'

She stared back with frank, unblinking green eyes. 'I knew this was going to be difficult. Nat, it's not as bad as it sounds. Just hear me out before you press the panic button. It won't mean moving to the States – at least, not immediately.'

'Well now, that's comforting!'

'Nat, *please*! Greg got them to agree a fantastic package. We get a Manhattan apartment and two free flights a month to London. And the salary is positively indecent.'

'We're not exactly living in penury now.'

'Sure, but this means realizing all those dreams we've

always had. We'll be able to do anything we want to do.'

'Except, apparently, live together. But that, I suppose, is a mere bagatelle.'

There was a sharp blast on a car horn. Nat looked in the driving mirror and saw that he was blocking the narrow lane. He transferred his foot to the accelerator and threw the Mercedes into the sinuous bends ahead at a speed that was rather less than safe.

'What about the boys? Have you thought how they'd feel having a mother living three and a half thousand miles away?'

'It'll be very exciting for them to have two very different homes.'

'Nonsense! Children have to have stability. They want their parents to be there for them when *they* need them, not when it suits their business convenience to be available.'

Kathryn held her breath as the Mercedes sped past an oncoming milk tanker with inches to spare. 'I guess you'd prefer them to be orphans!'

'What's that supposed to mean?'

'The way you're driving you're going to get us both killed.'

'If you'd been ready in time there'd be no need to hurry,' Nat retorted but he eased his foot off the accelerator. He glanced sideways and saw that, though Kathryn's jaw was thrust defiantly forward, her eyes were moist.

After a long silence she said, 'Of course I care about Ed and Jerry – passionately. This is a once in a lifetime chance to give them everything they could possibly want. Think of the great holidays we can have together, the places all over the world we can take them to see.'

'Everything they could possibly want,' Nat echoed. 'When I was tucking Jerry in the other night he asked me for two things for his birthday. Shall I tell you what they were?'

'Sure.'

'A puppy and a baby sister. On mature reflection he said he realized that asking for both might be pushing his luck, but could we please get him one or the other? Looks as though it's going to have to be the pup.'

Kathryn hammered her fists on the facia. 'Oh, you . . . That is emotional blackmail!'

'T-junction,' Nat announced, slowing the car down. 'Which way?'

Kathryn grabbed up the Ordnance Survey map and peered at it blankly. Angrily she brushed away a tear that fell on to the paper. 'Oh, how the hell should I know! Left!'

After another long pause Nat tried a different approach. 'Had it occurred to you that this is a pre-emptive strike on Greg's part?'

'What do you mean?'

'Everyone in the journalistic world knows what you've done for *Panache*. It's only a matter of time before the headhunters start closing in. Greg's simply getting his bid in first.'

She looked thoughtful. 'No, that's . . . Anyway, I couldn't leave . . .'

'Couldn't leave the magazine but you could leave your family. That's what you're trying to say, isn't it?'

Kathryn flared up at that. 'Are you accusing me of being selfish?'

Nat did not answer.

'Things aren't tidily black and white. I suppose you don't think there's anything selfish in your expecting me to turn my back on something which I'll find fulfilling so that I can go on being a decorative wife in your dreary university social scene.'

'I'd no idea you found our life so uncongenial. I'm sorry.'

'Nat, I didn't mean . . . Oh hell!' She slumped in her seat and stared unseeing out of the side window.

Two minutes later Nat said, 'We've been travelling due

14

east for about five miles. That can't be right and it's now 6.16. We've about an hour and a half to find the hotel, change into our absurd costumes and get to Coln St Ippolyts. Perhaps we ought to concentrate for the time being on working that little miracle.' He pulled the car into the side and together he and Kathryn consulted the map. 'We'll have to cut through here to the M40,' he said. 'We've no choice.'

That was how they came to join the procession of impatient families in overpacked cars and caravans, snailing away from the torrid streets of the city and the suburbs, enduring the miseries of the motorway to spend a few hours in some rural Shangri-La, before embarking on a bad-tempered return journey. Inevitably, a couple of the holiday-bound vehicles had shunted into each other and the whole convoy came to a halt between the Lewknor and Wheatley interchanges. By the time the Gyes had escaped the mêlée, reached Burford, turned off its steep main street to head into the Windrush valley and located Parsifal Country House Hotel they were already late.

Twenty sweating minutes later they were back in the car. Nat was now dressed in the sombre black and white of a Bible-loving Puritan while his wife had opted for something more flamboyant. Nat looked at the stunning woman beside him, radiant in a revealing gown of pale blue satin that made her dark colouring appear even more dramatic. He reflected that the character he was representing would have branded Kathryn as a shameless hussy. He also realized that he could never face the thought of losing her. He thrust the Mercedes forward in a spurt of gravel.

Nat knew little about the elaborate housewarming for which they were headed or the couple who were hosting it. Sheldon and Juniper Myles were only acquaintances of Kathryn's. Both of them were London barristers who had, apparently, amassed a fortune between them, invested most of it in rescuing a Jacobean manor house and were now intent on displaying their impressive home to the *haut monde*. According to Kathryn it was a celebrity-feste, a bid to make an impact on society by bringing together as many as possible of the great and the good all togged up as Cavaliers and Roundheads.

There was no risk of any of the Myleses' guests getting lost; signposts to Coln St Ippolyts Manor were placed at every junction and fork, even the most minor, and when Nat swung the Mercedes round the last bend in the road he was confronted by tall iron gates flanked by blazing torchères. A man in a full-bottomed wig and a long coat gushing lace at neck and cuffs stepped forward, carrying a very twentieth-century ultraviolet scanner. This he passed over the invitation Nat handed to him. For good measure he checked the Gyes' names on a list before waving them on with the assurance that if they drove straight up to the house a colleague would take care of their car.

'Rather unnecessary security,' Nat commented as he put the preselector lever in 'drive'. 'There can't be many gate-crashers prepared to get togged up in all this gear just to swill Sheldon Myles's best Krug.'

Kathryn grimaced at her image in the vanity mirror on the back of the sun visor. 'It's not that kind of uninvited guest they're worried about. Sheldon's made quite a few enemies in his years at the bar.'

'I thought he specialized in commercial law. Surely disappointed takeover rivals don't hire assassins to get rid of the opposition's legal brains.'

'You'd be surprised what men will do when megabucks are at stake. Anyway, Shelley only switched to the commercial sector a few years ago. Before that he was a leading criminal prosecutor.'

'You've done your homework thoroughly, as usual.'

'Not difficult. He was involved in quite a few high profile cases. Remember the Forbes brothers?'

'No, I don't think . . .'

'You must do. They went down for slaughtering their

aged parents in order to lay their hands on the family fortune.'

Nat nodded. 'Yes, of course. Weren't they the ones who got out on appeal last year?'

'That's right. The leading prosecution witness was discredited.'

'And it was Myles who headed up the Crown case?'

'Uh-huh.' Kathryn muttered through pursed lips as she pouted to herself in the mirror.

'I suppose if I'd spent several years in the Scrubs for a crime I didn't commit I might think seriously about settling old scores. Well, here we are. Let battle commence.'

They had reached the end of a straight drive along which more flaming torches were set. Coln Manor stood before them, making the most of its modest splendour. The south front which faced them was symmetrical and of three storeys, beneath an undulation of Dutch gables. The entire façade was pierced by ranks of large mullioned windows, every one of which was ablaze with inner light. Low evening sunlight gilded the stonework. The effect was breathtaking.

Nat eased the Mercedes to a halt before a shallow flight of wide steps and immediately two period-costumed flunkeys darted forward to open the doors. Nat entrusted the vehicle to one of them and received a numbered disc in return. Then, Kathryn hooked her arm through his and for a moment they stood staring up at the Jacobean mansion and listening to the strains of lute and viol music coming from within.

Kathryn suddenly shivered. 'I'm cold! Quick, let's go in.'

Nat looked at her in mild surprise. The stones were still pulsing with the heat of the day and the motionless air was decidedly balmy. 'This way, then, milady,' he said and sedately they mounted the steps to the open front door.

Another liveried servant was on hand to guide them to the focal point of the festivities although they needed no help in finding their way. As they walked down a narrow screens passage the sounds of music, laughter and conversation were almost deafening. A turn to the right through an arched doorway admitted them to the Great Hall where dinner was in full swing.

'Hollywood meets Sir Walter Scott,' Nat muttered, taking in the lively scene at a glance. The room was not large as such impressive chambers went but it comfortably accommodated three long tables studded with flickering candles leading from the screens to the raised dais at the far end. These tables were filled with guests all obediently dressed in the garb of three and a half centuries before and some of them visibly sweating. Despite the large space beneath the ornately plastered ceiling and the open windows which pierced the upper part of the wainscotted walls, the atmosphere was stifling. The spaces between the windows were decorated with geometrical arrangements of shields, swords and pikes obviously inspired by displays in the Tower armouries or some medieval edifice where their context lent them more credibility. Straight ahead, however, the panelling behind and above the high table bore a row of painted portraits, stiff, flat copies of elegant originals by Mytens and Lely. Nat's gaze moved down to the top table. Seated centrally behind it were reincarnations of Charles I and his queen, Henrietta Maria.

It was his first sight of Sheldon and Juniper Myles and he was not impressed. Their host might, with his over-jolly demeanour, have made a passable Henry VIII but he lacked the aloof presence necessary to portray the dapper, melancholy Stuart king. As for Queen June, the animated face with its fringe of seventeenth-century-style ringlets was pretty enough but even Van Dyck would have struggled to draw out from her any sense of regality. She was laughing just a little too loudly and her gestures seemed nervous, even agitated.

The new arrivals were ushered to their places and the next twenty minutes or so were devoted to catching up with the other diners, introducing themselves to their

neighbours and offering light-hearted accounts of the mis-
adventures of the afternoon which had led to their late
appearance at the festive board. Music drifted down from
the ensemble in the minstrels' gallery above the screens.
Course followed well-presented course and Nat was
relieved to discover that the quest for period authenticity
had not extended to the culinary arrangements. He had
just begun to enjoy a raspberry bavarois accompanied by a
luscious Vouvray and the candlelight had started to assert
itself against the fading glow from the windows when the
first of the night's alarming events occurred.

There was a loud bang from somewhere outside, followed by three more. Conversation fell abruptly. A woman
squealed. Another giggled. One or two people stood up in
alarm but the majority were held in bewildered immobil-
ity. Now the first sounds were followed by others, less
distinct but equally puzzling – plops and whines and
fizzing noises.

Sheldon Myles stood in his place and held his hands up.
'Please carry on eating, everyone! Nothing to be alarmed
about!' But Nat thought as their host hurried from the hall
that he looked very alarmed – alarmed and angry.

The noises continued intermittently. Talk warmed up
again. Nat turned to his right-hand neighbour, the chief
executive of a major City bank. 'A hiccup in the impeccable Myles organization?' he suggested.

The man dabbed perspiration from his brow with a silk
handkerchief. 'Sounds like bloody Bonfire Night,' he
muttered.

'Of course,' Nat said. 'It's fireworks, isn't it? I knew
I ought to recognize it.'

'Fireworks . . . fireworks . . . fireworks . . .' The word
drifted along the table. Guests nodded and laughed. Diag-
onally opposite Nat a young actress, who, it appeared, was
currently enjoying celebrity in a TV soap and had been
disappointed to discover that she was quite unknown in
the present company, suddenly looked at him and

squawked, 'But the guy's in here.' She pointed an incarnadine finger. 'Nathaniel Gye, the television shrink. I saw that series you did on ghosts. What was it called?'

'*Is There Anybody There?*,' Nat muttered. He groaned as everyone within earshot turned or leaned forward to get a glimpse of him. Up to that point he had kept conversation away from his media work and talked only about university life. Now some of his neighbours said oh, yes, of course, they recognized him . . . fascinating programmes . . . did he really not believe in ghosts . . . well, what did he make of this? There followed a string of stories about spooky happenings and unexplained appearances and their narrators demanded Nat's diagnoses. It was all very familiar to him. Just as doctors frequently were made the recipients of the medical history of comparative strangers, so people who had seen his programmes wanted Nat's 'professional opinion' on their brushes with the supernatural.

'Don't you think some places have *atmosphere*?' The banker's wife – a spare woman with worry lines inadequately concealed by heavy make-up, who had only toyed with her food – asked intently.

'Oh, definitely.' The actress leaned forward revealing even more of a cleavage of whose contours the green silk of her Restoration gown left little to the imagination. 'I felt it as soon as I stepped out of my limo. I said as much to Mark, didn't I, Mark?' She turned for confirmation to the muscular, inarticulate black man beside her who Nat seemed vaguely to recall was a footballer. She did not wait for his reply which, judging by past form, probably would not have been forthcoming anyway, but rushed on breathlessly. 'Yeah, I said, "Mark, this house gives me the creeps. I bet it's got lots of dark secrets."'

Kathryn grabbed her opportunity to do some business. 'You're so right, Steph.' (The woman's stage name was Stephanie Pace.) 'I sensed it, too. Have you ever been told that you have psychic powers? I'm sure you have; it's very common among great actresses.' Steph took the bait. She nodded and tried to look profound. Kathryn reeled her in. 'I'm preparing a special feature on celebrity hauntings,' she said. 'We must fix up for me to come and interview you.'

At that moment a gong sounded. Everyone turned to the top table. Sheldon Myles had returned and was now on his feet. 'My lords, ladies and gentlemen,' he announced portentously, 'June and I hope you have enjoyed your dinner. Coffee and liqueurs await you in the Cavalier Chamber, through this door on my right, or in the Green Sollar which is at the top of the east staircase, also to the right. In those rooms you will find a list of the entertainments it has been our pleasure to lay on for you. The only alteration to the schedule is the firework display, which, unfortunately, we've had to cancel. June and I will be available to the ladies and gentlemen of the press for about twenty minutes in the Walnut Parlour down there beyond the screens passage. I'm not much good at speeches.' He waited for the ripple of polite laughter. 'And this isn't going to be one. All I – we – want to say is, enjoy your time at Coln Manor. Thank you.' He sat down to warm applause.

The company dispersed, drifting in the directions indicated by their host. Nat helped his wife unfold herself and her voluminous skirts from her chair. 'Are you off to the press briefing?' he asked.

Kathryn gave a horrified grimace. 'With all the society hacks and local media folk who've come for a free feed? No way! I've an exclusive session lined up with the Myleses later on. Let's go and adjust the caffein count.'

They climbed the broad staircase with its newel posts carved into the shape of grotesque beasts.

'You know, it's funny what Steph Pace said about Coln Manor having a sinister atmosphere. I genuinely *did* feel it when we arrived. It was as though the house was trying to ward us off.'

Nat opened his mouth to respond but Kathryn went on.

21

'Oh, I know what you're going to say: romantic old buildings have a powerful effect on the imagination. But I know what I felt. This place must have seen some pretty horrific events over the years. These things leave their imprints in the stones.'

Nat considered responding with some observations about psi effects and how they were taken seriously in academic circles but decided instead to make light of the matter. 'I expect you'll find that, like most houses, Coln Manor has a very humdrum history. No grisly murders in the attic, or nuns walled up in the cellar, or duels to the death fought on the terrace.'

The Green Sollar turned out to be a spacious chamber with bleached oak panelling and carpet and drapes in a matching lime colour. Extra chairs had been brought in to accommodate the large number of guests and the better pieces of period furniture had been tastefully protected with silk covers so that no glass or cup rings should mar their patinated surfaces. Some of these upmarket table-cloths were anchored by animalier bronzes which gleamed in the soft light from carefully placed lamps.

'Nice,' Nat commented, running his fingers over a figurine of a boy with two greyhounds on a leash.

'Should be,' Kathryn muttered, whipping out a digital camera and pointing it at the marble fireplace topped by a coat of arms radiant in heraldic blazon, 'all the decor was done by Sperantis of Milan.'

'I meant the bronze,' her husband said.

'Oh, yeah, pretty.' Kathryn honoured with a quick glance the crafted metal which seemed to ripple with eager strength, as though the dogs could at any moment leap from their plinth. 'June collects those things. Very knowledgeable about them, I'm told.'

They found two seats in a window alcove and were soon served with coffee and brandies. Nat picked up a gilt-edged card from the small table between them. 'Well, let's see what the nouveau mega-riche have laid on for our delectation.' He read out programme items. ' "A Consort of Seventeenth-Century Music presented by the Steiner Ensemble of Vienna." That's in the Great Hall at 10.15. From 11.30 into the small hours there's dancing – also in the Great Hall. Dear God, I hope we're not expected to prance around doing galliards, gavottes and farandoles.'

Kathryn was casting speculative eyes over the other guests and calculating who might be good for a picture or a few words. 'You like dancing,' she observed abstractedly.

'Not in all this clobber, I don't.' Nat unbuttoned the heavy fustian of his jacket. 'Let's see if there's anything less energetic. "Tours of Coln Manor (approx. 30 minutes each)," ' he read out, ' "will begin at 10.00, starting from the Walnut Parlour." '

'Who's leading them?'

'The guides are listed as Dr Paul Greer (whoever he may be) and the mistress of the house herself, Juniper Myles. But there is more: the programme goes on to say, "The fascinating story of the restoration of Coln St Ippolyts Manor has been recorded on a 35-minute video tape and this will be shown in the King James Parlour at 11.15. Entertainments in the park will include The Siege of Coln St Ippolyts Manor (1643) re-enacted by the Civil War League at 9.45; Madrigals on the Lake by the Carnforth Singers at 11.00–11.45; culminating in a Grand Firework Display at midnight." Well we know that's off. I wonder what upset Mr Myles's *pièce de résistance*.'

'I guess some of the set pieces went off by accident.'

At that moment there was a sudden lull in the conversation. Looking up, the Gyes saw their host and hostess enter the room. Juniper, a diminutive figure in pale gold silk which glowed in the lamplight, with pearls at her neck, woven into her hair and threaded through a girdle of rich blue around her waist, came first, smiling and greeting individuals. Sheldon followed, looking taller than he was in his steeple hat and slimmer than he was in the black velvet cloak with the massive splash of a silver embroidered star on one shoulder. Someone started to applaud and the clapping was taken up rather uncertainly by half the room.

The Myleses made their royal progress. When they reached the Gyes Nat felt an almost irresistible urge to bow. He resisted it and said instead, 'I'm afraid we arrived rather late for dinner.' He explained about the congestion on the motorway.

June frowned, an expression, Nat realized, which came very easily to her. 'This probably wasn't the best day of the year to hold our little house-warming. We had problems booking all the necessary hotel space for everyone. Where are you staying? I hope they're looking after you.'

'Parsifal Manor,' Kathryn explained. 'It's very comfortable, thank you.'

'Ghastly place!' Sheldon scowled. 'Don't put up with any nonsense from the manager there. He's a jumped-up East End oik and I've strong suspicions about where the money came from to buy that monstrous pile. If you get anything less than the best attention from his staff just let him know that he'd be ill advised to cross me.'

Kathryn quickly checked the arrangements for her interview at ten, then the King and Queen moved on. The Gyes socialized with other guests. The party was warming up nicely, fuelled by the Myleses' lavish hospitality. Just before ten Kathryn slipped away to have her private tête-à-tête with the founders of the feast and Nat decided to take the first tour of the house.

He arrived in the Walnut Parlour just as the guide was introducing himself to his flock of about twenty sightseers. Paul Greer was a stocky, bespectacled man of middle years, dressed in simple Puritan garb. He explained that he was a historical author who lived locally and specialized in seventeenth-century studies. He began his lecture with a brief summary of Cotswold life in the Jacobethan period and the circumstances which had led to this 'little known architectural gem' being built. The mastermind was, apparently, an upwardly mobile London mercer who bought himself a baronage from James I and acquired an estate to go with it. This Lord Bygot created a mansion in the latest fashion, symmetrical, spacious and containing every mod. con. known to seventeenth-century man. The Walnut Parlour was the room he used as his estate office. This was where the tenant farmers would come to pay their dues.

The party ascended the west staircase as Greer explained that the house was built round a central courtyard which allowed most of the rooms to have windows in at least two walls. Did that mean that all the chambers were interconnected, someone wanted to know. Yes, indeed, the guide replied; privacy was little known four hundred years ago. It had been much later that corridors had been introduced, thus permanently changing the original concept. Nat gained the distinct impression that Dr Greer regarded the desire for some human activities to be performed in discreet seclusion as effete.

The next port of call was the library, an impressive room, fitted on three sides with eighteenth-century glazed bookcases. Greer informed his class that this was the creation of the Sumption family, who had owned the estate from 1673. The statement, Nat realized, was cunningly made in order to provoke a question. It duly came from a studious little man who had already engaged the guide several times in learned debate in order to demonstrate his own knowledge. 'What happened to the Bygots?'

Greer rested his bottom against one of the mahogany library tables and beamed at his charges, who stood before him in a wide semicircle. 'Ah, that's the most interesting part of Tripletree's history.'

'Tripletree?' someone queried.

'I'll come to that in a moment,' the historian said mysteriously and paused to make sure that he had his audience's full attention. He need not have worried; the company were hanging on his words. 'The first Lord Bygot was, as far as we can tell, an amiable enough man, content to sit back and enjoy his new-found wealth and status. His son, Simon, who inherited in 1630, was a bird of a very different feather, a harsh landlord and an even harsher magistrate. Woe betide anyone brought before him on any charge – petty theft, poaching, witchcraft, affray. The records tell a sorry tale of men and women handed over to the hangman on the slenderest evidence. If you'll look closely at the eighteenth-century painting on the wall behind me,' he indicated a large panoramic depiction of the house and its parkland, 'you'll see that there is a gallows very clearly shown on the hill above the house beyond the lake. That was the work of Lord Simon. That's why the manor house became known in the neighbourhood as "Tripletree House". "Tripletree" is an old word for gallows.'

'I knew it!'

Nat recognized the voice and turned to see Steph Pace staring wide-eyed at their guide.

'I knew there was something sinister about this place. I just felt it. Tell me, Mr Greer, are there ghosts here? There must be ghosts.'

The doctor smiled the smile of a raconteur who has his audience in the palm of his hand. 'The story gets worse. When the First Civil War broke out Simon Bygot declared for the King and set about with his accustomed ruthlessness to stamp out any sign of sympathy for the Parliamentary cause. The year 1643 saw a great deal of fighting in this area with fortunes flowing to and fro. In June Tripletree House was subjected to a short siege. But this military action had little to do with the great issues dividing the nation. It was a local revolt against Lord Simon's tyranny. It seems that, when it came to it, Bygot defended his family and household bravely. But they were all doomed. The attackers broke in after dark and slaughtered everyone they could lay hands on – men, women and children. For Lord Simon they reserved another fate. You can probably guess what it was.'

'Strung up on his own gallows,' Nat suggested.

'Exactly. With Simon the dynasty became extinct. The house was empty and fell into decay.'

'Who'd want to buy a place with that kind of history?' Steph asked in a horrified tone.

Greer nodded. 'It wasn't till Charles II was restored and there was a rush of ruined royalist families looking for land that Tripletree found new occupants – the Sumptions, who lived here for over two hundred years. Their main contributions to the building were this library and the adjacent Sumption Suite. Now, if you'll follow me . . .'

'Was it still called Tripletree House?' the studious man wanted to know. 'And how long did the gallows stay there?'

As they passed through into the next set of rooms Greer explained, 'The name stuck for a very long time. In fact, you'll still hear some of the locals using it. As far as I can tell the gallows stayed there till well into the eighteenth century and were still used from time to time. They must have fallen down eventually. In 1840 Sir Bernard Sumption (rather a squeamish fellow by all accounts) planted three cedars on the hilltop so that people would come to think that they held the explanation of the name. Two of his trees are still there.'

As the tour continued Steph Pace attached herself to Nat. 'I told you there was an atmosphere here,' she insisted. 'I've heard that horrid happenings like murders and massacres impregnate the very stones of buildings. That is true isn't it, Professor Gye?'

'Dr Gye or just plain Nat,' he corrected. 'As to places "remembering" past events, there is a theory – it's called the conscious universe theory – which suggests that we have not yet begun to understand the connection between mind and matter.'

'Aha . . .'

'But it is only that – a theory,' he added hurriedly.

'Well, it may be only a theory to you,' she said, gripping his arm tightly, 'but I certainly wouldn't like to spend a night here alone.'

At the end of the tour Nat managed to detach himself from the actress. He strolled out through the front door in search of fresh air and liquid refreshment. With the darkness had come a cool breeze and he stood for some moments filling his lungs before setting off for the marquee which according to the programme had been set up on the West Lawn to provide a continuous service of drinks and light snacks. Once there he obtained a bottle of mineral water and a glass full of ice and found an unoccupied stone bench in a hedged arbour where he could drink in peace.

His seclusion lasted less than three minutes.

'Ooh, that's better!' A basket of oranges was plonked on the bench beside him and beyond it a buxom young woman plonked herself. 'My feet are killing me,' she said. Then, in response to Nat's polite smile, 'Are you staff or guests?'

Nat looked at his new companion. Mid-thirties, luxuriant tumble of red hair which decidedly did not go with the yellow and green of her dress. 'Guests,' he said.

'Oh!' She pulled a face. 'We're not supposed to fraternize with the gentry.' She half rose then fell back with a chuckle and a distinct waft of gin. 'You ain't going to tell old Po Face, are you?'

'Po Face?'

'Mr high and mighty Myles.'

'You don't care much for the lord of the manor?'

She cackled. 'Me and all Coln.' She leaned close to him 'There's things I could tell you that you'd never believe . . .' The woman turned towards him a face that had once been pretty but was now rather bloated. She was more drunk than Nat had at first realized. 'But that's not what I'm paid for, is it? I'm supposed to do my Nell Gwyn bit

28

and be specially nice to the men. Do you want me to be specially nice to you?'

'You're being very nice by talking to me,' Nat said with a smile. He thought but did not say that the original Nell Gwyn was unlikely to have worn a silver ring through her left nostril.

'You're sweet,' she simpered, peering at Nat closely. Then, suddenly she said, 'I know who you are. I've seen you on the telly . . . talking about the super . . . whatsit. Spooks! Oooh!' She made a wailing sound and waved trembling hands in the air. 'Well, you've come to the right place here.' She looked away briefly. When she turned to face him again she had a puzzled frown on her face and seemed to be struggling to focus on him. 'You're sweet,' she said. Then, with a surprisingly quick motion, she put a finger to her overpainted lips, then pressed it to Nat's. 'You a friend of Shelley-welly?'

'Not really.'

'Don't be. Keep well clear. He's going to get his come-uppance.' Mistress Gwyn hauled herself to her feet. 'Must go, dear. Important things to do. Very important things.' She swayed away across the grass, humming, of all things incongruous, a Gilbert and Sullivan tune. Nat was about to call after her to point out that she had forgotten her basket. He decided against it. He looked at his watch. 10.47. Either video or madrigals shortly. Time for a leisurely stroll around the grounds.

Lines of flares snaked their way through the parkland, helpfully indicating the easiest routes from one attraction to another. Nat descended to the lake at the rear of the house. It was shaped rather like two balloons with a foot-bridge crossing where the connecting 'string' would be. From there an illuminated path led to the top of Tripletree Hill and the giant cedars that stood outlined against the moonlit sky. Nat decided, like other guests, to climb to the top for a view of the manor house. Half-way up he encountered Sheldon Myles. Or rather, he did not encounter him. The master of Coln Manor was striding downhill with angry, jerking movements and a face full of fury. He did not acknowledge Nat but rushed on past towards the lake and the house.

Near the summit and a little to the left of the path three men were working by the light of torches to dismantle the scaffolding to which the fireworks had been attached. Nat walked over to them. 'Shame about the display,' he said. 'You must have put a lot of work into it.'

A young man who was kneeling down and wielding a spanner glared up at him. 'Piss off!' he yelled.

'Sorry.' Nat turned.

Another voice said, 'Easy, Tom. No point taking it out on all and sundry. Don't mind him, sir. We've had an earful from Mr Myles. He's putting all the blame on to us for what's gone wrong. Could cost us our jobs. I'm afraid you missed one of our best displays.' The speaker was a grey-haired man in overalls, who was packing equipment into a long wooden crate.

'What went wrong?' Nat asked.

'That's what we'd all like to know,' the older man replied. 'We were set up in good time. Went down to the refreshment tent for supper. Next thing – whoosh! Bloody kids, I reckon.'

'There's more to it than that, Ned. You know damned well there is.' The third member of the group came from the back of the long, smoke-blackened stand. 'Kids would've set off one or two pieces then done a bunk. This bastard went along the whole row. Bloody dangerous. He could have killed himself.'

'Wish to God he had!' the young man muttered. 'Old Price will bloody slaughter us when he hears about this. Fifteen thousand quid down the drain.'

Nat gave an understanding shake of the head. These men obviously wanted a sympathetic ear and he had nothing better to do than provide it. 'There are sick folk about who get a buzz from this sort of thing. People with

30

empty lives who think that vandalism makes the world sit up and take notice of them.'

The third man, balding and wearing a check shirt with the sleeves rolled up, perched himself on the edge of the crate. 'I still reckon it was that bugger Myles who was the object of this. Too many funny things going on. I think someone was out to spoil his party for him.'

'What sort of funny things?'

'Well, first there was that business at the motorway services. We was coming down the M40 from Birmingham and happened to get talking in the caff with some of the girls from the choir . . . What do they call themselves?'

'The Carnforth Singers,' Tom supplied.

'Right. Well, it turned out they was booked to perform at the same gig. They're down there on the lake. Doing their bit any minute now. Only if it wasn't for us they wouldn't be here. They'd been given the wrong directions. They'd have ended up miles away the other side of Oxford.'

'And according to the caterers they had the same problem,' Ned added. 'The manager was telling me this afternoon that they'd had a right mix-up over the arrangements. Fortunately, one of his girls has an aunt who lives in the village and knew the way here.'

'Who'd want to sabotage the party?' Nat asked.

Tom stood up and threw down his spanner. 'Just about half the county from what I hear. Myles gets on everyone's wick. You should have heard him ranting at us. I told him straight that we weren't responsible for his lousy security. He went ballistic! Going to report me to my superiors for insolence, he is.'

Nat stayed chatting with the firework crew for a few more minutes, abandoning his plan to go the hilltop. Then he set off back to the house. He had decided on the spur of the moment to head for the King James Parlour and the videoed account of what the Myleses had done to the mansion. He had no particular interest in architectural restoration but he was becoming more and more intrigued about the owners of Coln Manor.

By the front door he met June emerging from the house, with a couple of lady guests. She looked extremely strained.

'Lovely party,' he said brightly and received a wan smile in reply. 'You haven't seen Kathryn . . . Kathryn Gye recently, have you? I believe she was doing an inter –'

'No, no, I'm afraid not. Sorry, you must excuse me. Something's cropped up . . .' She hurried down the steps.

The King James Parlour – so named because of a full-length portrait of the monarch above the fireplace – was a long room occupying one corner of the ground floor. A large TV screen had been erected at one end and several chairs had been arranged cinema-style before it. Minimum lighting was provided by table and standard lamps so arranged as not to shine on the screen. The room was quite full when Nat arrived and he slipped into a seat on the back row. He looked at his watch. Half a minute to go. Would the film start on time? Would it start at all? Nothing would have surprised him. The Myleses and their house seemed to be jinxed. But, dead on time, the screen flickered into life and the story of Coln Manor's transformation began to unfold. Seventeen minutes later it came to an abrupt stop. The image vanished. The soundtrack fell silent. All the lights were extinguished. The King James Parlour was plunged into complete darkness.

There was no panic. For a few minutes the audience waited, expecting light to be quickly restored. Then singly and in pairs people began to stumble from the room. Someone produced a torch and that helped everyone to find their way into the Great Hall. Some of the candelabra that had graced the tables were found and lit. Most guests moved into the comparative light of the outdoors. Some demanded flustered servants to have their cars brought. Then the lights came back on.

Nat immediately spotted Kathryn and went over to her.

'How did the interview go?' he asked.

She shrugged. 'I've had better. They both seemed pre-occupied.'

'Hardly surprising, the way things appear to be falling apart. Do you want to leave?'

'Well, I don't suppose the dancing will be much fun with everyone wondering if the electrics are going to go AWOL at any moment. What else is there on offer?'

'The madrigals have finished and the firework spectacular which should be starting about now is off.'

'I heard Shelley say he'd try to get the Carnforth Singers to extend their programme.'

Nat laughed. 'The way things are going the performers could all have ended up in the lake by now.'

'Shall we go and see?'

They wandered down towards the wide expanse of water. There were no sounds of music but a few other guests were headed in the same direction and a small crowd had already gathered at the lakeside. Not, however, a crowd of people come together for an aesthetic experience. Something was wrong. As the Gyes reached the outer ring of the little gathering a gap opened. Four men came through carrying something between them. They laid it on the grass close to where Nat was standing. He looked down. The first thing he saw was a tangled, sodden mass of yellow and green material. Then wet strands of red hair spreading out from a very pale face.

Explanations

The BMW purred up Trumpington Street, turned right along Fen Causeway, over the river with its summer throng of punts, and then right and into the shaded stretch of Queen's Road, running parallel to the Backs. But instead of taking the first road on the left, leading to the Library, Sheldon Myles eased the car into a parking space.

'Let me buy you a drink,' he said, and promptly began walking back in the direction of the traffic lights. Five minutes later he and Nat were seated on the terrace of the Granta Inn, overlooking the pool formed by one arm of the meandering Cam. The pub, a favourite with students, was discovered by few tourists and was therefore fairly quiet out of term time.

Nat watched a pair of cruising ducks drift up to the landing stage and cast calculating eyes at the occupants of the tables, then, realizing that no scraps were forthcoming, glide away towards the grassy bank opposite where two children under the care of an au pair offered better prospects. He took a gulp of his bitter and set the glass down on a garish table mat. 'Mr Myles,' he said, 'I do have work to do.'

The other man ran a hand carefully over his dark hair flecked with grey. 'Please call me Shelley, Nathaniel.'

'Most people know me as Nat.'

'Thank you.' The barrister looked genuinely grateful and much of the bluster had gone out of his demeanour.

'I realize this is an imposition but I really have no one else to turn to.'

Nat looked at the man opposite. On the surface he was an establishment figure, totally secure in himself and in his social position. Suit, tie, immaculately coiffed, luxuriant hair – all proclaimed unassailable British conservatism. The pale complexion and the lines dragging down the corners of his mouth told a different story. Nat guessed that Myles was sleeping badly. 'What's all this about your wife and the police?' he asked. 'I thought the death of that unfortunate woman had all been sorted out.' He cast his mind back to the disastrous end of the Coln Manor house-warming – the arrival of the police, the removal of the body, guests anxious to get away but being detained by CID officers until they had provided their names and addresses, the dispiriting drive back to the hotel to tumble into bed for what little remained of the night.

'There was never any doubt about the inquest verdict. The post-mortem showed that the stupid bitch was tanked up to the eyeballs with gin. She obviously slipped into the lake where the bank is steep. Unfortunately, there was no one near her at the time and, although she was found after only a few minutes, it was too late.'

Nat bridled at the word 'bitch'. He recalled vividly the sharp shock he had experienced on recognizing the dead woman. Their very brief conversation had somehow lifted the body out of the category of 'anonymous female'. She was someone who, less than an hour before, had been a living, breathing person with her own outlook on the world, albeit inebriated. Nat had been surprised at the acute sadness that had overwhelmed him. 'Terrible tragedy for her family,' he said. 'I gather there are two children.'

'Two *legitimate* children,' Myles corrected with a sneer. 'Tracy Pensham – what's the expression? – put herself about a bit. I'm afraid she had quite a reputation.'

'Still, she didn't deserve that.'

'Nor does June deserve to be pulled down with her.'

'What do you mean by that?'

Myles rubbed a weary hand over his eyes. 'It's all down to stress. June's been pushing herself hard for several years. That's OK when you're younger – thrusting ahead eagerly, competitively to make a successful career. But if you try to maintain the pace, well . . .' he shrugged, 'it's bound to catch up with you. Looking back to 1994 I can see that we bought Coln Manor at the wrong time.'

'You must have got it at the bottom of the market.'

'Oh, yes, it was a snip, especially as it was in pretty poor shape. We fell in love with it as soon as we saw it and I thought the renovations would give June another interest – something to take her mind off her work.'

'So what went wrong?'

Myles sighed. 'I don't know. Sometimes I wonder if it's true what the local old wives say about what they call Tripletree House.'

'What's that?' Nat asked, interested despite himself.

'That there's a curse on the place. What I do know is that I heartily wish we'd never set eyes on the bloody house.' He took a long pull at his beer. 'June got really wrapped up in the restoration project. She talked about little else. At first I was delighted. What I didn't see was that Coln Manor was becoming an obsession. By the time she began telling me about the "happenings" it was already too late. The builders were in full spate. We couldn't possibly have sold at that stage. And, anyway, June wouldn't have heard of it.'

'What do you mean by "happenings"?'

Myles's mouth creased in a mirthless smile. 'I thought that would interest you. It's quite in your line. Of course, I don't buy into this paranormal mumbo-jumbo. It's all in the mind but obviously some places do exert a power-ful influence over the imagination and if, as with June, that imagination is already overwrought, and then if mali-

36

cious people start playing tricks for their own twisted motives –'

'Suppose you just tell me what happened,' Gye suggested quietly.

'They were mostly trivial things. Mentioning them like this in the cold light of day makes it seem stupid that one would be bothered by them. That's why June kept them to herself for a long time. She thought I'd just laugh, and, God help me, I did – at first. Then she started having nightmares and even daytime hallucinations.'

'You still haven't told me what these incidents were.'

'Oh, voices, footsteps, sudden drops in temperature, furniture moving around – all the usual psychic phenomenon clichés.'

'Can you be more specific?'

'Well, I remember the first experience June told me about. She was working in what we now call the Green Sollar when she heard voices outside. It was as though a large, angry crowd had gathered. She went to the window to see what the fuss was about. No one was there and the noise stopped abruptly.'

Nat nodded. 'Interesting, but not a unique experience.'

'There you are, you see. You don't take it any more seriously than I did.'

Nat shook his head. 'I didn't say that. What else happened?'

'One of the decorators working alone on the moulded ceiling in the Great Hall fell from the scaffolding. He swore someone – or some *thing* – pushed him. We had a devil of a job with the insurance company over it.'

'Was he badly hurt?'

'A few broken bones. The trouble was that when he'd recovered nothing would induce him to come back to finish the job. I had to hire another firm half as good for twice the price.'

'It wasn't just your wife who had these experiences, then?'

'No, although she had the lion's share of them.'

'Did you consider doing anything to put a stop to what was obviously a very disturbing series of events? Exorcism, for instance?'

The barrister sat back with a forced laugh. 'That's rather a sign of weakness, isn't it? People with no religious belief, no concept of a "spiritual realm" beyond the here and now, throwing a wobbly and sending for a priest when they come up against something they don't understand.'

'Not necessarily. When a priest or a psychic researcher or a psychiatrist or any other expert performs some kind of ritual it often has a curative effect –'

Myles brushed the argument aside with an imperious wave of the hand. 'Let me make one thing clear. I'm a rational being. So is June – basically. We don't believe in magic, whether it's performed by priests or psychiatrists or witch doctors. Whatever June has experienced at Coln has its explanation inside her own mind or in certain evil individuals who are deliberately making trouble for us.'

'Who would want to do that?' Nat asked, and a picture of Tracy Pensham floated into his mind, alcoholically confiding that none of Coln's villagers had much love for 'Mr high and mighty Myles'.

'You'd be amazed what a backward and introverted little community Coln St Ippolyts is. Going there is like taking a step back into the Middle Ages. Superstition, gossip, prejudice and, of course, hatred of foreigners. It doesn't matter that we've created lots of employment, not to mention putting the village on the map, the yokels bitterly resented us taking over the manor and have tried their level best to make life unpleasant for us. You saw what they got up to at our party.'

'Did you ever get to the bottom of all that?'

Myles drained his glass and sneered over the rim. 'No point in trying. They'll shut up like clams, every one of them.' He stared moodily out across the water.

Nat prepared to steer the conversation towards its close.

'Well, Shelley, if Cotswold life is so unpleasant and if it's really affecting June's health, wouldn't the best answer be to sell up, move on, put all the unpleasantness behind –'

Myles brought his fist down heavily on the table making the glasses jump. 'What! Give in? Let those bumpkins think they've won? No way!'

'Well, I'm sorry to hear about your problems, Shelley.' Nat looked pointedly at his watch. 'But I really don't see how I can be of any help.'

Myles looked back in mild exasperation. 'That's because I haven't told you where you come into the picture. Stay there while I go and get these refilled.' He collected the glasses and went into the pub.

When he had returned with two fresh pints the squire of Coln St Ippolyts took up his narrative in an altogether brisker style. 'I don't suppose you've heard of a character calling himself Dr Caradoc Owen?'

Nat shook his head.

'No. I didn't think so. The man's a charlatan. Not in your league.'

Nat was not sure whether or not this was a compliment. He said nothing as Myles went on.

'A couple of weeks ago I had to go to Frankfurt on business. June was resting up in our London flat. This Owen character wheedled his way in and said he could help her by using regression therapy. Naturally, if I'd been there I'd have sent him packing but by this time poor old June was ready to clutch at even the most unlikely of straws. When I did get back I hardly recognized my own wife. She was hysterical. Told me that now she understood everything – especially how the Pensham woman died.'

'Did Owen regress her to a supposed past life?'

Myles nodded vigorously. 'It wasn't difficult. June has done a lot of research on the history of the manor house and its owners. She was carrying a great deal of information in her head.'

Nat agreed. 'Undoubtedly more than she realized, since some of it would be locked in her unconscious.'

'Precisely! So what happened? Under the fluence she produced this supposed past life experience. She believed that she had been a maid in the manor house at the time of the Civil War and she had become involved in some sort of love triangle with another servant girl. They had a fight and in the process June's alter ego killed her rival by drowning her in the well. She was subsequently tried and ended up on the gallows on Tripletree Hill.'

Gye said, 'One of the fascinating facts about supposed reincarnations is the intensely exciting lives subjects believe themselves to have lived. We very rarely hear anyone admit to the dreary humdrum existence of an obscure peasant to whom nothing remarkable ever happened.'

Myles scowled. 'This is my wife I'm talking about, not some interesting case turned up in your academic research. The point is she's now completely confused. She's mixed up the present with the fictional past and believes she murdered the Pensham woman.'

Nat considered this silently for several moments. Eventually, he said, 'Yes, I see why you're worried. Your wife certainly needs professional help. But I have to say again I'm not the right person to give it.'

Myles leaned forward across the table. 'I'm not sending her to a shrink! That would be round all the muckraking press in hours. You know what a field day the tabloid jackals had last month after the party fiasco. Anyway, June's not . . . mentally ill. Just confused. And you're the one who can sort her out; get her to start thinking straight. This sort of thing is right up your street. I won't pretend I've seen any of your programmes but I know your reputation for exposing spiritualist gobbledegook. You've had dealings with this regression therapy nonsense, haven't you?'

'I have done some work on it but –'

'Well, that's all that matters. Talk to June. She'll listen to you. She certainly won't take notice of anything I say. Talk to her, that's all I ask. You might also see if you can find out anything through your professional grapevine about this Caradoc Owen creature. If we can expose him for the fraud he is then we can let June down gently and put this wretched business behind us.'

Nat shook his head but Myles would not let him speak.

'Come down to Coln for the weekend. Just Saturday, if you like. If you visit us in the country it won't set the noses of the press bloodhounds twitching. Please!'

'Myles, I –'

'Please! I'm not accustomed to begging favours but I'm begging you now. Charge whatever fee you want, but come!'

To his surprise Gye found himself looking into the eyes of a man close to breaking point.

Victims

The circumstances of Nathaniel and Kathryn Gye's second visit to Coln St Ippolyts were very different from their first. For one thing, it was raining. An intermittent, gusty wind drove the flurries almost horizontally across the landscape and their first view of the house at the end of its long drive was as though through striated glass. On this occasion they were on time. Nat had agreed to come for lunch and the dashboard clock registered exactly 12.30 as Kathryn announced their arrival to the intercom and the tall iron gates swung noiselessly open. There was also a different atmosphere inside the car. An unspoken truce had settled over the couple on the subject of the New York job. Kathryn's appointment was due to take effect on 1 January. That gave them a few weeks 'cooling off' period before arrangements for the move had to be made, and they had tacitly agreed neither to discuss it nor mention it to the boys immediately. The subject hung between them like a black curtain which neither wanted to draw back.

'You know, this place still gives me the creeps,' Kathryn said, as the Mercedes slowed to enter the wide, oval space at the end of the drive.

'That's hardly surprising considering what happened on our last visit – plus the fact that you lost your juicy feature.'

'I've no complaints about that,' Kathryn replied, adjusting her rain hat before alighting. 'My exclusive on-the-spot syndication piece more than made up for it.'

The Myleses' butler descended the steps with an umbrella to escort them into the house. Having taken their coats, he led them up the west staircase to the library, where they found Sheldon waiting for them. He offered his guests drinks and suggested they sat beside a small fire glowing in the marble hearth.

'Very relaxing room,' Nat observed, when their host declined to set the conversation rolling.

Shelley smiled distractedly. 'Yes, it makes a good all-purpose room. We tend to use just the ones on this floor when there are only the two of us here.'

'Don't you find the house a bit, well, overwhelming?' Kathryn asked.

Myles said, 'We bought the place mainly for entertaining. It's nice to be able to accommodate all our guests in a degree of comfort. Though, as things have turned out, we haven't had many visitors – yet . . .' He sighed. 'We can only hope things get better when we've put all this behind us. I'm taking June off to the Caribbean for a couple of weeks. I'm hoping that'll perk her up.'

Kathryn looked around. 'Is June –'

'Resting at the moment. She finds meeting people a strain and I want her to be at her best when she has her chat with Nat,' Myles explained.

'I do hope you're not putting too much hope on whatever little I can do,' Nat said. 'As I explained –'

'Yes, yes!' Myles controlled his impatience carefully. 'I'm grateful to you for coming and I'm sure June will be relieved to be able to discuss her problem with someone who understands it.'

The butler glided in and stood beside the door. 'Lunch is ready, sir. Mrs Myles will join you in the dining room.'

A small table had been set in front of a south-facing window in the adjacent room and they had just taken their places when Juniper Myles came in. Nat looked at her and suppressed a gasp. It hardly seemed possible that so great a change could have come over someone in such a short space of time. Shelley's wife wore a simple flame-coloured dress, presumably to convey an impression of liveliness. The vivid hue had the opposite effect. It gave her pale, drawn face an almost jaundiced appearance. This was one very sick woman.

Throughout the meal June kept up a brittle chattiness and it was obvious to the others that it was a huge effort.

Afterwards they returned to the library for coffee and a few minutes later Shelley took Kathryn off ostensibly to show her a collection of early prints of the house.

'Not very subtle.' June stood by the fireplace and stared at the closing door. 'Funny, he's quite brilliant in court. Never at a loss for exactly the right word. But at home . . .' She turned her back on the room, her words trailing away. 'Have you seen this old painting?' She nodded at the eighteenth-century view of the manor house.

'Yes, I saw it last time I was here.'

She ran a finger over the gallows on the skyline. 'They used to call this place Tripletree House.'

'Yes.'

'Ah, you know the story, then. You've heard about the wicked Simon Bygot.' She turned to face him. 'He wasn't really as black as he's been painted.' She thrust out her little pointed chin, inviting contradiction. 'No one knew him better than me. We were lovers.'

'How fascinating,' Nat said. 'Won't you sit down and tell me about him?'

She perched on the edge of a bergère chair, her hands tightly clasped in her lap. 'Shelley says you're an expert on regression therapy and you won't tell me I'm potty. *He* thinks I am.'

'He's very concerned about you.'

She shook her head. 'He's concerned I'll tell everyone the truth. That's why he wants them to think I'm potty.'

Gently Nat asked, 'What is the truth?'

A long sigh shuddered through her body. 'That I'm a murderess and I must pay for my crime.'

'I see. Who did you murder?'

'Tracy . . . the slut!' June spat the words out with sudden venom.

'Why did you do that?'

'She was having an affair with my man.'

'Shelley?'

She nodded vigorously. 'Yes, Simon.'

Nat tried another tack. 'It was Caradoc Owen who helped you discover the truth, wasn't it?'

She smiled faintly. 'Yes, it was such a relief. I just couldn't remember . . . My mind was a complete blank. Then Caradoc came along. Wonderful man. He found the key to what my conscious was locking away.'

'I see. What did he do exactly?'

June looked slightly puzzled. 'Well, you know . . . hypnosis, questions . . . I thought you understood.' She tensed suddenly.

Nat was alarmed that he might have lost her trust. 'I do understand but, you see, different practitioners have different techniques and since I'm not acquainted with Mr Owen –'

'*Dr* Owen. He's very particular about having his qualifications acknowledged. Some people are, apparently, very critical of his work. Well . . . he conducted the sessions at our flat in town. He settled me in a comfortable chair and we chatted for a bit – I suppose that was to get me to relax.'

'Were you and he alone?'

June shook her head, firmly rejecting any idea of impropriety. 'Oh no, he always came with his assistant – a funny little woman with rather protruding eyes. She took notes.'

'Did he explain to you the nature and purpose of regression therapy?'

'Most certainly. Caradoc told me that anxieties and tension are often the result of suppressed memories of events in childhood or in previous existences. The healing process lies in recovering those events and dealing with them.'

'Good, that was very proper. Dr Owen is obviously a conscientious practitioner.' Nat noted that June relaxed in response to his words. 'Tell me,' he went on, 'before you met him, did you believe in reincarnation?'

She gave a faint laugh. 'No. I suppose like most modern people I preferred not to think about the "beyond". Funny, now it all makes such complete sense.'

'So, Dr Owen suggested putting you in a hypnotic trance and you consented. You had no qualms about it?'

June sank back in the chair. 'No, I was so miserable, so wretched. I would have plucked at any straw.'

Gye wondered what the cause of Mrs Myles's depression might be but decided not to pursue that for the moment. 'What memories did you unearth?' he asked.

'Oh, silly childhood things at first. My third birthday party. A kitten we used to have called Tabitha. The pattern of my nursery wallpaper. All the memories were so vivid – the colours, the smells, the sounds. It really was like reliving them.'

'And then?'

'Caradoc said I had memories that went even further back. I only had to let myself recall them.'

'Did he tell you how far back to go?'

June wrinkled her brow in concentration. 'I don't think so . . . perhaps he suggested a time of great trouble . . . but I may be wrong. What happened next was horrible!' She put a hand to her throat. 'I couldn't breathe. My body was heavy. Swinging. People . . . trees going round and round. I choked and Caradoc brought me back quickly.' She was breathing heavily and still clutching her neck.

Nat said, 'I'm sorry, this is distressing you. Let's talk of something else.'

June seemed not to hear him. 'That was the end of our first session.'

'You still wanted to carry on?'

'Caradoc explained that his subjects frequently experienced their own death in earlier existences. And, of course, that's what it was. My death, or rather Gunny's death on Tripletree Hill.'

'That must have shaken you very badly.'

'Yes, it did, but at the same time I knew I was getting very close. I had to go on.'

'You mentioned "Gunny".'

'That's right, Gunny Whiddon. That's who I was in the 1640s.'

'Strange name.'

'"Gunny"? Yes, it was a nickname. It meant bleary or weak-eyed. It explains why, when I was in her memories, I couldn't see very clearly. I think, now, that it must have been the result of a childhood disease.' June stared at him, dark eyes now bright and eager. 'You see, it's little details like that that prove what I experienced was true. "Gunny" is an archaic word. I've never heard it. There's no way I could have made up a half-blind fictional character and given her that name. No way at all.' She looked to Nat for reassurance.

He nodded. 'And what sort of a woman was this Gunny Whiddon?'

'A thoroughly bad lot, I'm afraid. She was the mistress's personal maid – and the master's personal mistress.'

'The master here at Coln Manor?'

June nodded, a half-smile coming over her face. 'Lord Simon Bygot, the notorious tyrant. My God, but he was a handsome devil – tall, very black hair, piercing eyes that looked right through you.'

'And he seduced Gunny?'

'Seduced? No, I was willing enough. Head over heels in love. And he was a great lover.'

Nat looked at this middle-aged woman and saw the ardent, glowing smile of a teenage girl in the grip of a grand passion. He said, 'But somehow this relationship ended unhappily?'

The radiance faded. June's face contorted with startling suddenness into pained, angry savagery. 'It was all revealed in our third session. First I was in the orchard. Happy. Enjoying a few rare moments of solitude on a hazy summer afternoon. Till I came upon *them* . . .' She broke off abruptly, her mind focused on some scene that was vivid to her.

Nat made no intrusion on a long silence whose seconds were sonorously measured by the thudding mechanism of a long case clock beside the door. Eventually he suggested, 'You saw Simon with another –'

'With *her*.'

'With who?' Nat gently probed.

'With the Pensham woman.'

'Tracy Pensham!' Nat exclaimed in alarm. 'But that's not –'

June interrupted. 'I know what you're going to say. But it *was* her. Oh, she had a different name then but there was no mistaking the hussy. I saw her quite clearly as she rolled around with him in the long grass, skirts up round her fat arse. Not love. Filthy lust!' She flung the words out with such venom that spittle flew from her lips. 'And she saw me. Oh yes, she saw me and grinned at me. A gloating grin. It was sickening. I just turned and ran.'

June Myles was breathing heavily now, staring into the fire through narrowed lids. Another long silence followed and this time Nat did not break it. He was thinking hard, trying to find some way of bringing June gently back from her fantasy land of black nightmare.

He was disturbed by a little cackling laugh. 'But I paid her back. No more orchard romps for Mistress Pensham – or him. My next memory was in the courtyard here. Now it's all neatly cobbled but then it was bare earth with a few flagstones to walk on. You can still just make out where the well was, by the old kitchen door. It was in that corner we fought. She was talking with one of her cronies when I passed. I heard her say, "What man would ever want poor blind Gunny Whiddon?" Stupid woman! She didn't realize my ears were as sharp as my eyes were dim. I flew at her. Very sudden. All at once we were rolling round in the mud – scratching, biting, tearing. And all the other servants gathering round to watch the fun.' Once again June was lost in the vividness of her recollection. 'I drew blood – two deep scars down her cheek. She screamed and pushed me away. She got to her feet and ran a few steps. But she only got as far as the well. Then I was on her again. She turned with her back against the low wall. I hit her with both fists in the stomach. Then, as she doubled up, I used all my strength to half push, half lift her over the edge. Down she went, arms waving but no scream, because I'd knocked the wind out of her.'

Nat stared at this well-bred, professional woman talking with the coarse breathlessness of a creature from some poorly scripted TV soap. Then the clock chimed the half-hour and June suddenly smiled at him. 'That's about all there is to tell,' she said in her normal, well-modulated voice. The spell was broken.

'It's a tragic story,' Nat observed, 'but it all happened a long time ago.'

June shook her head. 'Ah, but it's all locked up in these stones, vibrating in the very air of Tripletree House.'

'Strange that you should have come back here – and Mrs Pensham, too.'

She looked up sharply. 'Are you familiar with the latest theories concerning extra-cranial intelligence?'

Nat thought she had slipped into her well-practised cross-examining counsel mode. He nodded.

'Then you will be aware that the old distinction between objective and subjective knowledge is being seriously called in question. If we can no longer think in terms of truth as simply "out there" waiting to be discovered but all the time interacting with our own conscious and unconscious mental processes, then would you not say that the concept of people and places interacting ceases to be a difficult one to accept?'

Nat deliberately avoided an excursion into quantum mechanical theory and its application to consciousness. 'Did you discuss with Mrs Pensham your common association with Coln Manor's past?' he asked.

Another abrupt change came over his hostess. 'Time for tea, don't you think?' she said. She rose and pressed a button by the fireplace. The butler appeared within seconds and she briskly ordered, 'Tea in here, please, Brunnage. Perhaps you could find Mr Myles and Mrs Gye and let them know.'

Clearly the interview was at an end. Nat decided to take the bull by the horns. 'The coroner was quite satisfied that Mrs Pensham's death was accidental,' he said. 'Is that a verdict you dispute?'

'It must be wrong.' Her voice was flat, emotionless. 'I murdered her.'

'Three hundred and fifty years ago, perhaps, but not in 1999.'

'Yes, yes, yes!' she insisted. 'It was a re-enactment. Everything happened as it did before.'

'But you were nowhere near the lake when Mrs Pensham fell in.'

'Wasn't I? How do you know?'

Gye hesitated. 'I don't. But you do.'

'No!' she wailed. 'That's the point. I don't know. I can remember nothing for at least half an hour during the party. I don't know where I was, who I was with, what I did, what I said. That can only be because something terrible happened that my conscious mind is rejecting.'

'Not necessarily. Have you had temporary amnesia before?'

She shook her head. 'Never. But, anyway, it doesn't matter. It will all become very clear on Tuesday.'

'Tuesday?'

50

'I have another session with Caradoc and we're going to go through everything that happened at the party. Then I shall know, for certain sure, once and for all. And if I am a murderess, as I believe I am, I shall be clear about what course to take.'

Tea and the others arrived simultaneously and an hour or so later the Gyes took their leave. Sheldon saw them to their car. The rain had cleared and a drab, grey twilight was oozing over the landscape.

'Well,' Myles asked anxiously. 'What do you think?'

'I think you're right to be concerned. Something is disturbing June very seriously and this Caradoc Owen fellow is making it worse.'

'You agree with me, then, that this hypnotic mumbo-jumbo is all dangerous baloney?'

A curtain moved at a first floor window and, looking up, Nat saw Juniper Myles outlined against the light. 'No, I don't agree wholly. Hypnotic regression has a proven track record in the treatment of some forms of psychosis but its value is limited and it should only be resorted to under strict clinical supervision. The opportunities for manipulation – intentional or otherwise – are enormous.'

'Well, you needn't worry about that Owen charlatan. I'll make damned sure he keeps well away.'

Gye frowned. 'Your wife spoke of another appointment on Tuesday.'

Myles managed a slight smile. 'On Tuesday June and I will be in Barbados.'

'Does she know your holiday plans?' Kathryn asked.

'Not yet. I'm keeping her in the dark until the last moment. Best way to avoid a long-running argument.'

Nat held out his hand to the barrister. 'Thank you for your delightful hospitality, Shelley. I hope a rest and a change of scene will do the trick for June.' He paused, his fingers still clasped tight by Myles's large hand. 'Of course, there is one thing you could do but it's so obvious I imagine you've already thought of it.'

'What's that?' Myles's eyes glinted eagerly.

'Get her to realize that she was nowhere near the lake when that unfortunate woman fell in. Talk to some of your guests. Work out her exact movements for the critical period. June's emotions are carved up but she's a highly intelligent woman. I'm sure –'

'No!' Myles almost shouted the word and Nat felt the spasm that passed through the other man's body as his grip tightened. 'This must be kept confidential. I don't want rumours spreading.' With an effort he relaxed and put on a forced smile. 'I have thought of it, of course. But stories would only get back to June and that could make her worse. Well, goodbye, Nat, Kate.' He stopped to brush Kathryn's cheek with his lips.

Once again the barrister expressed his profuse thanks to Nat and offered to pay for his services. Gye politely declined and, a few minutes later, he and his wife were in the warm cocoon of the Mercedes and heading back down the long drive.

'Well,' said Kathryn, settling into the yielding leather, 'what do you make of all that?'

Nat stared into the dusk and only replied when he had formed his thoughts into carefully considered words. 'That woman is an emotional chameleon, which means one of two things.'

'Yes?'

'Either she is on the verge of a complete mental collapse or she is an extremely accomplished actress.'

Secrets

They had travelled no more than a couple of miles when Nat said, 'Would you like to drive for a bit? I want to make some notes while things are still fresh in my mind.'

He pulled the car into the side and he and Kate changed places. As they pulled away again and Nat was opening his laptop, Kathryn said, in a half-mocking tone, 'So, the Myles mystery is worthy of a place in the celebrated Gye Journal.'

Nat was very disciplined about taking notes. Whenever he came across material that might prove useful for lectures, books or television presentations he recorded it. Now he typed in the password 'Journal' and, when he had accessed his confidential record, he opened a new file headed 'Juniper Myles' and linked it to 'Hypnotherapy'.

'Everything that doesn't appear to fit accepted theory should always be examined carefully,' he replied, unaware that he had slipped into lecture hall mode.

'Well, don't leave the obnoxious Shelley out of the record. A dollar to a bag of beans says he's as unhinged as his poor wife. I don't wonder she's teetering on the brink, married to that monster.'

'Monster? That's a bit strong, isn't it?'

'Not at all. The man's ambition is truly frightening. You don't suppose he really cares about June, do you? You saw how he reacted to your suggestion about questioning partygoers to find out her precise movements at the time of Mrs Pensham's death. "It'll start rumours and they'll get back to poor June." Huh! The reason he wants to keep the lid on his wife's odd behaviour is that it'll put the brake on the Sheldon Myles bandwagon.'

'June accused him of wanting people to think she was . . . well, "potty" was her word.'

'Rubbish!' Kathryn emphasized the word with a fierce blast on the horn directed at a motorist who had the temerity to pull out in front of the Mercedes from a side turning. 'Everything has gone swimmingly for Mr Myles QC – until now. He came from nowhere, married the daughter of a wealthy judge, established a reputation at the bar for brilliance and unscrupulousness, made a few too many professional enemies in the criminal law field, switched to the commercial sector – with the help of June, who was already well established there. It's common gossip that he's set his sights on entering Parliament and ending up with a seat in the Lords. Having a wife in the funny farm wouldn't fit the programme at all.'

'Hmm!'

'What does "Hmm" mean?'

'It means what game is Mr Myles's wife playing?'

'You don't buy all this past life stuff, then? June looked convincingly fazed to me.'

'I don't know. There's a big question that's sitting up and begging for an answer.' Nat turned his attention to the screen. He typed in the date, 'Saturday 30 September', then:

Juniper Myles QC. Fiftyish. Wealthy. Successful. Marriage probably unsatisfactory. Why does she want to convince herself and/or others that she has committed murder?

Possible answers:
a) She *has* committed murder and can't cope with the guilt.

No. Deceased – Mrs Tracy Pensham – accidental death.

b) Suppressed hatred for husband. Wants to cause him serious embarrassment.

Possible. Perhaps long history of putting on a brave face. Well bred. Public image important.

The car stopped at a T-junction and a long column of traffic passed in front of it. Kathryn looked across at the laptop screen.

'She'd have to hate him a hell of a lot to risk prison.'

'If she knows there's no real chance of being found guilty she has nothing to lose personally. Any fresh enquiry would exonerate her while the publicity would achieve her desired result.'

'She didn't strike me as that devious.'

'Me neither. But there's nothing more cunning or terrifyingly single-minded than a vengeful woman. Anyway, whether she's manipulator or manipulated, there's something very wrong in the whole Coln St Ippolyts set-up. Remember all the things that went haywire at the house-warming?'

'You think June was behind sabotaging the fireworks, switching out all the lights and the other deliberate party-pooping?'

'Someone was.' Nat looked back at the screen and added a third 'possible answer'.

c) Person unknown undermining the Myleses?

Perhaps. The couple have made enemies locally and probably in the course of their professional lives.

Someone went to a lot of trouble to ruin their housewarming party.

Caradoc Owen, apparently practising as a hypnotherapist, may have messed up June's mind.

Incompetent or malevolent? Discussion with

the subject indicates he used auto-suggestion.
THIS COULD BE USEFUL MATERIAL FOR
PAPER TO MANCHESTER SEMINAR ON
CLINICAL HYPNOSIS.

Nat switched off the computer and stared out at the empty road illuminated by the car's powerful lights.

Kathryn said, 'I suppose your analysis doesn't include the supernatural?'

Nat laughed. 'You mean poltergeists setting off rockets and bangers?'

Kate turned and glared. 'You scoff as much as you like, mister, but that house has a bad aura and some pretty godawful things have happened there.'

'Oh, I certainly don't discount atmosphere. June has identified very closely with Coln Manor and steeped herself in its history. It would be very surprising if that had no effect on her.'

'But you don't buy the inexplicable happenings – the voices, the "presences", the man who said he was pushed off his ladder? You put all June's ghostly experiences down to the imaginings of an overwrought woman's mind?'

Nat pointed to an illuminated sign half a mile away. 'There's a wayside café up ahead. Let's stop for a coffee.'

Ten minutes later, as Kathryn depressed the plunger on a cafetière and poured the black liquid into cups, Nat took up the conversation. 'What you're really asking is two questions: do I believe in ghosts and do I believe in reincarnation? More specifically, do I think Coln Manor is haunted and was Juniper Myles genuinely regressed to a previous existence? You know my answer to the first. No, I don't think the house is possessed by some malevolent force. But June's mind might be. To the second I would say much the same. I have come across no convincing evidence that some or all of us have lived multiple previous lives but I've met scores of people who believe that they have been here before. Some of them have been the victims of

56

unscrupulous practitioners, bogus psychiatrists, "show-ground" hypnotists, criminals who, unfortunately, the law can't touch. It's possible Juniper Myles has fallen into the clutches of such a charlatan.'

Kathryn cupped both hands round her coffee and gazed across the half-empty café. 'Well, I guess we'll never know,' she said.

Nat shook his head and frowned. 'We'll have a damned good try.'

Kate raised her eyebrows in surprise. 'You mean this business has got under your skin? I thought you had no time for Shelley Myles and his problems. You refused his money and more or less told him that you could do no more for him.'

Nat drained his cup. 'I don't give a damn for Myles. Not because I go along with your description of him as a monster. Monsters are quite interesting. I see him more as a boring robot; a self-obsessed, amoral automaton. Someone set the switch to "Success" and he mechanically followed a preset programme. Now that an obstacle has appeared in the way he can only blunder around ineffectually making a great deal of noise. He wants someone to take the inconvenient blockage out of his path and I'm not going to be that someone.'

'What about June?'

Nat shrugged. 'She made her bed a long time ago and if she wanted to get out of it she could.'

'That's callous! The wretched woman's at the end of her tether! Anyone can see that.'

'You may be right. But I'm not convinced and I've seen a lot of disturbed people.'

'OK, so you want to wash your hands of the both of them. I don't see what's bugging you.'

'Someone, somewhere is playing mind games. That rouses my personal and professional ire.'

The truth was that Nat could not really explain to himself over the next few days just why the Myles affair had taken hold of him. It was not just that his mind was like a terrier that felt compelled to worry away at puzzling problems. He was always trying to impress upon his students the importance of intellectual rigour and he could be quite alarmingly fierce with what he dismissed as 'mental flabbiness'. Many a nervous undergraduate had seen the words scrawled in red across the bottom of an essay: 'Don't be satisfied with simple answers to complex questions!' Nat was equally hard on himself. But that did not explain his sense of unease with the events at Coln St Ippolyts. Nor did his indignation with charlatans and incompetents who preyed upon the fears and anxieties of vulnerable people. He had, in his time, tangled with many such. It came as no surprise to him that his enquiries through professional bodies and clinical directories drew a blank over the name of Dr Caradoc Owen. No, there was something else. Something that nagged insistently at him. Something that told him that whatever was going on between and around Sheldon and Juniper Myles had a greater importance than was immediately obvious. Nat knew, with growing certainty, that he would have no peace until he had paid a visit to the Oxfordshire village.

A new academic year was beginning, with its usual overload of activities – fellows' meetings, faculty meetings, sherry parties for the freshers, interviews with his latest crop of students, who seemed to become younger and more naïve year on year. But he deliberately kept a clear two days in every term-time week for his own research and it was one of these that he now devoted to a trip to Coln. He had no plan of action, no specific leads to follow, and the guilty feeling that he was wasting his time kept prodding at him.

Coln St Ippolyts was not a tourist village. Visitors either bypassed it on their way to Bourton-on-the-Water, the Slaughters and Stow-on-the-Wold, with their rows of pristine cream stone cottages, tea rooms, souvenir emporia, and overpriced antique shops, or, finding themselves among its jumble of council houses, mini-supermarket and slightly shabby older residences, clustered round the tiny green like distressed gentlefolk, hurried on in search of the 'real' Cotswolds. As Nat passed the 30mph sign he spotted a pub board hanging over the high street about a hundred yards further on and, as the dashboard clock told him that it was a few minutes past midday, he decided to try there for an early lunch. He was about to make for it when a brightly painted legend to the right caught his eye: 'Pensham's Garage'. He pulled the Mercedes up alongside the row of four petrol pumps.

He looked around at the premises as he refilled the car's tank. Mr Pensham, it was clear, dabbled in everything to do with motor vehicles. A row of second-hand Land Rovers and Japanese four tracks occupied one side of the forecourt, their prices displayed boldly on the wind-screens. Behind the pay kiosk-cum-shop was a large repair garage and, in the space to the left, stood two single-decker coaches, currently being hosed down by a youth in jeans and a grubby T-shirt. Nat entered the shop and presented his credit card to a twentyish girl who seemed absorbed in a magazine but who looked up with a welcoming smile. Any fresh face, Nat guessed, must relieve something of the boredom of her lonely vigil. Perhaps she would be more than ready for a little conversation.

'This seems to be a quiet place,' he offered.

'Oh, we're well off the beaten track here, sir,' she replied, tearing the pay slip from the till and holding it on the counter while he signed it.

'I'm surprised at that. Your manor house looks an impressive place. It is open to the public, isn't it?'

The smile left the young woman's face. 'No way, sir. Very very private, that place is.'

'That's a pity. I was hoping to get a chance to look round. Who owns it? Do you think if I go up –'

The girl shook her head very firmly. 'It's owned by London folk. They're not there very often. But you won't get anywhere near the house. They're paranoid about security – specially after what happened a few weeks ago.'

'Really?' Nat opened his eyes wide in fascinated interest. 'What was that?'

The cashier leaned forward, as though sharing a confidence. 'Someone was killed there,' she said.

'Killed! What, do you mean a bad accident?'

'That's what some people call it but there's those round here who'd give it a different name.'

'Well, who'd have thought it,' Nat said. 'Quiet place like this. Must have put the village on the map well and truly.'

A woman came in manoeuvring a pushchair through the narrow door. Nat's informant glanced at the newcomer and lowered her voice. 'No, sir. It was all brushed under the carpet.'

Nat realized that this source of information had dried up. He tried a different tack. 'I've just noticed a knocking noise under the bonnet. Is there any chance of getting someone to look at it for me?'

'If you pop round the back and ask for Mr Pensham I'm sure he'll help you out.'

As Nat thanked her and turned away she said suddenly, 'Haven't I seen you somewhere before?'

Nat grinned. 'I hope you don't say that to all your male customers.'

The girl giggled and Nat stepped quickly outside. In the large workshop one man in overalls was working underneath an old Ford which was on the ramp and another was on his back beneath a tractor. A corner of the building was partitioned off and the door to the room thus created bore the faded legend 'Office'. Nat knocked and put his head round the door. The interior looked as though it had been struck by a tidal wave of paper which had retreated leaving pools of letters, bills, pamphlets, old envelopes and sheets of newspaper on every flat surface, including the floor. A desk slewed across one corner had been even more heavily inundated than the stack of shelves beyond it. A large man sat behind it in an old swivel chair. Nat took him in at a glance: mid-forties, dark hair drawn back in a pigtail, rings through both ears, shirtsleeves rolled up to reveal heavily tattooed arms. He was speaking on a mobile phone.

'You tell him sixty grand cash or I go . . .' The man swung round and saw Nat. He held the instrument away from his ear. 'With you in a tick, mate.'

Nat hovered in the doorway. On the wall beyond the proprietor's head was a framed certificate proclaiming that Thomas Pensham was the south of England amateur middleweight boxing champion. Nat could not read the date but doubted whether the bulging form before him had been light on his feet for many a long year. Pensham was now staring at him, heavy brows raised.

'In a tick,' he repeated and waved towards the door.

Hastily Nat withdrew. He heard the chair creak and the tread of Pensham's feet as he crossed to the door and pushed against it to make sure that it was firmly shut.

He emerged a couple of minutes later, all smiles. 'Right, mate. I'm all yours. What's your pleasure?'

'It's my Merc,' Nat explained. 'It doesn't seem to be running as smoothly as usual. I'd rather not continue my journey till I know that it's OK.'

'Well, let's have a listen, shall we?'

They walked over to the car and while Pensham lifted the bonnet Nat turned the engine over. It purred into life with its usual Teutonic efficiency.

Pensham leaned over. 'When was she last serviced?' he asked.

'I can't remember,' Nat lied.

The mechanic nodded. 'Trouble with these German engines is they run sweetly but they expect to be pampered. Ah, there's your problem – camshaft.'

'Oh dear, is that bad?'

Pensham shrugged. 'Can't tell till we get the cover off and have a look. But you were certainly right to stop as soon as you were aware of trouble.'

'Can you fix it? Is it a long job?' Nat asked anxiously.

'In a hurry, are you?'

'Well, I'd like to be in Oxford sometime this afternoon.'

Pensham rubbed his hands on a rag. 'Well, tell you what, mate; you go and get yourself a bite of lunch and I'll put Steve on the job straight away. Come back in an hour or so and I'll have some news for you.'

'Well, that's very good of you.'

Pensham's large face creased itself into a smile. 'That's what we're here for. If I was you I'd try the Bull, just along the road. They do quite a good menu. Publican's name is Jack Lang. Tell him I sent you.'

Voluble in his thanks, Nat almost bowed himself out of the garage proprietor's presence.

The Red Bull was clearly a pub that catered more for locals than for passing trade. The only three customers were gathered together at one end of the bar and they all looked up with mild interest when Gye entered. He ordered a half of bitter from the man he assumed to be Jack Lang. 'Mr Pensham at the garage told me I'd get a good lunch here,' he suggested brightly.

By way of reply the barman, a thin, bald little man with a wistful moustache, waved a hand at a blackboard over the hearth in which the gas flames of an imitation log fire flickered weakly, and then returned to the conversation he was having with his regulars. Nat read the scrawled menu of largely microwaved items and decided that a ploughman's lunch was probably the safest choice. He walked along to the group in order to place his order which the landlord noted on a pad with what was apparently his habitual air of indifference, before passing it through a hatch to some unseen minion in the kitchen. Nat took the opportunity to accost his fellow customers.

Opening gambits about the weather and road conditions and the unreliability of modern motor cars brought little response. The locals remained in a tight, inward-facing group, excluding the foreigner as much by their body language as their taciturnity. Nat decided to be bolder. 'That's a fine-looking manor house you have here. I'm surprised it's not better known.'

The atmosphere changed dramatically. If cool before, it now became positively arctic. 'The folk at Tripletree don't have much to do with us or we with them,' an elderly man in tweeds announced in a tone designed to close that conversational avenue.

Nat declined to take the hint. 'Not exactly the local "big house", then? People there not major landholders any more?'

'The estate's big enough,' a man in cord trousers and red sweater replied, 'but common or garden folk like us don't get any access to it.'

Nat nodded knowingly. 'Ah, I see. It's the old story of townies coming in and buying up major properties. These people just don't understand the ways of the country, do they?'

'Don't understand and don't want to understand,' Red Sweater agreed. 'There was a plan . . .' He immediately fell silent as his companions frowned and the older man gave an almost imperceptible shake of the head.

'Have the present owners been here long?' Nat asked the question but sensed that it was a bridge too far.

At that moment the landlord reappeared. 'I've put your ploughman's on that table by the fire, sir,' he announced. 'It's a bit chilly today. I don't suppose you'll want another beer, being as you're driving.'

Nat had no alternative but to retire into splendid isolation to eat his solitary lunch. Moodily he reflected that all his foray into Coln St Ippolyts had achieved was confirmation of the ill-feeling that existed between the village and the Myleses and the likelihood of being ripped off by the local garage owner. He had almost finished his meal when he sensed a change in the room's atmosphere. His back was to the door but he heard it open and someone walk in. All conversation stopped and an almost tangible silence descended on the bar. Nat turned.

In the middle of the room two women were standing. One was a dumpy figure in her fifties, a thatch of wiry white hair out-thrust from beneath a green woollen hat, her body swathed in a large, floor-length black cloak. Her companion was a diminutive creature, some twenty years younger, more conventionally though less becomingly dressed in a belted raincoat which made her appear more shapeless than she presumably was. The elder woman commanded the room. She stood stock still, her head swivelling, her gaze sweeping round in an arc like the beam of a lighthouse. It fastened on Nat and stopped. With three strides she reached his table, plucked out the chair opposite him and sat down. Behind her the buzz of conversation resumed. Her acolyte moved to the bar. Everything seemingly returned to normal.

'Won't you join me, Ms . . .? May I get you a drink?' Nat remembered the advice his father had dinned into him years before: 'When in doubt fall back on good manners'. He smiled and observed the woman's face. It was the colour of parchment and the black eyes and brows, and even the layered lines across the forehead, gave the appearance of having been drawn upon it.

The eyes now fastened, unblinking, upon his own. It was, Nat thought, rather like the game children play to see who can outstare the other. He won. The newcomer cast a quick glance behind her. 'Mildred will fetch me a drink. You are Dr Nathaniel Gye.'

Nat nodded. 'Unmasked,' he said. 'And that means you have the advantage of me.'

'You may call me Morgana. I wrote to you after your disgraceful programme on wicca. All I received by way of reply was a churlish note from one of your underlings which quite missed the point.'

'We receive hundreds of letters. It would be impossible to respond to every complaint and query in detail. And I didn't do a programme on witchcraft. I was comparing the survival of several ancient beliefs. Earth magic was just one.'

Morgana waved a hand. Her companion appeared silently beside her, placed a double gin on the table and as noiselessly withdrew. 'It's of no consequence. What I've come to tell you is that I know why you're here.'

'Then you know more than I do. I was beginning to think I was wasting my time.'

'Don't play with words. That's a foolish academic exercise. There are spiritual forces at work here which you don't even begin to comprehend. Leave it to those of us who have the power to counteract this great evil.'

Nat stared back thoughtfully. 'And what exactly is this evil?'

The white witch swallowed half of the spirit at a gulp. 'Tripletree House has been possessed for centuries by negative powers. They were only kept within bounds by members of the Craft. Those who went before us maintained a ring of protection round the manor and the village. But now they have gained control of the new owners and the warfare has intensified. You've already seen that it has led to denial of the life force. That should warn you not to become involved.'

'By denial of the life force I take it you mean death.'

'I mean what you would call murder. There has been one. If you persist in probing it with your puny, earthbound intellect, there will be more.'

Nat had the rare experience of being fazed. 'May I ask how you claim to know so much about my affairs?'

The parchment face crumpled into a smile. 'So, the great psychologist is baffled.' Morgana sneered at him. 'There are more things in heaven and earth, Dr Gye, than are dreamed of in your modern so-called science.' She tossed back the rest of the gin and rose abruptly. Seconds later she and her human shadow had left as suddenly as they had arrived.

Nat concluded his meal very thoughtfully and, with a nod to the landlord, took his leave. As he stepped back into the village street he had a sense that the atmosphere of Coln St Ippolyts had somehow changed. Grey clouds were now massed overhead, the pavements were deserted and no vehicles passed the door of the Red Bull. He strained his ears to catch the comforting sounds of daily life. Nothing. No voices, no bustle of human activity, not even any birdsong. It was as though the entire community had withdrawn into itself, determined to have nothing to do with the intruder.

Nat shook his head. 'Don't be stupid,' he muttered to himself as he turned to walk briskly back to the garage.

Pensham dispelled the mood of foreboding. He was still his hail-fellow-well-met self as Nat went up to him in the doorway of the workshop. The overweight proprietor was munching a sandwich and behind him one of his mechanics was bent over the open bonnet of the Mercedes. 'Good job you stopped when you did, mate,' Pensham mumbled through a mouthful of bread, ham and lettuce. 'She wouldn't have taken you much further.'

'Oh dear, can you fix it?'

The large man looped a thumb through the belt beneath his overhanging belly. 'They haven't invented the engine yet that Tom Pensham can't fix. Don't you worry, mate. We'll have you on the road as soon as we've fitted a replacement gasket. I've already sent over to Chippy – Chipping Norton – for one.'

'Will it be an expensive job?' Nat asked anxiously.

Pensham dropped the crusts of his sandwich into an old oil drum serving as a dustbin. 'Well,' he said slowly, 'it's not so much the parts – though they're pricy enough on these foreign cars – it's the labour. Right bugger these Merc camshafts are. Dead difficult to get at. Still,' he beamed reassuringly, 'young Steve here has very nimble fingers. You give us another hour, mate, and we should be done.'

Nat used the time to take in the 'sights' of Coln St Ippolyts. The village had shaken off its lunchtime slumber. Customers passed in and out of the shop and the post office. Three small children played with a puppy on the diminutive green under the watchful eyes of two young mums who chatted while they slowly propelled their pushchairs. It was all reassuringly normal and Nat thought how fanciful his earlier impression had been.

There was little to see. The church was locked and the churchyard was too overgrown and sad to invite inspection. The classical façades of three of the houses fronting the green had some pretensions to architectural distinction but the columns flanking their doors were pitted and peeling and the ornate capitals crowning them had weathered to a smoothness. One dwelling had been divided into flats and the ground floor of its neighbour was now a doctor's surgery.

Nat walked the length of the main street to where it ended abruptly and ploughed fields began. To the left was the opening of what had once been a drive, now closed by a gate of new iron and strands of barbed wire. The stone gateposts were topped by carved lions holding heraldic shields and Nat recognized the Bygot arms displayed in several of the rooms in the Myleses' residence. This was obviously a disused entrance to the Tripletree estate. Near the gate an old billboard lay on its side in the hedge, as though blown over by the wind. Nat craned his neck to read the lettering, partly obscured by mud and leaves. It announced that this was the site for a development of fifty-five, three and four-bedroomed houses to be built by J. Holt and Sons.

He had just begun to retrace his steps when his own car approached and pulled up beside him. He looked at his watch and saw that scarcely half of the hour had elapsed that Pensham had indicated would be necessary for the work. Steve, the mechanic, lowered the nearside window and called out for him to jump in.

'That was quick,' Nat said, as he slipped into the passenger seat.

The young man merely nodded by way of reply. He drove on to where a farm entrance allowed him to do a three-point turn and headed the Mercedes back towards the garage. As they approached Pensham's business premises Nat saw a figure stride across the forecourt, a long black cloak billowing around it. Steve pulled in beside the pumps, jumped out quickly, removing the protective plastic cover from the driver's seat as he did so, and disappeared towards the back premises. At the same moment Tom Pensham emerged from the shop.

'There you are, mate, all done,' he said, in a tone that was almost dismissive.

'Thank you very much.' Nat smiled. 'How much do I owe you?'

Pensham shrugged. 'Oh, let's say a tenner, shall we?'

'Ten pounds? But I thought –'

'Yeah, well, when we had a closer look we realized it was only a matter of some adjustment.'

'Oh, that's good, I –'

'You can pay Amy in the shop.' Without another word Pensham turned and hurried away.

Nat settled his bill and drove out of Coln St Ippolyts, several questions blundering around in his mind.

68

Concerns of a Lawman

Thursday 12 October
General opinion in Coln: Tracy Pensham was murdered.
Why's that?

Nat stared at the Juniper Myles file on his computer screen,
the only pool of light in his study. He rubbed his eyes and
leaned back in the chair. He was tired but unwilling to give
up until he had reduced all his impressions of the day to
some sort of order. His fingers moved over the keys.

a)   Resentment against new people at manor.
     The Myleses thoroughly detested. Any reasons for
     this other than blind prejudice?
b)   Was Tracy a popular woman in the village?
     Don't know. Myles says she was a tart. Something
     going on between the two of them? Tom Pensham
     a grieving widower? No evidence of it. Every-
     thing seems like business as usual at his garage.
c)   Could there be any truth in the rumours?
     Amy, the garage attendant, says suspicious nature
     of death covered up.
     Morgana, presumably leader of a local wicca
     coven, claims to know Tracy was foully done to
     death. Identifies spiritual forces at work in Coln
     Manor. A powerful woman with a lot of clout in
     the village.
Local folk seem paranoid about keeping lid on the affair.

If convinced one of their own has been deliberately drowned why don't they want the crime investigated?

a)   Whether there was a murder or not, they want to keep the police out of their hair.

Other guilty secrets? Morgana says any attempt to probe Tracy's death will lead to other fatalities. Melodramatic nonsense, perhaps, but fear, hate and suspicion have created a toxic atmosphere.

   T FIELDS*

b)   Could it be

'You coming to bed?' Kathryn slid into the room, wearing a bathrobe and smelling of jasmine. She rested her hands on his shoulders. 'This Myles business really has got under your skin, hasn't it?'

Nat yawned. 'There's something about that place. Something very wrong. Something . . .'

'Evil?' She spun the chair round and moved on to his lap. 'Surely the great rationalist hasn't come round to believing in *dark* forces.'

He put his arms round her. 'I met a witch today but her spells were nothing like as powerful as yours.'

Kathryn pouted and pressed her nose to his. 'Sounds as though I have a rival.' The words came in a half-whisper, half-growl.

Nat laughed. 'If you could have seen Morgana you'd have realized you have nothing to fear from that direction.' He shook his head at the recollection. 'Extraordinary woman, though.'

'In what way?'

Nat described his encounter with the witch.

'Hmm, spooky,' Kathryn responded. 'What do you think she meant about more deaths?'

'Oh, just being theatrical, I guess. Her whole life's a

---

* T fields = psychological/emotional vibrations supposedly resonating through matter.

performance. You should see the way she sweeps majestically round the place in her enormous cloak. Very Margaret Rutherford.'

'Yet she did know who you were and why you'd gone to Coln.'

'Not much mystery to that. She knows me from the box. She's convinced that I'm the arch enemy of her and her kind. Doubtless she saw me in the village and grabbed the opportunity for a showdown.'

'Oh, and how do you explain her knowing why you'd gone to Coln?'

Nat shrugged. 'She must have heard that I was at the party back in August and put two and two together.'

'Isn't that what you academics call tinkering with the facts to fit the hypothesis?'

'Only if the alternative hypothesis is untenable. Since I don't believe that Mistress Morgana, or whatever her real name is, used some form of magical divination to discover my whereabouts and probe my mind, I prefer my rationalist's explanation.'

'Well, seems you've run into a brick wall. If the folk at Coln are giving you the big freeze there's no way you can probe their guilty secrets.'

Nat was silent for a moment. 'I was just thinking . . . Do you remember the name of that policeman who led the investigation at the manor? The one who gave us all a little lecture before setting his minions to take down our names and addresses.'

'Dave Mitchenor,' his wife replied promptly.

'That was quick. He must have made quite an impression on you.'

'Well, he was rather gorgeous – thick blond hair and dark, come-to-bed eyes. I remember thinking that he was remarkably young to be a chief inspector. Actually, I felt rather sorry for him, out of his depth among the celebs and the legal top brass.'

Nat grinned, recollecting the scene. 'Yes, all the

impatient, self-important people wanting to scurry away and demanding to know how long they were to be kept waiting. I thought he coped very well.'

'So, what do you want with the Adonis of the local CID?'

'Oh, I just thought I might have a word.'

Kathryn shook her long hair so that it brushed against his cheek. 'Nathaniel Gye, you are an impossible man. When something's elusive you go after it like a stag in rutt. But if it's right under your nose you don't even see it.'

'What don't I see?'

She took his hand and pushed it inside her robe. 'Me! Now for God's sake switch that machine off and come to bed before I explode with desire.'

Their love-making was energetic, frenzied, desperate – bodies asserting what minds had begun to question. For a long time afterwards both of them lay silently sleepless, embracing their own thoughts.

Nat's father, currently canon residentiary at Wanchester Cathedral, had always collected aphorisms – short-cut sermons, as he called them – and frequently quoted them to his children as signposts pointing the way to a happy life. They were a standing joke between Nat and his sisters but many of them had done their work very effectively in that all three of them remembered the pithy sayings dinned into them since childhood. One epigram the Reverend Edmund Gye had repeated often, with particular earnestness since his son had become something of a mini-celebrity, was an *obiter dictum* of Einstein, 'Try not to become a man of success but rather try to become a man of value.' Yet, as Nat increasingly discovered, success could be a very useful commodity. It was certainly a master key that opened a great variety of doors. So, when he wrote a carefully worded note to DCI David Mitchenor of the Oxfordshire Constabulary reminding him of their earlier brief encounter and asking if the inspector could spare him a little time to assist with a new TV series that he was preparing, the reply was prompt and affirmative.

They met at one of the county's rural restaurants, a mecca for gourmets who appreciated the food and wine created by one of Europe's master chefs and for expense account businessmen who were ignorant of the nuances of haute cuisine but enjoyed the prestige conferred on them by their patronage of a five star, exclusive establishment where they were served with flattering deference in an ambience of hushed luxury. Nat booked a lunch table by a window overlooking a tranquil autumn landscape of turning trees reflected in a wide pool. He arrived early in order to be ready to receive his guest, who appeared with precise punctuality.

'Often passed this place,' the detective said as he shook hands and took his seat. 'Never thought I'd actually ever eat here. Bit beyond a humble copper's means.'

Nat surveyed his guest approvingly. He was certainly, as Kate had suggested, a man of physical presence. Mitchenor had the litheness of a sportsman or, at least, someone who took regular exercise. But more than that, he came across as a man who was very straightforward, who knew his mind and spoke it. 'The least I could do in return for your giving up your time was to offer you a decent meal.' Nat said.

'Why me, Dr Gye?' Mitchenor asked frankly.

'Most people call me Nat – short for Nathaniel. You're David, aren't you?'

'Dave.'

'Well, Dave, first let me test a theory on you. I believe that there are, broadly, two kinds of criminal mind. I'm talking here about deliberate criminality, not crimes of passion and impulse offences, which obviously make up a large part of your case load. Some thieves, murderers, arsonists, fraudsters and what have you know perfectly

73

well that what they do is wrong. Either they don't care or they actually get a kick out of defying the law and the standards decent people try to live by. I guess most hardened criminals come into that category.'

Mitchenor nodded.

Gye went on, 'What interests me is the other kind – the man or woman who really believes that the appalling act he or she is committing is morally justified: it's normal, an expression of their persona, something they have to do, it's predestined or even dictated by some higher power.'

'Nutcases, you mean?'

Nat smiled. 'Ah, now that's the point. Society has this tendency to label as mentally disturbed or ill those who flout its conventions. We give them names – psychopath, paedophile, satanic ritualist, religious fanatic – as though that explains the phenomena, and we shut them away for as long as the law allows.'

'Quite right, too.'

'I agree with you. I'm no wishy-washy liberal who wants to go easy on people who are a menace to their neighbours. On the other hand, I do think we should fall over backwards to consider the ways in which people become alienated from society. When a middle-aged man, to all outward appearances normal and mild-mannered, rapes and murders a five-year-old girl, then proceeds to dismember her and turn her into stew for his supper, we all recoil with horror. But he, quite sincerely, only regards his taste for human flesh as "a bit unusual". Now how do you begin to get inside such a mind? And how do you relate such aberrant behaviour to changes in social attitudes? For centuries we locked up or lynched homosexuals but regarded incest as a less serious crime. Now, society's judgement of such behaviour has come full circle. We used to burn witches and religious heretics. Such people still exist among us but now we regard most of them as harmless oddballs.'

At that moment the head waiter presented them with

menus and a wine list encased in heavily embossed covers and there was a long pause while they made their selection and ordered. Throughout this process Nat was aware that his guest was observing him closely; weighing him up as he might a suspect in the interview room. He realized that it would be no easy task prizing the information he wanted out of this canny professional.

Eventually Mitchenor remarked, 'What you were saying is all very interesting but I'm no theorist. I don't have the leisure to sit back and think about why a con-man swindles old ladies out of their life savings or a sexual pervert preys on small children. I just try to bang them up so that they won't do it again for a long time. We coppers enforce the law; we don't make it.'

Nat nodded enthusiastically. 'Exactly! You're at the sharp end, dealing with all those undesirables the rest of us would rather not soil our hands with. In my opinion that's something the viewing public can't be reminded of too often. The impression most people have of you and your colleagues is what they pick up from the soap operas that pass for TV crime series, and, let's face it, they don't exactly show the police in a very favourable light – all those sexual predators, bullies and coppers on the take.'

Mitchenor shrugged, relaxing. 'I suppose it makes good fiction – as long as people understand that's all it is.'

'Well, you're more indulgent than I am. Now, I can't pretend that my proposed programmes are going to set the record straight but what I want to do is explore a few specific cases with intelligent, hands-on experts, like yourself. It could be that one result will be that viewers will appreciate how tough it is doing what you say: interpreting what society really wants of its police force and trying to deliver the goods.'

Conversation now flowed easily, ranging over a variety of topics from the policeman's unhappy lot to psychological profiling of suspects; from the shortcomings of criminal legislation to some of Mitchenor's more successful

75

cases. They were part-way through their main course before Nat cautiously broached the death of Tracy Pensham.

'That sad business at Coln St Ippolyts must have been a tricky job for you to cope with – all those bigwigs to handle with kid gloves. I thought you and your team managed it remarkably well.'

Mitchenor agreed enthusiastically. 'It wasn't my favourite assignment of the year. No investigating officer likes having his superiors breathing down his neck and that night I had to cope with the chief constable and most of the local magistrates, not to mention several circuit judges and that bloody Myles man trying to tell me how to do my job.'

'You share the widely held opinion about Sheldon Myles, then?'

'He and his wife seem to have done just about everything they could think of to alienate the locals.'

'Such as?' Nat tried not show his eagerness.

'Are you a friend of theirs?'

'No, I was at the party because they wanted my wife to do a prestige piece about it in her magazine.'

'In that case I don't mind telling you that a lot of people at Coln have got it in for the Myleses. There's Jack Holt, for example. He's the wealthiest man in the area, ex-chairman of the parish council, runs a big building firm based in Oxford. He'd set up with the previous owner of the manor to buy a chunk of the estate for a new housing development. It would have meant a lot for the village, as well as putting another million or so in Holt's pocket. He thought he had the deal all sewn up, nice and legal. He didn't reckon with Myles's knowledge of the law. As soon as Myles took over, he pulled out of the contract. Holt took him to court – and lost. Cost him a packet one way and another.'

'I see.'

The inspector was now warming to his subject. 'Then

there was a set-to Myles had with Estelle Simpson.' He put down his knife and fork and leaned forward. 'This will interest you, seeing as you're into the supernatural. Ms Simpson calls herself Morgana and claims to be an "earth priestess" or some such. She publishes her own books on magic – does quite well out of them, I believe. It's amazing what rubbish people will read. Locally she runs a witches' coven. Harmless bunch of cranks. She's never given us any trouble, apart from sometimes offering her services to solve crimes.'

'Offers which you refused?'

'What do you think?' Mitchenor grinned.

'So how did Myles get up her nose?'

'Morgana and her faithful followers used to carry out their midsummer ceremonies on Tripletree Hill – that's the one behind the big house. Perfectly peaceful bit of non-sense; no blood sacrifices or ritual deflowering of maidens. They just dressed up in funny clothes and greeted the dawn with chants and incantations. Or they did – until last year. That was when Myles and two of his retainers burst in in the middle of their goings-on waving shotguns. There was a scuffle and a couple of Morgana's people got hurt. She tried to bring a charge of criminal assault. Myles counteracted with an action for trespass. No prizes for guessing who won.'

'I see what you mean. The Myleses don't seem to have any interest in winning friends and influencing people.'

'You can say that again. The situation's been getting worse month after month. The local cop shop has had it up to here with Coln St Ippolyts. If it's not someone in the village complaining about Myles it's Myles complaining about someone in the village. The locals wasted no time in hitting back.'

'In what way?'

'Oh, petty things for the most part: hedges broken down, slogans painted on walls, and there was a very unpleasant business with a cat.'

'Cat?'

'Someone strung a dead cat up to one of the trees on Tripletree Hill with a placard round its neck. I won't repeat what it said about the lord of the manor but it was very explicit. It takes a lot to shock the boys in blue over at Chipping Norton but that incident turned a few stomachs. Myles complained directly to the chief constable that time. Said he was fed up with people prowling his grounds and getting into the house, and he demanded police protection. All he got was a sympathetic ear and the offer of a visit from our security advice officers.'

'*Were* people breaking into his house?'

'We never found any evidence of it but Myles insisted someone was getting in and upsetting his wife.' The policeman drained the last of an excellent Gevrey-Chambertin from his glass and a waiter immediately stepped forward to refill it. 'Of course,' Mitchenor went on, 'he wasn't at loggerheads with everyone. There were rumours about him and Tracy Pensham.'

'Oh?'

'When the new owners started work on the house and they hadn't taken on any staff they employed Mrs Pensham to keep an eye on the place while they weren't there; supervise the builders and the landscape gardeners, deal with tradesmen, that sort of thing. According to the wagging tongues, she and Myles had more than a master-servant relationship. I don't suppose there's anything to the story and, if there is, it's probably a matter of six of one and half a dozen of the other. Our Tracy wasn't exactly the faithful little wife.'

'Did her husband know about the rumours?'

Mitchenor laughed. 'What, Tom Pensham? Probably.' He was suddenly serious. 'Now, there's a collar I'd like to feel. Tom's the local wheeler-dealer. He's into anything and everything that might make money and he's not fussed whether it's legal or not. So far he's been very clever but, one of these days, he'll step over the line and then we'll have him.' He yawned. 'Sorry. Too many late nights recently. We're short-staffed as ever. If you could see the pile of paper on my desk . . . Where was I?'

'Tom Pensham.'

'Oh yes. I'd love to believe he'd done his old woman in in a fit of jealous rage. That would suit my book very well.'

Nat looked up sharply from his plate. 'There was no question of Tracy Pensham being "done in", was there?'

Mitchenor frowned and concentrated on plying his knife and fork. Nat was afraid he had pushed his luck too far. However, after a long pause, the policeman muttered, 'Not according to the coroner.'

'Are you not happy with the official verdict?'

The inspector stared for a long time across the table. Nat could see that he was considering carefully how much to say. Eventually, he shrugged. 'Of course I'm satisfied with the verdict. Young women don't get murdered in the presence of the chief constable and the cream of county society, do they?'

'You tell me.'

'There was no sign of anything suspicious on Tracy's body except the mark of a blow to the front of the head. Forensics couldn't say how she came by it. She could have sustained it when she fell into the water.'

'But you'd have liked more time to investigate?'

'Not at all. Like I say, my desk is inches deep in paper. The words "case closed" are as music to my ears.' Mitchenor worried the last morsel of *gigot à l'Avignonnaise* around his plate and Nat knew that he was lying.

Later they said goodbye in the car park, Nat promising to keep in touch with the inspector about his progress on the new series. Mitchenor nodded with a wry smile on his face. They were standing beside his car when he took a business card from his wallet and scribbled a number on the back.

'That's my mobile,' he said. 'Don't ever hesitate to call

me.' He slipped into the driver's seat and switched on the engine. Then, just as he was about to pull away, he lowered the side window. '*If* I'd investigated the Pensham case further, you're one of the witnesses I'd have wanted to interview. Tracy's conversation with you. All that stuff about Myles getting his comeuppance. Interesting.'

'Yes I was intrigued by it,' Nat said.

'Well, perhaps there's not so much paper on your desk. Anyway, your hands are less tied than mine. Thanks again for the lunch.'

The car reversed out of its parking spot, then headed down the drive towards the main road.

Visiting the Past (1)

The following Monday Nat had a meeting arranged in London with his television producer, Malcolm Glover. He drove to Cambridge station, dropping the boys off at their junior school en route. Edmund, as the elder, claimed the passenger seat and was in talkative mood.

'After school Christopher's mum is taking us swimming and then we're all going to judo.'

Nat slowed for traffic lights. 'I think the judo's tomorrow.'

'We had a competition last week and Christopher won but Mr Hapgood said I was very nearly as good.'

'Well, Christopher is a bit bigger than you.'

'Yes, but I beat him sometimes. When I'm as big as him I'll always win.'

'Sure you will.' Nat turned the car into the quiet road where the private school was situated. 'Right, have you got everything ready?'

'I'm better at swimming than Christopher is.'

The car pulled into the kerb and Nat concentrated on extracting his sons together with all their belongings.

As they joined the file of children and parents passing through the gateway, Edmund looked up. 'When we go to live in America can Christopher come, too?' Then, spotting a friend, he ran off without waiting for an answer.

When he reached King's Cross station and went in search of a taxi Nat was still angry. He had tried to use the one-hour train journey to do some marking of student essays but all he could think of was that Kathryn had broken their pact to say nothing to the children about her possible transfer to the Manhattan office. Was she trying to force the pace, make him discuss something he shrank from facing? Very well, then, they *would* talk about it and he would be calm and rational and together they would weigh up the pros and cons of Kate taking the new job. Better still, he would phone Greg in New York and have a frank man-to-man chat. Kate might accuse him of going behind her back but, what the heck, she was the one who had broken the truce.

With an effort he pushed these thoughts aside as the taxi reached Soho. Black Box Productions occupied first floor offices overlooking the square, and Malcolm, a bulky, bearded man of infectious enthusiasm, welcomed Nat effusively into his sanctum. It was neo-1920s, all chrome and black leather and elemental curves. They sank into armchairs that were more comfortable than they looked and were joined within a few minutes by Malcolm's assistant producer, Susan Avery-White, earnest-looking and hugging a clipboard to her chest. She poured coffees from a machine in the corner and they settled down to business.

'I'm sure we'll have no difficulty selling a third series,' Malcolm began. '*Is There Anybody There?* went down a bomb in the States and we've virtually tied up contracts in Canada and Australia. Translation deals notoriously take forever to fix but our people tell me that talks are going well in Frankfurt, Tokyo and all stations to God knows where. Of course, we've still got to get the concept right for another batch of programmes. It's always true what they say in this business: it doesn't matter how impressive your record is; you're only as good as your next idea. So, Nat, what brainwave have you got to share with us?'

'Evil,' Nat said succinctly. Then, as the others looked at him enquiringly, he continued. 'We've touched on it here and there in earlier programmes and I think the time is right to sharpen our focus.'

Malcolm nodded vigorously. 'Like it! What do you think, Sue?' He turned to his auburn-haired assistant. 'Sue's great on concepts; she knows instinctively what Joe Public will latch on to,' he explained.

Susan tapped a pencil against the end of her nose. 'Mmm,' she mused thoughtfully. 'Could be good as long as it doesn't get too philosophical. How do you see the series breaking down, Nat?'

'First we'd have to explore what we mean by evil. What evidence is there for the existence of objective evil forces? Poltergeist activity, demon possession, voodoo and so on. We could use some of that Haitian footage we couldn't fit into the last series. That would lead us naturally to satanic rituals. We ought to revisit the notorious Orkneys case of a few years ago. There are still some big question marks there.'

'ITN has archive footage on that,' Susan said. 'We could trace some of the victims; see if they're ready to talk more freely after all this time.'

'The second programme I'd like to devote to what I call "mind games". People's fears leave them exposed to exponents of so-called "cures". I'd examine exorcism, white witchcraft and the pseudo-science of hypnotherapy. There's a lot of evidence now on the use and misuse of hypnotic regression and the dangers of implanted memories – practitioners "discovering" repressed recollections of childhood abuse. I want to expose that as a definite modern evil.'

'That's sure to provoke a lot of interactive response,' Malcolm said. 'You're happy to be on a chatline again?'

Nat nodded. 'Of course. Susan, on the business of regression therapy, could you set your bloodhounds on the scent of a character who calls himself Dr Caradoc Owen? It's a bit of a challenge, I'm afraid. You won't find him on any professional register; he's not a graduate of a British university; and he's almost certainly working under an assumed name.' He grinned. 'Apart from that, tracking him down should be a doddle.'

Susan made a note on her pad and Malcolm said, 'Our Sue loves a challenge. If anyone can find your Dr Owen, she can.'

'Certain avenues do suggest themselves,' the assistant commented with a serene smile. 'How important is it to find this character, Nat?'

'I'd say very. I suspect that he's typical of the worst kind of shady, pseudo-scientific operator. I'd love to pin him down in an interview situation.'

'OK, leave it with me. Where do we go from there, programme-wise?'

'Crime, I think. Let's look at convicted men and women most people would happily label as evil. How do paedophiles justify their actions? What has gone wrong in the minds of psychopaths? Is psychological profiling all it's cracked up to be? There are several police officers who have interesting cases to talk about.' Nat paused. 'Those, it seems to me, are the three obvious subject areas. They would leave us a final programme to tie up any loose ends.'

They spent an hour discussing fine detail, after which Nat, having declined Malcolm's offer of lunch, went to the British Library to consult a deposit of papers concerning the work of Thomas Lethbridge, pioneer researcher into the paranormal. He crossed the wide forecourt in front of the impressive new building's brick façade, passed through the glass doors and headed for the reading room. It was at the last moment that he changed his mind and turned towards the cafeteria. He would, he decided, have coffee and a sandwich now, in order to be able to put in a couple of hours uninterrupted on the manuscripts afterwards. It was while he was paying for his modest lunch that he heard someone speak his name.

'Dr Gye, isn't it?'

Nat turned, tray in hand and saw a rotund, bespectacled figure standing, somewhat apologetically, before him, in jeans and a well-worn tweed jacket.

'I don't suppose you remember me. Paul Greer. We met –'

'At Coln Manor. Yes. Of course. You gave us that excellent guided tour.' Nat smiled. 'It took me a moment to recognize you out of Puritan garb.'

'What a terrible night that was.' The historian's eyes were rheumy behind the lenses. 'I've a table over here. Would you care to join me?'

'Do you do a lot of research in the British Library?' Nat asked, depositing his tray.

'It's become a second home over the years. I miss the old British Museum reading room, of course. It had a wonderful atmosphere. But I must admit it's a lot easier to work since the library moved here. And you?'

They talked scholars' talk for a while but it took very little time for the conversation to drift back to the night of the party.

'Everything seemed to go wrong, didn't it?' Nat observed. 'The lights, the fireworks. It was as though the event was jinxed.' He went on, hoping to provoke a reaction, 'There seem to be some places which attract trouble, just as there are some people who are apparently doomed to suffer every kind of misfortune.'

The response was stronger than Nat had expected. Greer seemed suddenly annoyed. He held his cup half-way to his lips. 'That ghost stuff and nonsense! It was all over the local papers after Mrs Pensham's death. I had sensation-seeking journalists on the phone for days. Idiots! People imagine that because of the dreadful goings-on at the time of the Civil War the place must be haunted. Well, I've never seen any chain-rattling spectres there and the Johnsons certainly weren't bothered by "things that go bump in the night".'

Nat hastened to set the record straight. 'I wasn't suggest-

85

ing anything of the sort. It's just that someone was obviously out to sabotage the party.'

'That's possible, I suppose, but if they did, it was from this side of the grave.'

'You mentioned the Johnsons,' Nat said. 'Were they the family who lived at Coln Manor before the Myleses?'

'That's right. They inherited it from Mrs Johnson's aunt, who was the last of the Denvers who bought the estate from the Sumptions in 1867.' Greer was now in his element and Nat was happy to let him continue his telling of the Tripletree story. 'Charming people, the Johnsons. They had quality, breeding. Roger was an airline executive and they had three children. I knew them well. They let me potter around the place at will and were always interested in the snippets of information I came up with.' His face took on a sad smile. 'They really cared.' Greer finished his coffee before continuing. 'Of course, they couldn't afford to live at the manor but they loved the place too much to contemplate selling it. The children in particular adored it. I can see them now, playing hide and seek around the cellars for hours on end. The family spent all the school holidays at Tripletree, and Roger and Amanda went down most weekends, usually spending all their time on decorating and running repairs.' He sighed. 'I'm afraid the place ruined them. Well,' he corrected himself, 'of course, one can't blame what happened on the house.'

'Another tragedy?' Nat asked.

Greer nodded. 'They poured all their own money into Tripletree. Then they sold off some bits of land. Then the pictures went up for auction one by one, followed by the furniture. It was no use. The estate soaked up every penny and still demanded more. Eventually they offered it to the National Trust but they won't take on historic buildings without massive endowments.'

'So the place became a real millstone. Was that when the Myleses appeared as saviours?'

Greer gave a cynical laugh. 'Oh, no. Far from it. No, if

there was a shining white knight he appeared in the unlikely shape of Tom Pensham, Tracy's husband. Tracy got on well with the Johnsons. But then,' he added ambiguously, 'she got on well with everyone. You couldn't really help liking her. She was very friendly – but shrewd with it. Definitely a cut above her husband when it came to intelligence. She acted as a sort of chatelaine for the Johnsons; looked after Tripletree when they were away. Where was I? Oh yes, Tom Pensham. He came up with a business proposition. I don't know all the details but he has wealthy contacts who were prepared to put up capital. Roger interested his own company, Euroair. Jack Holt, the local great panjandrum, and some of his cronies were in on it, too. The idea was to turn Tripletree into a luxury conference centre which would be hired out to multinationals, foreign embassies, and the like.'

'Sounds like a good scheme.'

Greer sniffed. 'Seemed sacrilegious to me. Still, I suppose corporate financiers are the new aristocracy. Anyway, it all came unstuck.'

'How so?'

'The partners invested heavily in setting the thing up – planning permission, lawyers, architects, and so on. Then, just when the deal seemed all done and dusted, Euroair pulled out. It was devastating for the others, especially poor Roger. He'd mortgaged the house up to the roof and now he was left with a worthless pile and a debt he hadn't the slightest hope of servicing. *That* was when Mr Sheldon Myles stepped in.'

'And bought the estate for a song?'

'Exactly so. The price he offered was derisory. It didn't cover half the principal and interest weighing down on Roger's shoulders. But the poor devil had no choice but to accept.'

'What happened to him?'

'Depression. Collapse of the marriage. Then, one winter's day, he drove off without telling anyone where he was going. Weeks later the police found the burned-out shell of his car at the foot of a Cornish cliff.'

'How awful for the family.'

'Yes, but the final tragedy was that the insurance company refused to pay up on Roger's life policy for seven years until what they call "presumption of death" can be established. There was no sign of his body, you see, and though the tides had washed over the wreckage scores of times – quite enough to remove all traces – the insurers could wriggle out of their commitment. Bastards!'

'You were obviously fond of the Johnsons,' Nat responded.

The historian nodded.

'And the Myleses?'

Greer shrugged. 'She's a real lady. Comes from a long line of high court judges. Knows the meaning of "noblesse oblige".'

'But not him?'

The other man scowled. 'He's no gentleman. Not to mince words, he's a crook. He doesn't deserve Tripletree.'

'But you keep up your association with the place.'

'Difficult to tear myself away after all these years, and Mrs Myles has been glad of my help.'

'You've tutored her on the history of Coln Manor, I assume.'

'Yes, she's a very enthusiastic student as well as having an extremely keen mind. I've never known anyone master the intricacies of seventeenth-century legal scribing and secretary hand as quickly as her. The instruction hasn't been all one way by any means. She has unravelled a number of obscure passages in the archive that have puzzled me.'

'There are a lot of estate documents, are there?'

'Boxes and boxes of them. That's mainly what I've been working on over the years – preserving and cataloguing the muniments. It should really be a full-time job for someone but I don't see Mr Myles paying a qualified person to do it, not when he has Muggins here who's silly enough to do it for love. Actually, I shouldn't complain. I live in the next village and the Myleses let me come and go as I please, so it's scarcely an arduous chore.'

Nat saw a possible new line of enquiry. 'Do the names of servants ever appear in the records?'

'They're listed in the account books. Why?'

'I suppose you don't happen to recall whether the name Whiddon features on any of the lists? She may have been a maid to the mistress of the house sometime in the 1630s or '40s.'

Greer pondered. 'Whiddon, Whiddon . . . No, doesn't ring a bell. It's certainly not a local name. Most of the servants came from surrounding villages. Is it important? I could have a trawl through the relevant documents next time I go to the house. Can you give me any more to go on?'

'Mrs Myles told me a story about this woman known as Gunny Whiddon. She apparently got involved in a fight with another servant and it had fatal consequences – for both of them.'

'How strange. Mrs Myles has never mentioned it to me. I wonder where she came across it. Spats between below-stairs staff weren't usually considered worthy of note.'

'Might there be any contemporary court records? According to the story, this Whiddon woman was put on trial for murder.'

'Quarter sessions papers would be in the Oxford Record Office but I know they're incomplete.'

'I suppose that's where Mrs Myles found the information.'

Greer shook his head firmly. 'I very much doubt that. When I said that she is a keen student I didn't mean that she pursues her enquiries far and wide. She confines herself to the Tripletree documents. If there's anything that needs checking elsewhere I always do it. Shall I –'

'No, no,' Nat said quickly. 'It was just idle curiosity on my part.'

Later, as he sat at his appointed desk waiting for the Lethbridge papers to be brought to him, Nat went over the scant details of June's Gunny Whiddon story. Such events when vividly recalled under hypnosis were almost always the product of information emerging from the unconscious. Someone read a tale in childhood which made an impression at the time but was subsequently forgotten. In a hypnotic state memory was unlocked and the details re-emerged, fresh and vivid. That was the source of virtually all supposed past life experiences. The alternative was that the therapist deliberately encouraged his patient to fantasize. If that was what Caradoc Owen had been up to, he had a lot to answer for. Nat hoped fervently for an opportunity to confront that gentleman.

He set off for home early to avoid the rush of northbound commuters heading out of the City. As the train rattled through the suburbs the cloud of his own problems settled over him again. All thought of what he had unexpectedly learned about the Juniper Myles case was banished by the depressing realization that he would have to speak to Kate that evening.

There were few lights showing in the house as Nat garaged the car. He collected his briefcase, locked the Mercedes and trudged through into the living room. The scene that met him brought a sudden lump to his throat: Kate and the boys curled up together on the sofa watching one of the children's favourite videos.

'Hi, everyone,' he said, walking up behind them.

Ed and Jerry looked up briefly, then returned their gaze to the screen, but Kate extricated herself and came round to give him a quick hug.

'Useful day?' she enquired.

'Yeah. All well here? How did the swimming go?'

Kathryn pulled a face. 'Traumatic. Ed and Christopher had a falling out.'

'Oops!'

'Oops indeed! Christopher's mum was in hysterics. Accused Ed of trying to drown her darling boy. I think I managed to pacify her but, frankly, I'm drained. Give me a primadonna starlet or a posturing politician rather than an outraged parent any day. Still, that's best forgotten. Are you ready for supper? It won't take a moment.'

Nat followed his wife through into the kitchen area. 'Kate,' he began firmly, 'there's something –'

'Ssh!' She put a finger to his lips. 'Before you say another word I've got a present for you.' She picked up a box file from the table and thrust it into his hands.

'What's this?' Nat opened the cover and saw a thick pile of photocopied newspaper cuttings.

'I knew there was no way you were going to let this Myles business drop so I had my gofer do a bit of beavering away in the national newspaper archive. *That* is the result. It was biked up from the office this afternoon. It's just about all there is on the unhappy couple in the public domain. I hope it gives you some interesting ideas.'

Nat sat at the table and began leafing through the pages. They covered more than a quarter of a century and most of them seemed to be from court reports and gossip columns. The earliest, however, was a small item from the news pages of the *Northern Courier*. Under the headline, 'Court Triumph for Durham Trained Barrister', it garishly related Sheldon Myles's successful prosecution of a high profile fraudster in March 1972. 'Mr Myles,' it announced with proprietorial pride, 'was the leading law graduate of his year when he left St John's College in 1962. At that time, a brilliant career was forecast for the young graduate. His masterly cross-examination in this case indicates that such prophecies were well founded.' Nat frowned. Something about the three column inches before him seemed odd.

'What was it you wanted to say just now?' Kathryn asked as she opened the microwave.

'Hmm?' Nat mumbled, his concentration broken. 'Oh,

91

nothing that can't wait.' He returned his attention to the *Northern Courier* but failed to re-establish contact with whatever it was that had roused his curiosity.

Later, while Kathryn put the boys to bed, he took the file to his study and went through it, extracting details and entering them into his computerized Journal.

Monday 23 October
Bios of Sheldon and Juniper Myles
Sheldon – a brilliant and turbulent lawyer.
1st class law degree from Durham 1962.
Membership of Middle Temple 1966– Why the gap?
Married June 1969.
No children.
Controversial reputation as criminal prosecutor in 70s and 80s.
Twice up before Bar Council for browbeating witnesses.
No disciplinary action.

At this point Nat scanned in a fragment from a *Daily Mail* report dated 26 February 1990. It was headed 'Forbes Case – Judge v. Crown'.

Mr Justice Scanley, who had twice during the trial called the prosecution leader into his chambers, came as near as the etiquette of the legal profession allows to issuing a public reprimand. In his summing up he urged the jury to concentrate on what prosecuting counsel said and not how he said it. 'You may be familiar with Hollywood versions of American courtroom techniques but in the real world we do not award points for histrionics. The facts – and the facts alone – are all that must concern you.'

The point of the judge's remarks was not lost on all those who have been following this sensational trial. Sheldon Myles QC, widely known as the 'Robespierre of the Old Bailey' because, like the demagogue of the

92

French Revolution, he is both a snappy dresser and a vitriolic hounder of defendants, has looked at times during the last eight days as though he were auditioning for the Royal Shakespeare Company. At one stage he pointed the murder weapon, a twelve-bore shotgun, at the jury, squeezed the trigger and shouted 'Bang!' When cross-examining Peter Forbes, he produced a succession of photographs of the 17-year-old co-defendant's slaughtered parents, shouting over and again, 'Did they deserve to have their heads blown apart?' Clearly Judge Scanley . . .

Myles gave up criminal advocacy in 1991.
Specialized since in company law.
Retained by, among others, bankers Compton Fulbright, food and drinks conglomerate Drew's, Euroair (!), and Santando, the chemical giant.
A man the gossip columnists love to hate.
A conspicuous donator of funds to the Tory war chest.
Famous for parties thrown in his Thameside flat for political leaders.

Juniper Myles (née Grant-Selby) – clever and studious legal expert.
Only daughter of Austin Grant-Selby, Lord Justice of Appeal.
1st class hons from Lady Margaret Hall, Oxford, 1967.
Enrolled Gray's Inn same year.
Engaged to the Hon. Simon Everett, 1968.
Married Sheldon, 1969.
Society press made much of a 'whirlwind romance' and the breaking off of her previous engagement.
Sole heiress of her father's estate, 1975.
Low profile specialist in commercial contract law but involved in several publicized takeover battles and (1986–9) adviser to the Treasury on arbitrage law.

Prominent patron of children's charities.
Chairman Campaign for the Rights of Women (CROW),
1993–

Before he closed the Journal, Nat entered the information that seemed relevant from his conversation with Dr Greer. It was gone midnight by the time that he had finished but Kathryn was still reading.

She put her book aside as he slipped in beside her. 'So, how's the great Tripletree mystery coming along?'

'Mysteriously.'

'Tell me more.'

'Well, everyone, but everyone, believes that Tracy was murdered. Mitchenor came as close as a policeman can to actually inviting me to investigate. But what doesn't make sense is that we're talking about the wrong murder.'

'What do you mean?'

'Well, if anyone was to be bumped off it should have been our friend Shelley. I've never come across a man so wholeheartedly hated by so many of his fellow human beings, many of whom had what they might have considered good reasons for killing him.' Nat repeated the gist of his conversation with Greer.

'I see what you mean. How reliable do you think the tubby historian is? What did you make of him?'

'Awful snob and a thoroughgoing busybody but there's not much about Coln St Ippolyts that he doesn't know. He's a useful source of information, so I shall have to make a point of being nice to him.' Nat yawned, turned on his side and pulled the duvet up round his shoulder. 'It's like one of those puzzle boxes our ingenious ancestors used to make. I'm still staring at it, trying to find a way in. The trouble is if I'm successful, I don't think I'll like what I find inside.'

He woke suddenly at 2.36 by the bedside clock and remembered what he had found strange about the *Northern Courier* article. He immediately dismissed it. Could be any one of a dozen perfectly ordinary reasons, he told himself. Then, tidy-minded as usual, he thought, still, easy enough to check. He was just turning over and burrowing his head deep into the pillow when he was aware of a heavy vehicle engine running outside. With a groan, he eased his feet out of the bed's warmth and ambled across to the window. Great Maddisham was a prime target for burglars and residents were urged to be vigilant.

What he saw as he pulled the heavy curtain to one side and peered out on to the green was a white van standing near one of the village lampposts, its engine running. His angle of vision showed him the front of the vehicle but he had no clear view of the driver who was in shadow. However he could read part of the number plate which was not hidden behind a gatepost. He was concentrating on memorizing the letters when the vehicle suddenly moved forward. It circuited the green, presenting Nat with a side view, before speeding out of the village. He gasped. The legend in black letters was quite clear: 'J. Holt and Sons – Builders – Oxford'. A telephone number followed.

For several seconds he gazed down on the empty circle of tree-edged grass. Everything was quiet and still. Iridescent haloes ringed the road lights and the first slight autumn frost lay over the empty green. He sensed a movement on the far side; was it a flitting figure in a long overcoat or cloak? He rubbed his eyes and stared hard. Nothing. Only the motionless shadows of the plane trees.

Persuasion

In the morning Nat dismissed the sequence of events as a dream, the result of puzzling too hard over the Coln St Ippolyts affair. He was, in any case, too busy to give it any further thought. Kathryn worked in London from Tuesday to Thursday and usually arrived home late. So, as well as managing a full timetable of lectures and supervisions, Nat had to look after the boys. He did, however, spend a few minutes in the college library consulting *Who's Who* and the Law List. These sources confirmed that Sheldon Philip Myles had, indeed, studied for his degree at Durham and subsequently taken his bar exams as a member of Middle Temple. They revealed, further, that he was the only child of Michael and Sarah Myles (both deceased) of Northowram, near Halifax, in the hills of West Yorkshire.

'Does the name Sheldon Myles mean anything to you?'

It was Wednesday and Nat was having a light lunch in Beaufort's fellows' parlour. He found himself seated in the oriel window overlooking the circular lawn of Simeon Court and sharing a table with Barnaby Cox, an emeritus fellow who still lived in Cambridge and occasionally dropped into college for meals.

The silver-haired ex-law faculty lecturer, immaculate in dark suit, striped shirt and neat bow tie, peered at Nat over the spectacles perched on the end of his long nose. 'Since there can be only one member of the esteemed legal profession with that name you must be referring to a highly successful young barrister – too successful to be much loved by his peers.'

'The man I'm thinking of is scarcely young,' Nat said with a smile.

Cox shrugged. 'At my age all the world is young – young and bewildering; alien almost.' He leaned forward and, in a mock confidential whisper, said, 'Have you noticed how many of our fellow citizens have developed a strange physical excrescence? It's attached to one of their ears and it's obviously painful because you see them walking the streets with a hand clapped over the afflicted part of their anatomy and muttering to themselves.'

Nat grinned. 'You don't approve of mobile phones?'

Cox raised his eyes to heaven. 'Oh, is that what they are? How bizarre!'

'Come on, Barny,' Nat said, laughing. 'It's not like you to be maudlin. Let me give you some college claret to mellow you a bit.'

When Nat returned from the buttery counter with their glasses he said, 'So you do know this brilliant *middle-aged* barrister.'

The older man wagged a finger. 'I didn't say "brilliant"; I said "successful".'

'And thereby hangs a tale?'

Cox sipped his wine and frowned. 'I see we're still drinking the '88. I hope Charles hasn't got too much of it left. It hasn't any staying power. When *I* was steward I managed to find a hoard of '61 Marquis d'Alesme. Stood us in good stead for years.'

'All gone before my time, I fear.'

'Ah, your loss, my boy.'

'So, Barny, what of Myles QC?'

The retired academic stared out into the quad. On the chapel steps opposite a male and female undergraduate were passionately entwined. He shook his head. 'In Dean Moffat's time that would probably have been a rustication offence. Myles? I knew his head of chambers, Monty Pym. He took Myles in as a favour to one of the judges.'

'Grant-Selby?'

'Very possibly. I don't recall. Anyway, Monty was never altogether happy with his protégé. Thought he lowered the tone.'

'In what way?'

'Do you know what someone said of Harry Truman? He couldn't tell the difference between history and histrionics. Well, it was rather the same with young Myles. He made his reputation in front of the jury but he was never reckoned as much of an original legal mind. Rumour has it that he used to pay hacks to do his research for him; had a corps of 'em beavering away on his briefs in a garret somewhere. All he had to do was learn his scripts and turn them into high drama in court.'

'That sounds a bit far-fetched. He got a first class degree.'

'Did he now? Well, he certainly didn't shine in his bar finals. I remember Monty saying that was why he thought more than twice about taking him on. Anyway, Nat, what's your interest in him? Hardly your line of country I'd have thought, unless some of his old victims have come back from the grave to haunt him.'

Nat laughed. 'That may not be so far from the truth. Someone seems to have it in for him.' He gave Cox a scaled-down version of the events at Coln St Ippolyts.

The old man drained his glass thoughtfully. 'And it's your considered opinion that because this poor woman posed some kind of a threat to him, friend Myles, instead of disposing of her in some discreet fashion, bludgeoned and drowned her at his own party, when there were scores of guests wandering freely through the grounds and then persuaded the local constabulary to hush the matter up? My dear boy, what sort of tenth rate crime fiction have you been reading? I said that Myles isn't brilliant but I certainly don't think he's a fool.'

98

'Yes, I've come up against the same brick wall, or perhaps "fog" would be a better metaphor. Myles obviously has something to hide and so do lots of other people.'

The old lawyer gave his friend a pitying stare. 'You mind doctors always want to make things more complicated than they really are. Any half-way competent advocate would tell you this is an open and shut case, the sort of crime of passion the courts are dealing with every day.'

'Impulsive murder by a jealous wife?'

'Exactly. Poor woman, driven to distraction by her husband's infidelities. Under additional stress planning this elaborate party. And what does she see at the party? Her man's latest playmate of the month flaunting herself as Nell Gwyn – a royal mistress no less! She encounters this floozy down by the lake and something inside her head goes "snap". She already has motive and now suddenly she's presented with means and opportunity. It's all over in seconds. The only unusual aspect of the case is that she gets away with it. By some strange fluke there are no witnesses.'

'So why does she deliberately try to get the case re-opened and plan to go to the police with a confession?'

'Guilt!' Cox said firmly. 'Very common reaction for a normally decent, balanced person who commits a totally uncharacteristic crime. She can't live with herself –'

'But –'

'I know what you're going to say: "What about all that hypnotic hocus-pocus?" Well, remember she is a barrister. She knows all about the susceptibilities of juries. They're always sympathetic to the wronged wife and, if her counsel can plant even a suspicion that she acted under the fluence, well, she'd probably get away with a plea of diminished responsibility.'

'But the prosecution would bring in expert psychiatric witnesses to show that people can't be hypnotized into performing desperate acts which go completely against their nature.'

'Doubtless. It would be a fascinating case. I rather hope it comes to court. I should follow it with great interest.'

'Hmm!' Nat gazed into his empty glass. 'I wish I could believe it was as simple as that. But I'm sure Myles does have something to hide and so do several of his neighbours in the village. They're all half obscured in the mist and I'm damned if I know what's going on.'

'Intriguing. Coffee? Allow me.' Cox rose stiffly, went over to the corner where a machine dispensed filter coffee and came back carefully carrying two cups. 'So, dear boy, can I be of any further help; offer a lamp to show you a path through the Stygian gloom?'

'That's kind of you, Barny, but I don't want to trespass on your time.'

'Huh!' The old man snorted. 'Time? That's something I've plenty of.'

Nat looked at the retired academic and realized, almost with a shock, that behind the dignified offer of assistance there was a cry for help. The old man was bored, perhaps even frightened of what might happen to an active brain that found itself underemployed after decades of decision making and wrestling with knotty legal problems. 'Well,' he suggested, 'perhaps a few discreet enquiries among your friends at the bar. Find out if there are any rumours about Myles; if anyone has heard the odd rattle of bones in his cupboard.'

Cox beamed his pleasure. 'What a delicious prospect! Yes, I shall enjoy that. Quite a challenge. Thank you, dear boy, thank you. I'll be in touch, as they say.'

Back in his rooms Nat immersed himself in some urgent paperwork. Or tried to. It turned out to be one of those afternoons when the phone never stopped ringing. There were matters of college and faculty business that, it seemed, could not wait till a more convenient time. Kathryn called to say that something had 'cropped up' which would delay her in London till after the last train had gone. 'See you tomorrow, darling,' she cooed. 'Kiss the boys for me. Tell them I'm bringing a new computer game back for them. And make sure Ed takes his clean rugger kit to school in the morning.' The flustered secretary of SODS (the Senior Officials' Dramatic Society) was devastated to inform him that the read-through of Wycherley's *The Country Wife*, their next production, would have to be postponed for a week because the producer had gone down with flu. She was having to phone all the cast to tell them, but it was so difficult getting hold of everyone, and she was so glad she had caught Nat, and he did understand about the change of plan, didn't he?

But there were two other calls which did not come within the category of provoking mild irritation. The first was from Susan Avery-White. She was her usual bright, brusque self.

'Bingo!'

'Which, being interpreted, is?' Nat enquired.

'We've found your Dr Caradoc Owen.'

'That was quick work.'

'We strive to please. I played a hunch that he might have done a stage act at some time and contacted some of the sleazier theatrical agents. Eventually, I hit pay dirt. Owen – real name George Williams – performed on the club circuit until about four years ago. Now he calls himself a therapist and works from a Birmingham address: 4a Commercial Street, Aston. Are you planning to call on him soon?'

'Yes, I think so.'

'Do you want me to set it up?'

'Good idea. He's more likely to respond to you. In fact, it might be advisable to keep my name out of it for the time being.'

'Fine. I'll do my standard, charmy-smarmy routine. Tell him we're looking for leading experts in the field. Offer him his brief moment of fame. Seldom fails. Cheers, Nat. I'll get back to you.'

It was just as he was picking up his briefcase and making for the door at the end of a frustrating couple of hours that the telephone rang one more time. Nat almost ignored it, then, on impulse, picked up the receiver.

'Hello?'

George Bramley's voice came on the line from the college switchboard. 'Dr Gye, I have a call for you from a Mr Myles.'

'OK, George, put him on.'

'Putting you through now, sir.'

Nat heard the connection made and said, 'Shelley, good afternoon. How was Barbados?'

'Is that Mr Gye?' It was a man's voice, deep and with a suggestion of a Birmingham accent. Certainly not Sheldon Myles.

'Dr Nathaniel Gye speaking. Who's that?'

'We've not met, Mr Gye, but we ought to. My name's Jack Holt. That should tell you what I'm phoning about.'

'Yes, I get the message, Mr Holt. But there are better ways of going about things than masquerading as someone else. What do you want?'

'You're not in any position to lecture me on underhand behaviour, Mr Gye.' The words were slow and measured, with more than a hint of menace. 'What me and my brothers want is a meeting.'

'Yes, well, I suppose that could be arranged. If you'd like to hang on a moment while I get my diary out –'

'No need for that. We'll see you tomorrow afternoon at about this time.'

'Really, Mr Holt, I'm afraid I can't –'

The voice interrupted, calm but insistent. 'There's a Travellers' Oasis hotel just outside Huntingdon, on the Kettering road. That's not too far from you. We'll meet you there.'

'Look here, I can't just drop everything and –'

'Mr Gye, you found time to stick your nose in our business. I reckon you can find the time to meet us face to face.' The line went dead.

Nat hurried out before the insistent bell could start ringing again. He went to the fellows' car park and collected his Mini, the vehicle he and Kathryn used for local journeys. With mounting impatience he negotiated Cambridge's one-way system. Queens' College boasts a wooden structure spanning the Cam and known as the Mathematical Bridge. According to legend it was constructed by a seventeenth-century engineering genius who built it entirely without nails or pegs, its timbers locked together by precisely calculated interdependence. Two hundred years later inquisitive theorists dismantled it in order to discover how the trick was done. Having completed their researches, they found that they could not put the bridge back together again and had to resort to crude screws and metal supports. Nat often felt that the city council's tinkering with what they euphemistically called 'traffic flow' had produced the same dire result. For long centuries citizens and university residents – 'town and gown', as they were usually referred to – had presumably managed to manoeuvre their way around the compact medieval streets to their satisfaction but the inner core of thoroughfares had successfully resisted modernization and the unmanaged Victorian sprawl which later enwrapped it was equally hostile to the needs of the motor car, the omnibus and the delivery van. Nat inched his way through the congestion of shoppers, tourists and bicycling students, taking his mind off the urban chaos by brooding on his more pressing problems.

Holt had a nerve, *demanding* his attendance at such short notice, and Nat was tempted to ignore the summons but there had been a hint of 'come or else' about it. There was also the matter of Monday night's visitation. If Nat had not dreamed about the van then he certainly had to find out exactly what the angry Mr Holt was playing at. He sensed that he had reached a point of no return. Up till now the puzzling events at Coln had been little more than an intellectual exercise, a piece of intriguing research that could be dropped if following its labyrinthine channels became too arduous or time-consuming. Now it was obvious that most of the people involved knew of his interest and were reacting to it. He had lifted the curtain to see what was inside and whatever it was was now reaching out to draw him in. He wondered who Jack Holt's 'brothers' were. Genuine siblings? Or did the word imply something more sinister? Visions of a kind of Cotswold Mafia floated into Nat's mind and he recalled the chilling, almost tangible feeling of hostility he had experienced in Coln St Ippolyts.

Nat jammed his foot on the brake as a bicycle was thrust off the pavement right in front of the Mini's bonnet. He also called a halt to the impetus of his imagination. Criminal gangs did not stalk the streets of quiet English villages. Coln was no Naples or Palermo where drug dealing underlay politics and rival suppliers regarded murder as a legitimate commercial activity. Whatever evil lurked in Coln was personal, quirky and limited in scope – though none the less unpleasant for that.

Meanwhile, he had more immediate matters to deal with. He collected Ed and Jerry from a neighbour's, settled them down to do their homework, then went to his study and put a call through to New York.

'Nathaniel, hi!' Nat pictured Greg Polowski, balding but muscular, swivelling in his executive chair to gaze out over the Manhattan skyline or pedalling monotonously on the exercise bike which he kept in a corner of his office and called his 'inspiration machine'. 'How's things in the old UK?'

'Could be better.' Nat came straight to the point. 'I imagine you know why I'm calling.'

'I guess so.' Nat could almost hear the wide smile on the tanned face. 'But, hey, you don't have to thank me. Katie deserves the promotion. She's worked her butt off for the company and it's time we showed our appreciation.'

'Thanks wasn't exactly what I had in mind.'

'So,' the American was cautious now, 'do you have a problem, Nathaniel?'

'I think we all three of us have a problem. I don't want Kathryn relocating to New York.'

There was a brief silence before Greg said, 'Surely that's her decision. I got the impression she was very happy about it.'

'I can imagine the sales pitch you made to her, dazzling her with a huge salary and gilt-edged perks. It's the sort of thing you're very good at.'

'Nathaniel, I can assure you that every cent I offered her is no less than she richly deserves. The board backed me one hundred per cent and these guys don't throw their money around.'

Nat took a couple of deep breaths to keep his voice calm. 'Oh, I've no doubt she would repay your investment, Greg. It's just that you and I see Kathryn from different perspectives. To me she isn't a commodity you can put a price on. She's my wife and the mother of our children.'

'Well, now,' Greg's New England drawl made him sound more relaxed than he was, 'aren't we being just a bit the Victorian paterfamilias? Katie's a modern woman, emancipated. She has the right to choose her own career path. I'd have thought you'd want to see her –'

'Spare me the sanctimonious feminist lecture, Greg!' Nat knew that he was losing control but could not stop himself. The thoughts and feelings he had bottled up for weeks now broke free. 'You're not interested in Kathryn fulfilling herself. You know she's damned good and you're scared of losing her to a rival outfit. That's why you want her under your thumb in America.'

'Nathaniel, listen –'

But Nat's anger was in spate now. 'No, you listen,' he shouted. 'Take the dollar bills out of your ears and perhaps you'll actually be able to hear what someone else is saying for a change.'

'OK, Nathaniel, calm down. I'm listening. I'm listening.'

The American sounded infuriatingly cool and Nat took a moment get a grip of himself. Then he said in a voice he struggled to keep steady, 'Kathryn's been balancing family and career most of the time we've been married – and doing a damn good job. I think we've always known that one day the balancing act might become tricky; that she'd be faced with making tough choices, even sacrifices. I suppose we should have discussed the possibility more frankly. We just never got round to it. But we sure as hell do have to discuss it now – *before* any final decision is made. That's why I don't take kindly to your bouncing her into a "yes" or "no", "take it or leave it" situation.'

There was a pause before Greg responded. 'I see. Thank you for sharing that, Nathaniel. Now, perhaps you'll listen to how things look from my end. For the last six months we've been staving off a takeover by one of America's biggest media conglomerates. We're desperate to keep our independence but these big boys speak the language of power – money. The only way we can keep the big bad wolf from huffing and puffing and blowing our house down is by building a stronger house. We've had to take a long, hard look at all our magazines, revamp where necessary, bring them up to date and keep them up to date, get the most talented staff we can lay our hands on, boost circulation by every means we can think of. *Panache* is our flagship. We have to exploit its popularity and also widen its market appeal. That's why we're restructuring, putting a new team in place. It's meant tough decisions. I've had to let some people go – talented people, but not talented enough. I've poached shamelessly from our rivals. But I also have to maximize the gifted people we have in house. And, frankly, our biggest asset is Katie. That's why I want her in the international editor's chair. It's a hell of a responsibility – and a hell of an opportunity; one that, under normal circumstances, wouldn't come her way for many years, if ever. So, Nathaniel, I'm sorry if you think I came on too strong to your lovely wife, but . . .'

'All's fair in love and war?'

'That's not quite what I was going to say. It's more a question of the damsel in distress and the knight in shining armour. Only this time I'm the damsel. But, look, this is no way to handle things, Nathaniel. Let's talk it through, *mano y mano*. I've got Katie's contract on my desk right now. I was going to fax it for her approval by why don't I bring it over myself? I could fit it in on . . . let me see . . . Wednesday and drive out to Cambridge. I love that town. Have done ever since I did a post-grad year at Trinity. We can spend as long as you like. Look at the problem from every angle. How does that sound to you?'

Nat agreed, despondently, outmanoeuvred by the American's sweet reasonableness. He felt like a beleaguered general who has obtained a much-needed truce but still can see no way of avoiding ultimate defeat.

'Fine,' Greg said warmly. 'I'll get an email off to London right now. If you like I'll tell Katie it's my idea and leave you to report on our little chat – or not, as you please.'

The depression that settled on Nat after that conversation had not lifted by the time he drove out of Cambridge along the A14 on Thursday afternoon. The Travellers' Oasis was a small, undistinguished, functional building set back from the main road, next to a filling station. It was one of a chain of cheap hotels that had sprung up all over southern England in the last couple of years, unimaginative, uniform edifices designed to provide economy accommodation for long-distance drivers. Most of the parking bays were empty as Nat brought the Mercedes to a halt close to the entrance. There were, however, two gleaming cars, a Lexus and a Rolls Royce, standing side by side, their chauffeurs seated nearby on the low wall. Nat noticed the number plates of the vehicles: JQH 1 and JQH 3. As he entered the foyer, a brass plate to the right of the entrance caught his eye. It read, 'Travellers' Oasis Hotel, Huntingdon' and, in smaller letters underneath, 'A Holt Hotel'. He began to revise his ideas about the non-existence of an English rural Mafia.

His misgivings increased moments later with his first sight of the Holts. A bar area opened off the foyer and was occupied by three men in dark suits. They sat in armchairs by the window, the air above them blue with cigarette smoke.

The tallest of the trio stood as soon as Nat entered and crossed the room to shake his hand. 'Jack Holt,' he announced. 'Come and meet my brothers, Harry and Quentin.'

As they rose to offer a cautious greeting, Nat was struck by the family resemblance. Jack, slim with luxuriant, swept-back grey hair, was obviously the eldest. The others, both in their forties, were fuller of figure and their dark hair had not yet begun to turn, but all three had flushed complexions, full lips and bottle-brown eyes that suggested shrewd calculation.

Nat smiled. 'Good afternoon, gentlemen.' He waved a hand. 'So this is another of the Holt enterprises.'

Jack explained succinctly. 'I'm in the construction business, Harry's interest is hotels and catering, and Quentin has one of the biggest car dealerships in the country. Together we control the second largest family commercial empire in the Midlands. Would you like coffee, Mr Gye?'

'Thank you.'

Jack called out to the bar steward who was slouched over a newspaper. 'Coffee for four in the office, Sam.' To Nat he explained, 'It's more private there. We won't be disturbed.'

The room they went to was small. There were only three chairs but Nat was offered one of them and Jack leaned against the desk. Clever use of body language, Nat thought: he has taken the stance of authority and power.

As soon as they sat down the younger Holts both lit up cigarettes.

Without further formality, Jack said, 'OK, Mr Gye, we're all busy men, so let's get down to it. I take it you're a friend of Mr Myles.'

Nat smiled faintly and shook his head. 'Then you take it wrong, Mr Holt.'

'You were at his big party back in the summer.'

'So were over a hundred other people but they weren't all Myles's friends. In fact, I doubt whether he has that many friends.'

Quentin sniggered. 'You can say that again.'

Harry blew out a long column of smoke. 'Since then you've been nosing around in Coln. Why?'

Nat was determined not to be intimidated. 'I didn't realize taking an interest in the village was an infringement of the by-laws. Anyway, you haven't been reticent about exploring my neighbourhood.'

Jack was not remotely fazed. He stared evenly back. 'Mr Gye, our sister met a violent death at Myles's party, so we're rather sensitive about strangers who come probing our family tragedy.'

Nat gaped, momentarily dumbstruck. 'Are you telling me Tracy Pensham was your sister?' he gasped.

'Don't pretend you didn't know!' Quentin's sneer radically distorted his features and Nat guessed that he was less in control of his emotions than his siblings.

The brothers' anger and distress now began to make sense to Nat. He said quietly, 'I'm very sorry for your loss. But, really, I had no idea . . .'

'Tracy was our kid sister,' Harry explained. 'Three years younger than Quentin. The only girl in the family. Our mother doted on her. She hasn't recovered from Tracy's murd– Tracy's death. Probably never will.'

'So,' Jack said, 'that brings us back to what the hell you think you're doing keeping these sores open, Mr Gye.'

At that moment the coffee arrived. The intervention gave Nat time to consider his response.

As the barman withdrew, Jack said, 'Quentin, you pour.'

His brother grimaced but obeyed. Nat accepted his cup and sipped the black liquid slowly, aware that three pairs of eyes were fixed upon him.

He began cautiously. 'I'm a lecturer in parapsychology. That means –'

'Ghoulies and ghosties and things that go bump in the night,' Harry ventured.

'Yes, among other things.'

'You expect us to believe that you came nosing around in Coln just to find out about the Tripletree ghosts?' Quentin demanded. 'The psychic research people have been over every inch of the place and interviewed everyone in the village who's seen the ghosts. Is that the best excuse you can manage?'

Jack threw him an impatient glance. 'Shut up, Quentin! I want to hear what Mr Gye has to say for himself.'

Grateful for the intervention, Nat improvised. 'Several strange things happened on the night of party, culminating in the tragic death of your sister. Naturally, some people put it all down to evil spirits and since I have a professional interest in that sort of thing I hoped to find out what the locals thought about it. If I've trodden on corns I'm sorry.'

'Don't give us that load of shit!' The youngest brother jumped up and stood over Nat menacingly. 'You've been talking to the police.' He smiled at Nat's surprise. 'Yeah, that shook you, didn't it? Thought we country bumpkins didn't know what was going on? Well, for your information, Harry belongs to the same golf club as Dave Mitchenor and he just happened to let slip something about your recent tête-à-tête. So, you'll have to come up with a better story.'

Nat looked at the three angry faces. Now there was no

attempt to restrain the belligerent Quentin. He wondered how far the brothers would dare go and knew that he did not want to find out. 'Look, gentlemen, I realize how very upsetting that business at Coln was for you and if I've inadvertently made things worse I'm sorry. But I didn't come here to be browbeaten. So, unless there's anything else . . .' He made to get up but Quentin stood also and placed himself squarely in front of him.

Jack Holt surveyed Nat calmly. 'You must see what this means to my family, Mr Gye. Our sister's reputation is at stake. We have to know what Myles is up to, who you've been talking to and what they've told you.'

Nat took a deep breath. 'Look, you really have got hold of the wrong end of the stick. For a start, I'm not acting on behalf of Myles. Any "nosing around", as you call it, has been entirely on my own account. Yes, I was interested in Tracy's death. I met her – very briefly – at the party. In fact I may well have been the last person she spoke to. She struck me as a very vibrant personality.'

'What did you talk about?' Quentin demanded.

'Tracy really did all the talking. She was in high spirits and said some pretty uncomplimentary things about Myles. Then she indicated that he was about to get his "comeuppance", as she called it.'

The brothers exchanged quick glances and Jack asked, 'What exactly did she tell you about Myles?'

'Nothing, really. She wasn't all that coherent. To be frank with you, she'd had a bit too much to drink. I got the impression that she knew something about him that would be damaging but she certainly didn't tell me what it was.' The brief encounter in the garden came back to Nat with a new vividness and he tried to remember Tracy's exact words. Perhaps there was something important in them that he had missed. Obviously her brothers were very worried about what she might have revealed. He decided to risk a veiled question of his own.

'I understand she worked at the manor. Could she have overheard something . . .'

Jack waved a hand. 'It's possible. Tracy loved Tripletree – ghosts and all. She knew a hell of a lot about the place and worked there, on and off, for many years. She was a very clever girl, Mr Gye. Better educated than the rest of us. We boys were trained for business but our father always wanted something better for his daughter. She should have gone to university. She was bright enough. But then . . .'

Then, Nat thought, as Jack snapped quickly out of his reverie, she fell in love with a muscular boxer and married beneath her.

As if reading Nat's thoughts, Jack continued, 'You talked to Tom Pensham. What did he have to say?'

'Absolutely nothing. He struck me as the sort of man who doesn't take to strangers and I certainly wasn't going to intrude on his private grief.'

Quentin uttered a snort of a laugh. The others ignored him.

'So,' Jack said, 'that just leaves your cosy chat with DCI Mitchenor. What was that all about?'

Nat thought carefully. Since he did not know what the policeman had passed on to his golfing associate he was not sure how frank he could be. 'I was following up a hunch, a crazy idea that occurred to me. Bearing in mind what Tracy said to me and the fact that, less than an hour later, she met a violent death . . . well I wanted to make sure the police had looked at the possibility . . .'

'That her death was no accident? That, perhaps, Myles murdered her to shut her up?' It was Harry who made the suggestion. 'And what did Dave say?'

'That he was satisfied with the coroner's verdict and that the case was very definitely closed.'

'Good. Good.' Jack nodded thoughtfully. After a long pause, he smiled. 'Well, Mr Gye, I think that concludes our business. We're very grateful to you for coming and for your co-operation. I'm sorry if our manner seemed a little brusque but I'm sure you understand that we all feel our sister's loss very deeply.' He reached out a hand and Nat, rather reluctantly, shook it.

The senior partner of the Holt empire took two strides to the door. 'I take it we can assume that your interest in the matter is now at an end?'

Nat nodded as the three men watched him anxiously.

'Good. Good.' Jack paused with his hand on the door-knob. 'Since you've been frank with us, I'll tell you some-thing in confidence, just to satisfy that scholar's curiosity of yours. Sheldon Myles did murder our sister. There was an eyewitness and there's absolutely no doubt about it.'

Nat stared. 'In that case, why –'

'Because, Mr Gye, we have our own way of obtaining justice. It's an older, surer way and it can't be perverted by Myles and all his legal friends.'

That was the moment at which Nat resolved to walk away from the Tripletree affair.

But events were already in train which would make any such decision irrelevant.

Visiting the Past (2)

Whatever throbbing entrepreneurial activity had once given Commercial Street its name had long since departed. It now presented to the world a face of small shops and offices, some patched with graffiti-scrawled plywood, and Victorian terraces subdivided into flats. On a Monday afternoon of late October drizzle it was not looking its modest best. Susan Avery-White hugged her raincoat around her, pressed the remote button which locked her red MX5 convertible, and looked anxiously up and down the glistening pavement. Twenty yards away three youths huddled in a doorway were staring at the car with undisguised interest.

'Perhaps we should have parked in the city centre and taken a taxi,' she said.

Nat stretched his cramped limbs. 'Certainly not a very salubrious area,' he commented, automatically raising his voice above the steady growl of traffic on the nearby motorway spur. 'Still, I doubt whether this charlatan will detain us long.'

Susan had made the appointment with Caradoc Owen in her own name in case he was frightened off by the prospect of coming face to face with Nathaniel Gye, the exposer of fraudulent mediums, hoaxers and supernatural-ist cranks. It was four days since Nat's uncomfortable encounter with the Holts and his determination to let sleeping Coln St Ippolyts dogs lie, but he saw no reason to cancel the interview with the self-styled 'hypnotherapist'.

Owen might have a useful contribution to make to the TV series he was planning and there was now no reason to pursue the man's connection with June Myles. Nat was, he told himself, working on a fresh line of research that had only a tangential connection with a murder in the grounds of a Cotswold mansion.

Susan looked up at the street number over a newsagent's door. '4a must be this way,' she announced, setting off in the direction of the main road.

Fifty yards farther along they found number 4. Its facia board read 'The Unicorn Bookshop' and its window was littered with trays of crystals and charms and books on subjects ranging from astrology to voodoo. There was no door next to it bearing the legend '4a', so they entered the shop. The only occupant was a young woman with an untidy aureole of frizzed ginger hair and wearing a shapeless, floor-sweeping purple dress down the front of which hung several strands of charm necklaces. Nat recognized images of the Hindu god, Siva, zodiacal signs and St Christopher. That's what you call playing the field, he thought to himself. The woman turned from her desultory task of dusting shelves bearing such labels as 'Herbology', 'Eastern Religion', 'UFOs', 'Occult Science' and 'Astrology', put on a hopeful smile and said, 'Good afternoon. Can I help you?'

When Nat asked for Dr Caradoc Owen the smile vanished. The guardian of arcane mysteries gave an orange nod towards a doorway covered with a bead curtain and returned to her work. The visitors passed through into back premises which consisted of a kitchen-cum-storeroom, with a deep, old-fashioned sink, above which was an equally antique Ascot gas water heater, and piles of cardboard boxes, some empty, some unopened. A door to the right bore a printed sign: 'Dr Caradoc Owen, Consulting Room, First Floor'. Nat opened the door and discovered a narrow, ill-lit staircase which he and Susan ascended in single file. The only door at the top carried another notice which indicated that they had reached journey's end.

The room which they entered covered the whole of the first floor but was divided in two by a curtain drawn across the rear half. Nat was immediately struck by the theatricality of the premises. The drapes were of maroon velvet, suggesting the existence of a stage beyond, and the 'auditorium', in reality Dr Owen's office, was appointed in plush vulgarity. Flock wallpaper patterned in dusky red and gold was in constant dispute with a carpet of green and lemon yellow swirls. Venetian blinds kept out the harsh realities of the inner city and were in their turn softened by more swathes of velvet.

There was even something *deus ex machina* about the 'entrance' of the principal actor in this scene. Across one corner of the space ahead of them was slewed a mahogany partners' desk, its tooled leather top studded with neatly arranged books, papers, telephone and an elaborate gilt inkwell. A green-shaded desk lamp made a pool of light on this surface and left the area beyond in partial shadow. It was from this semi-gloom that Caradoc Owen now emerged, standing behind the desk and extending his arm in what might have been a gesture of welcome or benediction.

'Ms Avery-White,' he intoned in a voice that was deep, Welsh and musical, 'it is a pleasure to meet you.'

'Very good of you to see us,' Susan responded, reaching forward across the desk to shake the outstretched hand. 'This is Dr Gye, who is scripting and fronting our programmes. I thought it would save your time if he came along to outline what he has in mind and ask a few preliminary questions.'

'Dr Gye, your fame goes before you. I'm honoured to have you under my humble roof – honoured and a mite apprehensive. You have a fearsome reputation, sir.' The voice was mellifluous – honey and cream – but the eyes reflecting the lamplight were bright, hard, probing.

The visitors sat in upright leather chairs and Nat left Susan to do most of the talking while he watched Owen watching him. The therapist was a small, dark man with patent leather hair brushed back from a high forehead. He wore the black jacket, dove grey tie and striped trousers favoured by bankers and Harley Street doctors of an earlier generation and looked every inch the trustworthy, conscientious professional. Gye could see how he might inspire confidence in hopeful 'patients' who came to him with their problems. But had he really bamboozled June Myles? If she had taken him at face value she really must have been plucking at straws.

Suddenly Owen's features tensed. If Nat had not been watching closely he would not have noticed. Something had alarmed the man. Nat turned his attention to what Susan was saying.

'I'm sure you have a professional opinion on that, Dr Owen.'

'Oh, indeed. Every occupation has its rogues and I'm afraid ours is no exception,' Owen replied gravely.

'I'm sorry; I'm afraid my mind was wandering.' Nat smiled at his companion. 'What was it you were saying?'

'I was just explaining to Dr Owen that one of the areas we want to explore is the way hypnotism is used and misused in connection with crime. For example, there was that case in Canada last year when a man was driven to suicide because his daughter under hypnosis had apparently "recalled" experiences of childhood abuse. Later it was discovered that the therapist had implanted false memories.'

'Of course,' Owen said, 'it's always that sort of case that makes the headlines. Like doctors and hospitals, we only hear about them when something goes wrong. What doesn't get reported are the more frequent examples of hypnotherapy being used to help in the detection of crime. I was involved in one such incident only a year ago. Young woman – nineteen-year-old – witnessed a brutal raid on a jeweller's. She was so traumatized that her conscious mind refused to recall the details of what she had obviously seen. I was able to relax her and allow her unconscious to release the vital evidence the police needed to make an arrest.'

'That's a great story,' Nat said. 'We must definitely use it. Are you much involved with the police?' Again he watched the other man's face closely.

There was the slightest twitch of the lips as Owen replied. 'No, Dr Gye, most of my work is far less dramatic than that. People round here come to me with a variety of very ordinary problems – they need easing through pregnancy or they want to give up smoking or they're nervous about a forthcoming interview, that sort of thing.'

'What are your views on regression therapy, Dr Owen?' Nat asked, making the question sound as casual and disinterested as possible.

'You mean regression to childhood?'

'Or beyond.'

Owen sat back in his chair, appearing to give the matter careful consideration. 'I would say that the two are quite different and that each has its own pitfalls. Helping patients to come to terms with unhappy experiences buried deep in the unconscious can be very therapeutic but, as Ms Avery-White has pointed out, there are several recorded instances of this kind of treatment being mishandled, with unfortunate results.'

'And past life experiences? Do you believe in reincarnation, Dr Owen?'

'Since you ask the direct question, yes, I do. You won't need me to point out to you that some of the experiments carried out by Ian Stevenson, Arthur Guirdham and other pioneers in the field are very difficult to dismiss.'

Nat smiled a half-distracted, musing kind of smile. 'But then, of course, you'd have to believe that your patients have been here before. Otherwise you couldn't in all conscience encourage them to revisit their earlier identities, could you?'

Owen responded sharply. 'I didn't say I had involved myself in past life regression, Dr Gye. I'm a practising hypnotherapist, not an experimental psychologist.'

Nat waved a hand dismissively. 'Of course, and we're wandering from the point. Our programmes will be very firmly anchored in the present. One avenue I'm anxious to explore is whether very suggestible people can be induced to commit crimes.'

Owen shook his head emphatically. 'Impossible! Quite impossible! One cannot, by hypnosis, make someone do something which otherwise would revolt them.'

'Yes, that is certainly the received wisdom but how does the practitioner know what would revolt his subject? Suppose, for example, that I hated someone, that I wished that someone were dead. And suppose that, under hypnosis, I produced the fantasy that that person was . . . what shall we say . . . having an affair with my wife. Might that not result in a post-hypnotic trigger, so powerful that the next time I encountered my *bête noire* I might make a savage and irrational attack upon him?'

Owen shrugged. 'An interesting theory, Dr Gye, but I don't think I can be of much use to you on such hypothetical questions.'

Susan re-entered the conversation. 'Do you see all your patients here, Dr Owen? I'm afraid I don't know the form. Do hypnotists make house calls?'

The little man gave a low chuckle of a laugh. 'You must let me give you a session, young lady. You really should discover what it's all about before you make your programme. But, to answer your question, yes, I work almost invariably from these premises. It's important that the subjects should have no distractions. In their own homes there are far too many things for them to think about. Here the ambience is more . . . conducive.'

Conducive or not, Nat thought, you'd never get June

Myles to this seedy, phoney stage set. She'd get your measure straight away if she saw you in your own habitat. I wonder what plausible line you spun her. How on earth does an intelligent woman like her get hoodwinked by a blatant, cheapjack fraud like you? Then he looked at Susan – sane, sophisticated, seen-it-all, woman of the world Susan – and realized with a shock that she was hanging on Owen's words. Her facial expressions were responding to every nuance of what he said. Her head was almost moving with the cadences of his speech.

Nat felt a sudden surge of anger. Determined to break the spell, he stood abruptly. 'Perhaps we could see where you treat your patients,' he said with a forced smile.

The next moment he almost burst out laughing. With a slight electrical hum the curtains screening the area behind him parted. He turned to see a dimly lit 'stage set', comprising an expensive leather sofa with a matching armchair, a long coffee table and a standard lamp. Two walls were adorned with reproduction old masters in sombre colours. Concealed lighting, controlled, Nat guessed, by a dimmer, enabled Owen to adjust the ambience.

'This is very impressive,' Susan said, rising and walking on to the inner stage. 'Could we film here?'

Owen was cautious. 'That depends –'

'Of course you have very proper professional concerns, Dr Owen,' Nat interposed hastily, 'but Sue has an excellent eye for production values. She can intuitively "see" what makes good television.'

'Yes,' Susan added enthusiastically, 'if we could film you actually in operation with a patient – whose anonymity would, of course, be absolutely safeguarded – that would be so much more immediate than simply interviewing you.' Noting the hypnotist's hesitation, she added hurriedly, 'Use of your facilities would, naturally, be reflected in whatever fee we negotiated.'

Nat observed the gleam in Owen's eye at the mention of

money. He said, 'So, I assume you would sit here and your patient would lie on the sofa. Is that right?'

'Not necessarily,' the little Welshman explained, moving round behind the furniture. 'The important thing is to ensure that the patient is completely relaxed. Some prefer to sit, some to lie. And I should point out that there is always a third person present, either a friend brought by the patient or an associate of my own.' He winked and again produced his deep chuckle. 'Could lay myself open to all sorts of hysterical accusations if I were to entertain ladies here unchaperoned.'

'So,' Nat said, 'there would normally be three people in here, just as there are now. How would the consultation proceed? Perhaps you could give us a practical demonstration. Sue, you wouldn't mind being the patient, would you?'

'Not at all,' Susan said, spreading herself on the sofa. 'I've always wondered what it would be like to be hypnotized.'

Owen's face wore an anxious frown. Nat hurried on, giving him no time to think. 'Having made the patient comfortable, you relax her with soothing words, I suppose.'

'There are various techniques,' Owen explained. 'Music. Visual images. I've a small console here, behind the sofa.' He fiddled with the out-of-sight apparatus and the sound of gentle, meandering Muzak filled the air. He clicked another switch and a concealed projector threw on to the blank wall a series of psychedelic shapes and colours which gently swirled and swayed and merged and separated.

'Mmmm, that's very soothing,' Susan murmured. She stretched out her long, jeans-covered legs on the smooth leather.

'That obviously works for Sue,' Nat observed. 'Let's leave those patterns up for a moment.' He watched the other man carefully and read uncertainty in the eyes

121

beneath thick, black brows. He resents not being in control, Nat analysed, but he's balancing that with the thought of a fat cheque and the chance of appearing on TV. The man's a natural performer. He can't resist showing off. With an effort Nat suppressed his feelings of contempt. Here was someone, he reminded himself, who had, very probably, planted murderous thoughts in the mind of a trusting woman. Could he be tricked into giving himself away? Could his own pathetic exhibitionism be used against him? One thing was for sure, Nat told himself: you'll never get another chance to find out.

He said, 'OK, let's see how this is going to look on the screen. Now, presumably you sit here, in the chair, facing the patient, while she's looking at the pretty pictures. So, would you mind?'

Hesitantly, Owen took his place.

'Good. Yes, that looks fine. You're immensely telegenic, doctor. Now give us an example of the kind of patter you'd use.'

Owen's brow cleared; his whole body language loosened as he slipped easily into his well-practised role. 'One has to establish rapport – complete confidence between practitioner and patient.' Smiling at Susan he said, 'Are you comfortable, Sue? I may call you Sue, mayn't I?'

'Please do and, yes, I'm very comfortable.'

'That's right. Good to relax. You've had a long drive in nasty weather. You must be tired.'

'Mmmm!' Susan yawned.

'There's warm and soft, the sofa, isn't it?'

'Very soft,' Susan responded languidly.

'So soft it feels as if you're sinking right into it, deeper and deeper. If you close your eyes it will seem as though you're floating. That's right, eyes gently closing. And you're floating on clouds. The room has dissolved and there's just you and the clouds and the warm sunshine and the sound of my voice. Nothing else at all.'

'Nothing else at all,' Susan echoed.

'Can you hear my voice?'

'Yes.'

'And you can hear nothing else. Nothing else at all.'

'Nothing else at all.'

'And you can only hear my voice when I call you by name; when I say "Sue".' Owen smiled at Nat and motioned to him to speak.

Nat said, 'Sue, this is Nat. Can you hear me?'

The only sound from the sofa was the woman's steady breathing.

'You and I can hold a conversation and she'll be quite oblivious,' Owen explained. 'Her unconscious mind has put on blinkers.'

Nat was genuinely impressed. 'That's remarkably good.'

Owen beamed. 'She's a very apt subject. It usually takes longer. Of course, she had already expressed a desire to be hypnotized, so there was no resistance to be overcome. I'll bring her back now.'

'Before you do that, can we take it a short stage further? We were talking about unlocking childhood memories. Why don't we try that with Sue?'

Owen frowned. 'That's dangerous territory, Dr Gye. I know nothing at all about the subject. For all I'm aware her early years may have been full of sadness and tragedy. The forgotten past is best left forgotten, unless there are impelling reasons for dragging it out.'

'Of course, but, you see, I'm a bit of a sceptic about regression. I'm not convinced that hypnotic memories are genuine. They could be implanted by the practitioner or invented by the subject. This seems like an opportunity for you to convince me. If you could get Sue to recall some pleasant moment from her earliest years – something we could afterwards verify – well, that would have to be reflected in the programmes.'

Still Owen looked worried. 'I don't have Ms Avery-White's permission . . .'

'Oh, you can take it from me Sue will be happy. She's a pro. Whatever will make a good programme she will do.'

'Well . . . But you must take the responsibility, Dr Gye.'

'Of course.'

Owen returned his attention to the figure on the sofa. Nat saw that he was perspiring. 'Sue, you're still floating on the clouds. You're happy. Blissfully happy. Now you're floating down to earth, very gently. Still happy. And you're five years old. How old are you, Sue?'

'I'm five but I'll be six in August.' The words were piped out with a childish lisp.

'That will be very soon, Sue. But today is almost as good as a birthday. You're very happy.'

Susan brought her hands together in a sudden, excited gesture. She gave a delighted giggle.

'Where are you, Sue?' Owen asked.

'Watching the witch!'

'What witch, Sue?' Owen pursued, gently.

'You know, the witch!' The reply was impatient, petulant. 'They've pushed her in the oven and she's going to be all burned up.'

Owen looked puzzled. 'Who's pushed the witch in the oven, Sue?'

'The children, silly!'

'Oh, I see. Sue, is this a picture in a story book?'

'No!' Susan now sounded quite cross. 'It's there. Everyone can see. You're silly. I don't want to talk to you!'

Owen turned to Nat. 'That's the trouble with early memories; they're often jumbled. Children don't distinguish between fact and fiction.'

Nat looked thoughtful. 'Maybe. Or she could have been telling us exactly what she saw. The problem is, we have difficulty interpreting it.' But his thoughts were far from Susan's real or imagined infant recollections. 'Now let's go a step further,' he suggested. 'Take her back beyond child-hood, beyond birth. Take her to an earlier life.'

Owen stared, open-mouthed. Now the sweat was hanging in droplets from the lines across his brow. 'I told you I don't dabble in that sort of thing! I'm bringing her back now!'

'You're lying!' Nat snapped. 'What can you tell me about Mrs Juniper Myles?'

Owen's eyes bulged. His mouth opened and closed several times. He pulled out a handkerchief and wiped it across his forehead. 'Who are you?' he gasped out at last.

'I am who I say I am,' Nat replied levelly. 'Which is more than you can claim, Mr Williams.'

Owen grabbed for his dignity. 'You'd better leave!'

But Nat persisted. 'I know about your "sessions" with Mrs Myles. What you've done to her is nothing short of diabolical!' Nat lowered his voice to a menacing whisper. 'Who put you up to it? How much did they pay you? How many clients do you have, for God's sake, who hire you to scramble other people's brains?'

Owen tried desperately to pull himself together. 'You're crazy,' he gasped. 'I don't know what you're talking about and I'll thank you to leave!'

'Oh, I'll leave.' Nat leaned forward and placed a business card on the low table. 'And I'll give you seven days to get in touch with me and tell me about your relationship with Mrs Myles and with any other wretched victims of your mind games. If I don't hear from you or if I discover that you have attempted to make further contact with Mrs Myles I will personally ensure that you're put out of business – permanently!'

'What went on back there?' The red sports car had threaded its way through the urban sprawl and out on to the motorway before Susan posed the question. 'Everything seemed to be going swimmingly. Then Owen put me under the influence. The next thing I know is we're almost being thrown down the stairs.'

'How did you like being hypnotized?'

'Don't really remember much about it. It was very restful. I felt as though I didn't have a care in the world. Then I came to to find the little Welshman screaming abuse at you. What on earth did you say to upset him?'

'Do you like opera, Sue?'

Susan pulled the Mazda into the outside lane to roar past a column of spray-spreading long vehicles. 'Will you stop answering questions with questions, Nat? You make me feel as though I'm being psychoanalysed.'

Nat laughed. 'Indulge me just for a moment. Opera? Are you a fan?'

'Enormous fan. I love it.'

'Do you remember the first opera you ever saw?'

'Vividly. *Aida*, Covent Garden.'

'How old were you at the time?'

'Let me see . . . fourteen? No, thirteen. Why?'

'And that was definitely your first experience of opera?'

'Definitely. I was knocked over by the sheer scale and magnificence of it all – and, of course the music. That's not the sort of thing you forget.'

'Have you ever seen Humperdinck's *Hansel and Gretel*?'

'No, my taste runs more to grand opera, especially Verdi.'

'You're quite sure about that?'

'Yes, of course I am. What's this all about, Nat?'

'Just a hunch of mine. Will you humour me a bit further? Next time you're on the phone to your mother ask her if you've ever seen *Hansel and Gretel*.'

'This has got something to do with Owen, hasn't it?'

'Possibly.'

'So, are you going to tell me what went on while I was out for the count?'

'I'm afraid I upset our friend. We had a little chat about the ethics of hypnotherapy and I suppose I let my academic cynicism run away with me.'

Susan laughed. 'Well, that wouldn't be the first time, would it? Remember that medium who brought her minder to the studio? He very nearly wrecked the set before we managed to pull him off.'

'This was not dissimilar. Owen took objection to some remark of mine and said he wanted nothing to do with the programme.'

'Does that mean I've got to phone him up and do my "sweetness and light" act?'

'No, I'll probably be in touch with him in a few days. Leave it with me for the time being.'

The File Refuses to Stay Closed

That evening Nat put a call through to Sheldon Myles. He had been meaning for some days to speak to the barrister but been deterred by his encounter with the Holts. How could one hold an honest, open conversation with a suspected murderer? But, then, he argued with himself, that was all Myles was – 'suspected' – and Nat had no means of knowing how reliable the business trio's proof was. And there was June to consider. She had to be his overriding concern and, following his head-to-head with Owen, Nat knew that he had to do all he could to obtain the right kind of help for her.

'Nat, hello. How are you?' The barrister sounded more relaxed than when they had last spoken.

'I'm very well. How did your Caribbean holiday go?'

'Just what the doctor ordered. Did June a power of good.'

'I'm delighted to hear it. What about the delusions?'

'Not completely dispelled yet, but if I keep her away from Coln for a few months and stop that pernicious Owen character getting to her I'm sure she'll mend.'

'I don't think you'll have any trouble from Owen.'

'You found him?' The voice was eager.

'Yes, or rather one of my television associates did some very clever sleuthing.'

'Excellent, excellent! Where is he?'

'He operates out of a grimy backstreet in Birmingham. Anyway, I've warned him off in no uncertain terms.'

'I was right about the little shit, wasn't I?'

'More or less. He's a charlatan of a type not altogether uncommon but I'm sure you've heard the last of him. But, look, you really should get June to see a top analyst. I recommend Ewen Macleod. He's the best there is. If you've got a pen there I'll give you his number.'

'Right. Fire away.'

Nat dictated the eleven digits but sensed that Myles would not make use of them. He added, 'Ewen's thoroughly professional, discreet and sensible. I've known him for years. You can trust him implicitly.'

'Right, point taken. While we're about it, you'd better give me the address of this Owen character . . . just in case.'

Nat provided the details and Myles said, 'Right, got that. Must dash, Nat, just on my way out to a dinner being given by the Lord Chancellor.'

'OK, have a pleasant evening.'

'That I doubt. Bit of a bore, really. Cheerio . . . Oh, and thanks.'

Nat was about to say, 'That's all right. Glad I was able to help.' But the line was already dead.

He shrugged and switched on the computer. He brought up the Journal file headed Juniper Myles and made a fresh entry.

Monday 30 October

Identity of the deceased: younger sister of Jack, Harry and Quentin Holt, wealthy, powerful, probably ruthless businessmen. Convinced Myles killed Tracy. Believe they have proof. Say they will take law into own hands.

Should I persuade them to take their evidence to the police? Non-starter. They have told me, in no uncertain terms to keep out of their business. Should I warn Myles?

a)   Are the Holts capable of planning and executing vicious revenge? Probably.
b)   Would Myles take the threat seriously? Probably not. He would regard it as just another attempt to drive him out of Coln.
c)   If Holts are intent on doing him a mischief difficult to see what steps Myles could take to protect himself.
d)   If they are right about Myles, warning him would put him on his guard. Could he get at the witness who apparently saw him with Tracy? (Wish I knew who it was)

Go to the police, then? Yes. Drop everything in lap of DCI Mitchenor of the county CID.

'Dr' Caradoc Owen, alias George Williams: ex-stage hypnotist, now an unqualified, backstreet 'therapist', making a living preying on the gullible. Prepared to sell his talent for nefarious ends. He ought to be put out of business but I cannot refer the police to him without involving June. Not an option. Who employed him to worm his way into June's confidence? I suppose I will never know. Anyway, I have warned him to keep away from Mrs Myles, which is what her husband wanted me to do. So my responsibility to him is at an end. Expose this potentially dangerous quackery in the next TV series. Perhaps Susan could track down three or four victims of unqualified hypnotherapists.

FILE CLOSED

After his Tuesday lecture, Nat strolled along Trinity Street to Heffers bookshop to check on some published American seminar papers that he had ordered. As he walked back up the wide stairs from the lower ground floor, his query having been dealt with, a voice hailed him. Turning, he saw the dapper figure of Barnaby Cox.

'Nathaniel, dear boy, I come, like Phidippides from Marathon, hotfoot with news.' The old man nimbly climbed the staircase. He beamed. 'Doing your detective work has been most stimulating – and illuminating. Come for a coffee and I'll reveal all.'

Nat stole a glance at his watch and thought of the pile of work on his desk. He wanted to put Cox off to a more convenient time but the old lawyer looked so pleased with himself that Nat knew he could not disappoint him. Certainly he could not tell him that his interest in Myles had waned.

Fifteen minutes later the two men were seated in a first floor café overlooking Market Hill and Cox was turning his nose up at the cafetière that a bored waitress set on the table between them.

'Whoever invented these diabolical machines should be drowned in a butt of the vile sepia liquid they dispense,' he grumbled as Nat depressed the plunger. He glared at the cup pushed across to him and sipped it suspiciously.

'You've enjoyed my little brain teaser, then?' Nat asked.

'Indeed I have. Apart from anything else it gave me an excuse to get in touch again with Monty Pym. I went and had lunch with him on Sunday. He lives over in Suffolk. Semi-invalid now, poor old chap. Had a stroke a couple of years back and never fully recovered but, mercifully, his mind's still clear.'

'So he could remember friend Myles?'

'Oh, certainly. Apparently they crossed swords on many occasions. A question of Old Guard versus Young Turk, I shouldn't wonder. Monty was always a stickler for upholding the dignity of chambers. He regarded Myles as brash and irresponsible, too much addicted to the high life. "Flash", he called him. Young Myles was one of the leaders of the bar social scene, a prominent member of the drama society, and attracted women like a magnet.'

'An actor, was he?'

'Indeed, and apparently quite talented. By all accounts his Iago is still talked of with hushed tones in thespian circles around Chancery Lane. Monty calls it type casting.'

'What of his early life? Do we know much about that?'

'That seems to be "a riddle, wrapped in a mystery inside an enigma". He rarely talked about his past. All Monty knows is that his parents were both dead – a plane crash somewhere in Asia, he thought – and that he had no immediate family.'

'I don't think the air crash story can be right. According to the press cuttings I've seen, his parents were stolid northern tradespeople.'

'Doubtless, that was why he was not anxious to discuss his origins. Difficult to cut much of a dash in the "right" circles if daddy was a shopkeeper. The only part of his past Myles did talk about was the years immediately prior to commencing his bar training. He claimed to have travelled widely in order to see the world before settling to a career.'

'That very conveniently fills the gap in his post-university years in a way that's very difficult for anyone to verify.'

'Still looking for a guilty past, are you? I doubt whether you'll find it in his adolescent naïvety. Many youngsters of his generation hit the hippy trail to the mystic East. It was part of the necessary rebellion against their parents' culture. Most of them came back sadder and wiser from their vain quest for Shangri-La.'

'But foreign adventure seems to have had just the opposite effect on Myles. He left Durham a serious, model law graduate with a first class brain and came back from his travels a young tearaway who couldn't be bothered to study properly for his bar exams.'

Cox held up a hand to decline a second cup of coffee. As Nat poured one for himself, the old lawyer said, 'You're the expert on human behaviour but is it really so odd for a bright young man in his early twenties to re-evaluate his lifestyle; to conclude that there is more to living than mugging up facts from dusty books? My guess is that he decided to gather a few rosebuds while he might.'

'And to pursue a career with ruthless aggression?'

Cox shrugged. 'He certainly did that. Cultivated the right people. Married the right woman. Got himself noticed. Went for high profile briefs and managed to make cases that weren't high profile appear so by exercising his theatrical skills to the utmost.'

Interested now despite himself, Nat suggested, 'Such a determined high flyer must have stretched the rules pretty often, trodden on toes, cut some corners.'

Cox laughed. 'My dear boy, when you mix metaphors you don't do it by halves, do you? But, in essence you're right. Friend Myles had a long run as a whizz-kid of the criminal bar. His differences of opinion with the bench were legendary. They would have sunk a less determined advocate without trace but Myles seemed to thrive on them and they only enhanced his reputation with the police and the Crown Prosecution Service, for whom he mostly worked. He certainly delivered the goods; got convictions where no one else would have done. The fact that a high percentage of those convictions were overturned on appeal didn't seem to worry the law enforcers unduly. They felt that here was a prosecutor with real "teeth", someone who could get the villains put away even if the evidence wasn't watertight.'

Nat mused, gazing out on the market stalls and their multicoloured awnings. 'Supposing he'd crossed the line at some point; colluded with less than scrupulous police officers to fabricate evidence. Would that be possible?'

Cox seemed shocked by the idea. 'Possible, certainly, but incredibly risky. Discovery would involve not only the end of his career, but criminal proceedings to boot.'

'Yes, but someone utterly single-minded, as Myles

clearly was, might not think he was being reckless. Such people are often blinkered to everything except success.'

'Ends justify means?'

'Precisely. Then there's Myles's sudden abandonment of criminal litigation. What lay behind that?'

'It wasn't all that sudden.' Cox leaned forward, speaking in a conspiratorial whisper. 'And this is where politics rears its ugly head. Our calculating friend made an uncharacteristic and fundamental strategical error. Not to put too fine a point on it, he backed the wrong party. Throughout the eighties he became increasingly involved with the Tory top brass. Deliberate calculation, of course. They were his armour plating and his meal ticket, if I may share your partiality for the scrambled metaphor. You see, he had made too many enemies in the judicial establishment to be sure of pursuing his upward path by purely professional means, so he counterbalanced that by cultivating important friends in higher places. By means of impressive donations, speeches at party conferences, selective entertainment of the "hang 'em and shoot 'em brigade", articles in the Tory press advocating tougher sentencing policies, and so on, he became one of the darlings of the far right. With that kind of support he could continue his outrageous courtroom antics unchecked.'

'But when the Conservatives were thrown out . . .'

'Exactly. In the mid-nineties it became obvious even to the somnolent British electorate that the Tories were hopelessly corrupt and incompetent. Myles could see that he could very soon find himself paddling a lonely canoe through shark-infested waters. The list of convictions he had secured that were found on appeal to be unsafe was growing embarrassingly long. Some of his recent cases had attracted very hostile press comment.'

'Like the Forbes murder trial?'

'Yes, and the Volnay fraud case that was taken up by the *Sunday Times* and the Williams incitement fiasco.'

134

'Williams?' The name triggered a quick response. 'What was that about?'

'Ah!' The lawyer's eyes glittered eagerly. 'Right up your street, dear boy. In fact it's the sort of thing we were discussing last week.'

'About hypnotism and crime?'

'That's right.'

'Good God! Was the defendant's name George Williams?'

'The very same. You've studied the trial?'

'No, but I'm beginning to get a nasty feeling about it. Can you go over the main points?'

'Well, it started with a case that Myles actually lost. Brutal assault by an unsavoury character called Briggs on his homosexual partner.' Cox paused in his narration. 'I do resent the way the word "gay" has been hijacked by that community. Very few of the homosexuals I've met could be characterized as "lighthearted and carefree".'

Nat struggled to conceal his impatience. 'About Briggs. Are you saying Myles failed to get a conviction?'

'For murder, yes. His defence brought psychiatric evidence to show that he was a mild schizophrenic and that the attack had been prompted by Briggs being subjected to hypnosis. It seems that the "couple" had been to a nightclub where this Williams character was performing and Briggs was one of the volunteers who went up on stage to be zapped. According to the defence, he underwent a character change and on the way home he picked up a brick and battered his chum to death.'

'Sounds a bit flimsy.'

'Perhaps, but it was enough to sow doubt in the minds of the jury. They accepted a plea of diminished responsibility and Briggs was referred to a mental institution. At that point the police decided to go after Williams for incitement to commit a criminal act and they briefed Myles, who was furious at having lost the Briggs case. It came to trial in Leicester crown court and Myles clearly threw himself into it body and soul. I read the transcript yesterday in the Law Library. The defence put Williams in the box – they really had no choice – and on cross-examination Myles tore the man into tiny, bleeding shreds. The defendant broke down twice and his counsel was up and down like a yo-yo raising objections. It was one of the most vitriolic performances in a court of law that I've come across. Despite an excellent summing-up in which the judge did his level best to reduce the impact of the prosecution's aggressive advocacy, the jury found for the Crown. Williams received the minimum sentence of three years. His lawyers immediately began work on an appeal but the poor man served a third of his sentence before the conviction was quashed.'

'Poor bastard!' Nat closed his eyes and saw again the diminutive Caradoc Owen, perspiring heavily and almost cringing as Nat lashed him with his tongue. What the charlatan had done to June was, by any standards, quite inexcusable but now Nat could understand the tortured logic by which he might have convinced himself that there was some kind of justice in his actions.

'Yes, indeed.' Cox continued with his bustling report. 'So there were compelling reasons for Myles to make a sideways career move. He mugged up on his company law and he had his wife on hand to fill in the many gaps in his knowledge. She's one of the leading experts in the field. Quite brilliant. So, for the last few years, Myles has enjoyed a lower profile and, doubtless, a higher income.'

The tables were beginning to fill with people coming in for early lunches and Nat was aware of the pointed looks the waitress was casting in his direction. He gathered his raincoat and briefcase from the seat beside him. 'Barny, I'm much obliged to you. You've put in a great deal of work on this and I certainly feel I know Sheldon Myles a lot better as a result.'

'My pleasure entirely,' the old lawyer replied, getting a little stiffly to his feet. 'I welcome anything to hold mental atrophy at bay. I'll keep a watching brief on the unadmirable Myles. If I succeed in digging up any dirt, you'll be the first to know.'

They parted and Nat made his way thoughtfully back to Beaufort.

Wednesday was the day that the Gyes were having dinner with Greg Polowski. When he was not teaching or in meetings Nat went over in his mind a score of times what he would say to the high-powered American and how he wanted the conversation to go. He knew the reality would be very different but that did not stop him trying to anticipate every argument Greg might advance nor worrying himself sick about the outcome. It would, he felt, be like going into a game of three-handed poker in which the other players were acting in concert and his own cards were innocent of pictures or aces. Confrontation would only strengthen Kathryn's resolve. If he lost control of himself he would lose everything. He would be reasonable and calm, he told himself. That way he might, just might, persuade two people totally dedicated to their jobs that there were things in life more important than making and selling magazines.

Kathryn returned early from London and spent twice as long as usual on her clothes and make-up.

'You look scrumptious,' Nat said, coming into the bedroom and eyeing appreciatively the loose shirt of rose shot silk over claret velvet trousers. 'Who are you planning to seduce?'

She smiled briefly but then her face clouded. 'Darling, you're not . . .'

'Not what?'

She turned away abruptly. 'Oh, I don't know. It sounds so silly I don't even want to say it.'

'Say it,' Nat encouraged. 'Better out than in, as my old gran used to say.'

'You're not jealous of Greg?'

'Jealous? You mean rival lover sort of jealous?'

Kathryn's free-flowing, midnight river hair gleamed as she shook her head. 'No, not that! That's silly!' She turned to face him but kept her distance. 'It's just . . . I want tonight to be positive, friendly. I don't want to feel like some maiden at a medieval joust with the black knight and the white knight fighting over me.'

Nat tried a casual laugh which did not quite come off. 'And which of us is the white knight?'

Kathryn pouted. 'Oh, don't twist my words. You know what I mean. It's important to me that you and Greg get on well.'

Nat crossed to the dressing table and busied himself brushing the lapels of his jacket. 'I don't dislike Greg. We live in totally different worlds, that's all. That makes it hard for us to understand each other.'

She came and put her arms round him. 'But you will try, won't you?'

He held her tight to him in a possessive, protective embrace. 'Kate, Kate, you're a fantastic woman and that's a secret I want to keep to myself. I can't bear the thought of someone else discovering it, especially if that someone is three thousand miles away.'

Kathryn clung to him for several seconds without making any reply. Then she pulled away and stared at herself in the mirror. 'Damn! Now look what you've made me do. My mascara's all smudged.'

The restaurant chosen by Greg overlooked Midsummer Common on the downriver side of Cambridge, where the Cam wanders lazily through water meadows, and the evening shadows were long across the drive as the Gyes arrived shortly after 7.30. They found their host waiting in the select establishment's bar.

'Katie, Nat, hi!' The American's personality filled the small room and seemed to make the other pre-diners cower at their little tables. He kissed Kathryn on both cheeks and gripped Nat's hand in a firm grasp. 'I hope you approve of this place. I asked my secretary to locate the best restaurant in Cambridge and this is what her Internet researches came up with.'

Nat sized up the opposition. Polowski's forty-something years sat lightly on him and if he was a worry-haunted executive, he certainly did not look it. His complexion was clear and he sported a trim beard, which was new since Nat had seen him last. Probably compensating for his spreading baldness, Nat thought uncharitably. He was a little under six foot and he did not need his finely tailored suit to emphasize that he was well on top of the middle-age spread problem.

Kathryn returned her boss's enthusiastic greeting. 'It's lovely to see you over here again, Greg. You should have let me send a car to Heathrow to bring you to the office. We could have travelled up from London together.'

'No, Katie, I didn't want to get bogged down in business detail.' He glanced quickly at Nat. 'This is strictly a one-meeting trip – a very important meeting with colleagues and friends. But it doesn't start yet, not till we've done justice to this place's excellent menu. I've had a quick preview and, frankly, I'm salivating already. Now, there's a bottle of Veuve Clicquot on ice at that corner table, so what say we go and join it.'

It was hard to resist being borne along on the tide of Greg's ebullience and the evening got off to a good start. Yet for Nat relaxation was impossible and, as the plates and glasses before him were emptied in slow succession, he concentrated more on keeping a clear head than on enjoying the food and the conversation. When desserts had been ordered he seized the initiative.

'I don't think we can put off any longer the purpose of this get-together.'

Greg nodded, immediately businesslike. 'OK, cards on the table. Our corporation needs Katie and we're prepared to do anything to have her at the helm of our flagship publication. There.' He sat back. 'I've just broken the first rule of business practice – "never let anyone see your vulnerability". You guys have me over a barrel. You can pretty well name your price.'

Nat saw the look of sympathetic concern on his wife's face and thought, Clever sod! He said, 'Greg, are you really telling us that there's no one out there in the wide world of international journalism who can hold a candle to Kate? That's very gratifying and I'm the last one to want to belittle her considerable abilities, but . . .'

The American stroked his beard and Nat recognized the comfort gesture that betrayed anxiety. 'Nat, how can I explain it? In your own line of country I'm sure you have some very bright students but sometimes one comes along who is, not just cleverer than the rest, he or she is in a different league, has an intuitive grasp of the subject, responds to your teaching with an enthusiasm that's almost electric. I'm sure you know what I mean. Now, how often does that happen? Once in five years? Ten?'

Nat nodded.

'Well,' Greg continued, 'that's how I rate Katie. Oh, certainly we could appoint someone else, probably at half the salary we're offering your charming wife. And perhaps in time that someone would make a damned good international editor. But, you see, Nat, we don't have the time. These are stormy days marketwise and we're talking survival.'

Nat stared back frankly. 'Survival. Yes, I reckon that's the key word. It's what interests me. Kate and I don't have a huge corporate ship to keep afloat; just a little boat with four people in it but it's as important to us as your ocean liner.'

'Well, of course, Nat, I –'

Kathryn slapped a hand down on the table. 'Just a minute, you two! Is anyone here interested in what I think?' She took a deep breath. 'My dad is a very successful businessman. He worked his way up from the bottom to the very top and he raised me on his philosophy. Do you know what it was? He summed it up in a few words and he dinned those words into me time and time again until they became part of my mental fabric: "Your only limitations are the ones you impose on yourself." So, that's why I've always believed the sky's the limit and never let anyone else stop me reaching for it.'

'Darling, I don't want –'

'No, Nat, I haven't finished.' She smiled faintly at him. 'What I didn't realize until years later was that my father was a fraud. No,' she hesitated, 'perhaps that's too hard. Let's just say he was inconsistent. You see, the one person he never applied his philosophy to was my mother. She was – is – a fine musician. If she'd had one ounce of dad's drive she could have made it to the concert platform. Instead, she became the corporate wife, the perfect hostess, the "little woman" who propped dad up, massaged his ego, soothed his fevered brow and, of course, bore his only child.'

Nat said, 'But your parents are a devoted couple.'

Kathryn nodded. 'Sure they are. Blissfully happy and still very much in love. But the reason their marriage works is that mom accepted the limitations dad imposed on her. But, darling, I'm not like that –'

Kathryn was interrupted by a buzzing noise. Nat thrust a hand into his jacket pocket and pulled out his mobile.

'Excuse me a moment.' He hurried across the room and went into the now empty bar to take the call.

He was away from the table for three or four minutes during which time the waiter arrived to serve the desserts. This effectively hampered further conversation. When Nat returned, steering his way slowly between the tables, something about his appearance made Kathryn jump to her feet.

'Darling, what's the matter? Bad news?'

Nat sat heavily and stared across the table at her. 'I think I've killed someone.'

Police Politics

The phone call was from Susan. As Nat listened to her in the comparative quiet of the deserted bar she sounded breathless.

'Nat, sorry to call you so late. We've been shooting all day and I've only just got back.'

'That's OK. What's so urgent?'

'I just thought I ought to warn you that you might be getting a call from the police.'

'Police!'

'Uh-huh.' The next sounds were muffled, then Susan said, 'Sorry, talking with my mouth full – grabbing some late supper. Yeah, some police sergeant from Birmingham called me this afternoon. It seems there was an accident last night at Dr Owen's place. A gas explosion, they think.'

'Oh dear. Anyone hurt?'

'The DS Baker who called me wasn't very forthcoming but I gather Owen was the only person on the premises and he didn't survive the blast.'

Nat gasped. 'Owen's dead?'

'I'm afraid so. Quite a shock, isn't it, when you've been talking to someone only a matter of hours before?'

'Yes, it is,' Nat said absently, his mind in a whirl. 'Why did the police call you?'

'They found my name and number in Owen's appointments book. I suppose it must have been in that massive desk of his and escaped the blaze.'

'What did they want to know?'

'Oh, Baker just said they were contacting anyone who had seen Owen recently. Purely routine, apparently.'

'And you gave them my name?'

'Just your name and college address. That was all right, wasn't it? I didn't mention your personal phone numbers.'

'Er . . . yes. Fine. Fine.'

Susan did not seem to detect the anxiety in his voice. 'Oh, while you're there, Nat.'

'Yes?'

'You were right about *Hansel and Gretel*. I phoned my mother and she told me that I'd been taken to see it when I was five. She says it made a great impression on me at the time but I've no recollection of it at all. How on earth did you know? Was it something I said when Owen hypnotized me?'

'What? Oh, I'll tell you about it next time we meet. Must go now.'

'Right.' Now she hesitated. 'You OK, Nat?'

'Yes . . . er . . . speak to you soon, Sue. G'bye.'

When he got back to the table Nat was in a daze. He told the others what Susan had said and Kathryn gave Greg a résumé of the events leading up to her husband's meeting with the hypnotist.

'I told Myles where to find Owen and the very next day Owen was killed.' Nat said bleakly.

'But the police say it's an accident,' Greg protested.

Nat groaned. 'Accident? Two people got on the wrong side of Sheldon Myles. One fell into a lake. The other was blown to bits in a gas explosion. What do you reckon the statistical odds are of those two deaths being accidental?'

Kathryn reached across the table to hold her husband's hand. 'Darling, even if we are talking murder you have nothing to reproach yourself for.'

'I should have been more careful. Not given Myles the address.'

'How could you know that he'd do something desperate – if, indeed, he did?'

'Because, if I'd put two and two together earlier, I'd have worked out something that I only discovered yesterday. Caradoc Owen was one of Sheldon Myles's victims. He was humiliated in court, had his career – such as it was – ruined and spent several months in prison, quite unnecessarily. That gave him ample motive for wanting to hit back at his persecutor. What better way than exercising power over June Myles? He'd been wrongfully condemned for inciting a man to homicide. OK, he'd get his own back by persuading June that she'd murdered her husband's lover.'

'But,' Kathryn protested, 'that doesn't hang together. Owen would have to have known that June was on the verge of a breakdown and he'd have needed a lot of information about the situation at Coln – much more than he could have read in the newspaper accounts of Tracy's death.'

'I agree. He needed accomplices.'

'And what was in it for them? Were they covering up for the real murderer? But that would mean the murderer wasn't Shelley.' Kathryn clasped her forehead with both hands. 'Oh, this doesn't make any sense. It just keeps going round and round.'

Nat nodded. 'This whole business has got loose ends all over the place. I'll have to go to the police. Tell them everything. Let them try to make some sense of it all.' He looked at his watch. 'I wonder if I can catch Mitchenor now.' He took out his wallet and found the policeman's card.

Greg had been fidgeting for some minutes. Now he pushed his plate away and said with manifestly controlled calm, 'Look, guys, I realize this is all very distressing for Nathaniel but I didn't cut into a busy schedule and fly the Atlantic to play Cluedo – who killed who in the conservatory with the candlestick.'

Nat stood abruptly. 'I'm sorry this has blown up, Greg, but I must get on to my police contact without delay. Why don't you two go through to the lounge for coffee? I'll join you in a few minutes.'

This time he went out on to the rear terrace and paced up and down while he tapped Mitchenor's number into his handset and waited for an answer. It was a mild night. The building and its flanking trees were floodlit. Wooden tables, used for pre-dinner drinks in summer, dotted the terrace. Nat took several deep breaths of the dank riverain air and tried to martial his thoughts clearly so as to give the inspector a concise report.

After what seemed an age he heard a breathless woman's voice on the other end of the line. 'Hello. Sorry, I couldn't find the phone. Kids!'

'That's OK. Is it possible to have a quick word with Dave Mitchenor? My name's Nat Gye.'

'He's just got back with Matthew from soccer practice, followed by a McDonald's. I think he's having a shower. Hang on a minute.'

Nat heard one half of a shouted conversation, then the voice returned. 'Mr Gye? Yes, he's in the shower right now. If you'd like to give me your number he'll get back to you in a few minutes.'

Nat slowly walked the length of the terrace. At the far end he found himself looking in through the window of the well-lit lounge. Kathryn and Greg were sitting in a corner by the fireplace and it was obvious from the American's body language that he was getting very impatient. He was a man used to setting agendas, not following other people's. Miserably Nat watched as Kathryn made soothing gestures, glancing every now and then at the door, willing her husband to come through it. Nat turned away. It had been a disastrous evening for everyone and he wondered what else could go wrong. Probably his attempts later on to pacify Kathryn. She would be embarrassed at having wasted her boss's highly valuable time and furious with Nat for being responsible for the fiasco the evening had become. Well, Nat thought, they're not the only ones to be frustrated. 'Damn! Damn! Damn!' he shouted to the empty garden.

At last the handset emitted its insect-like buzzing.

'Hello, Nat, sorry to keep you. What's on your mind?' Mitchenor sounded relaxed and friendly.

Nat got straight to the point. 'There's been another supposed accident, this time in Birmingham, and I'm sure it's connected with the business in Coln.' Briefly he gave Mitchenor the details of Owen's relationship with June Myles and his violent death.

Mitchenor listened in silence, then said, 'It would have been useful to know about the hypnotism angle earlier.'

'I would have mentioned it but you indicated that the case was very firmly closed.'

'Fair enough. Is there anything else I ought to know?'

'Well, I have found out one or two things,' Nat suggested cautiously.

'You'd better come over and tell me everything that might have a bearing on either of these deaths.'

'Yes, of course.'

'Meanwhile I'll get on to Birmingham CID and see what's going down there.'

They arranged a meeting for the following afternoon. Then Nat pocketed the phone and went back into the restaurant.

As he entered the lounge, he saw the American getting to his feet.

'Greg has to get back to his hotel to make some phone calls,' Kathryn explained, glaring at her husband.

'Have to talk to some folk in New York before they leave the office,' Greg added. He shook Nat's hand. 'Good to spend some time with you, Nathaniel.'

'I'm sorry our discussion was cut short.'

Greg fastened his jacket and checked his watch. 'Well, as I was saying to Katie, you two have to talk things over.

When you've done that, email me with your ideas. If I think we can live with them I'll see them incorporated in the contract. But I must finalize things by the end of next week, so you'll have to get back to me within seven days. Now I gotta run. My taxi's waiting.' He stooped briefly to kiss Kathryn. 'I guess you need to do some soothing of the fevered brow.' He turned and strode quickly to the door.

Nat took his place on the sofa beside his wife. She was sitting stiffly upright. 'I'm sorry the way things turned out, but –'

'Not a word!' Kathryn stared straight ahead. 'Not a single, sodding word!'

They drove home in silence.

They both spent a wretched night and, by the time Kathryn left for London the next day, she and Nat had still exchanged no more than routine domestic messages. Nat had a busy morning and it was not till midday that he had any time to himself. Then he firmly closed the inner and outer doors of his college rooms (known in university circles as 'sporting the oak') and stretched himself on the sofa to think.

He had made a mess of last night. Why? Because he had allowed the Coln affair to become an obsession. What had begun as a series of intriguing puzzles begging to be solved had become issues of morality, truth and justice. He had thought he could walk away from the facts and theories when they became too time-consuming but they had entangled his mind and refused to loosen their grip. Two people were dead, one of them as a direct result of his interference. Impossible to turn one's back on that. The culprit had to be brought to book and, whether he liked it or not, Dr Nathaniel Gye was involved in that process.

But not at the cost of destroying his marriage. Ever since Kathryn had told him about the promotion, Nat had accused her in his mind of putting her job before him and the children. Was he not, now, making the same mistake? If it were not for his own infernal curiosity he would not have been distracted last night. He and Kathryn might have been able to discuss their future with Greg like intelligent, grown-up human beings. Instead of which . . .

So, what to do? Nat explored the options and made some decisions. He put the first into operation immediately. Crossing to his desk, he switched on the computer and ran off a printout of the Juniper Myles file from his Journal. With this beside him he made a precisely worded report to give Mitchenor later that day. As he stared at the screen he still could not make everything fit. The pieces were like pottery fragments found in some archaeological dig which might or might not all belong to the same original artefact. However, Nat told himself, reconstruction was no longer his problem. When he had passed all the facts and theories he had gathered to the proper authorities he could, with a clear conscience, forget about the objectionable Sheldon Myles and his multitudinous enemies and concentrate on matters closer to home.

He arrived in Oxford soon after four o'clock for his meeting with Mitchenor and found the DCI in his shirt-sleeves in an overheated office.

'Thanks for your tip-off,' the inspector said when Nat was seated in front of the desk and had declined a mug of suspect canteen coffee. 'I've checked with our boys in Birmingham. They're waiting for the fire chief's report and forensics are still on the scene but at the moment it looks like the explosion was caused by a faulty gas water heater. However, I agree with you that two "accidents" suggest a coincidence that warrants careful enquiry. So, Nat, what else have you got for me?'

From his briefcase Nat produced two computer-printed sheets of paper. Mitchenor spent several minutes reading them carefully. Eventually he said, 'You have been busy.'

Nat was apologetic. 'I don't want you to think I'm muscling in on your job.'

'On the contrary. Crime detection today is an ever-widening partnership. I'll work with anybody and every-

148

body who can help in tracking down criminals – security officers, radio, TV, press, specialists in a variety of fields, the little old lady watching from behind her lace curtains. Just because we've got computer technology, psychological profiling and forensic detection techniques that, frankly, I don't begin to understand doesn't mean that we can shelter behind professionalism and pretend we can do it all by ourselves.'

'I hope those thoughts help.'

Mitchenor picked up a biro and marked some passages on the report. 'My first problem is going to be getting my super to agree to release manpower to open an old case. I'd better bring Jack Holt in and have a word. He didn't go into any detail about his evidence for his sister's murder?'

'No, just that someone had seen Myles go to meet her by the lake. He was rather "insistent" that I should keep that information to myself.'

The inspector smiled. 'I can imagine. A bit of a rough diamond is our Jack. So are the other two, if it comes to that. Holt Senior was a father of the old school. Brought up his boys with more stick than carrot. It certainly paid off. Jack turned a backstreet builder's firm into a major construction company and he and his brothers have diversified into other very lucrative concerns. The family's worth millions.'

'They talked about revenging Tracy's death in their own way. Do you think they might . . .'

'Do Mr Myles a mischief? I wouldn't put it past them. They've got underworld connections and they can certainly afford to pay a hit-man. But I'm not having that sort of thing on my patch. I'll make it known to Jack Holt that if anything happens to Myles his will be the first door I come knocking on.'

He stared at Nat. 'You look worried.'

'It's just that . . . I suppose there's no way that you can

question Jack Holt without him realizing that I've given you this information?'

'I certainly shan't tell him but he's not stupid. I'm afraid he'll put two and two together without much difficulty.'

Nat frowned thoughtfully. 'I see. Have you a local phone book I can have a look at?'

Mitchenor produced a heavy directory from the bottom drawer of his desk and Nat turned to the business section. He quickly found what he was looking for.

'Problems?' the policeman enquired.

'Just checking. One night last week I dreamed, or I thought that I dreamed, that one of Jack Holt's vans was prowling outside my house. When I hinted about it to Holt he didn't deny it.'

'So?'

'I made a mental note of the phone number on the van. It checks.'

'Meaning that Holt has had someone staking out your house.'

'There can't be any other explanation. What's he up to? You've just said he has connections with organized criminals and hit-men. Could he . . .?'

'Be planning to put pressure on you?'

'Or my family.'

Mitchenor gave the question careful thought. 'To the best of my knowledge none of the Holts have strayed that far outside the law. Sweeteners to the planning authorities, political pressure on local councillors, payments for favours – that's their style. I can't imagine them going in for gratuitous violence.'

'But there's always a first time and if they're determined to stop me getting in the way of their private vendetta . . .'

'Don't worry, Nat. I'll bring Holt in tomorrow. When I've had a little word with him he won't dare put a foot wrong.'

Nat looked at the self-assured custodian of the law and

thought of the three men who, just a week ago, had held him a virtual captive. He found Mitchenor's words remarkably uncomforting.

The inspector was oblivious to Nat's anxiety. He was busy mapping out his strategy. 'As soon as I can get the go-ahead I'll have someone sift through all the statements we took from people at the Myleses' party. I need to know who was where, when and what they saw. Let's start with you. As I recall, you had a brief encounter with Tracy round about 10.45. She was fairly drunk, talked about Mr Myles being very unpopular locally and hinted that something unpleasant was about to happen to him. Have you remembered anything in more detail about that conversation?'

Nat frowned deeply. 'No. I've been over it dozens of times. I'm sure there was something important but I'm damned if I can put my finger on it. She said she had to go and do something important.'

'Perhaps she had a meeting arranged with Myles. Was going to confront him with something. Let's say she threatened to go to the tabloids with juicy gossip about his sexual adventures. That would be motive enough for him to get rid of her.'

'In an impulsive attack? He looks round quickly, can't see anyone watching, grabs up a rock and – bang!, the deed's done.'

'Could be.'

'I can't help feeling there are a couple of things wrong with that. First of all, when Tracy hurried away from our impromptu chat she still had more than an hour to live. What was she up to in that hour? She can't have been with Myles all that time.'

'You've got me there. Yours is the last positive sighting of Tracy alive. No one else has owned up to seeing her after that. What's your other objection?'

'Not so much an objection. More a question. Was this an opportunist crime or was it carefully premeditated?'

'Surely,' Mitchenor looked puzzled, 'it must have been a spur of the moment thing. *If* Myles did for Tracy, he'd scarcely plan to carry out the deed when the grounds were swarming with potential witnesses.'

'I was thinking about that on my way over and it suddenly occurred to me that the murder could have been very precisely timed. In fact I'm sure it must have been.'

'I don't follow.'

'Poor Tracy met her nemesis around midnight.'

'As far as we can tell.'

'So, what was supposed to be happening at midnight?'

'The fireworks!'

'Exactly. That was the one event that everyone would be certain to be involved in. Throughout the evening guests had choices. They could have been anywhere – in the house, on Tripletree Hill, by the lake – but as the climactic moment drew near they'd all be making their way to the best vantage point – the terrace. The low ground between the mansion and the hill would be in darkness, all lights switched off so as not to detract from the pyrotechnics. What better moment for a secret assignation? He does the deed and he's pretty sure the body won't be found till the next day after everyone's gone home.'

'But the fireworks were cancelled.'

'That's right. But by now our murderer is all psyched up to do what he has to do. He's brought his weapon with him. Tracy turns up on cue, all unsuspecting, and the murderer realizes that he can still get away with it.'

Mitchenor considered the idea carefully. 'That's certainly one possible scenario.'

'And it has another advantage for Myles.' Nat was warming to his theme. 'It doesn't spoil the party. If the whole evening had gone according to plan the police wouldn't have been called in until the next day. All his high class guests would have gone home having had an enjoyable evening and when they read about the accident in the papers they'd just have thought, Poor old Shelley. What a rotten thing to happen.'

Mitchenor caught Nat's enthusiasm. 'And even if foul play was suspected we wouldn't have been able to fix the time of death so precisely. We'd have had getting on for a hundred and fifty suspects milling around the place for hours and no evidence.' He sighed. 'And that's still what we have – no evidence. Great theory, but nothing to back it up.'

Nat nodded in agreement. 'Well, at least both deaths connect with Myles.'

'Yeah, this hypnotist fellow may be our best bet for the moment. I'll have to find out as much as possible about him before I can even think of questioning Myles about his death. Was he a loner? If not, who might have put him up to offering his services to Mrs Myles?'

' I've thought a lot about that, of course. Many convicted criminals threaten to get even with the judges and barristers who put them away but, as I understand it, very, very few actually try to turn their threats into action. Owen didn't strike me as the sort of man who'd have the bottle for it. My guess – and it is only a guess – is that someone presented him with the opportunity to make Myles's life hell, and he jumped at it. I don't see him working out for himself what was, in fact, a very detailed plot. Anyway, someone must have provided him with the information about Myles's affair with Tracy Pensham, which was the basis of the fantasy he created in June's mind.'

'We don't even know for sure that they were having an affair.'

'June believed they were. If you'd heard her describing her supposed regression, mixing up Tracy with the rival in her fantasy world and exulting in her death, you'd have been in no doubt that she felt violent hatred towards Tracy. It was something that no hypnotist could have induced. If you need corroboration of the affair, you should be able to

153

get it from local gossip and, perhaps, Tom Pensham or the Holts.'

'Hmm! So, let me get this straight. In your opinion,' Mitchenor referred to the notes, 'Owen was acting out of sheer malice; doing to Mrs Myles what Myles had accused him of doing to this Briggs character?'

'Yes, if I'm right he wanted Myles to know what it was like to be close to someone wrongly accused (in this case self-accused) of homicide. But what he didn't know was that Mrs Pensham *had* actually been murdered – by Myles.'

Mitchenor looked across the desk with a sceptical frown. 'So, we have this couple living under the same roof and she believes she's committed a crime that, in fact, he's committed?'

'And he thinks he's got away with it because the police have accepted the coroner's verdict of accidental death. Imagine the shock, therefore, when she insists on giving herself up to the police. That may mean the case being reopened. What does he do? He's desperate to stop her. Desperate to hush everything up. Answer, he comes to me in the hope that I'll quietly sort his wife out.'

'And track down Owen so that he can silence him.'

'Don't rub it in, Dave.' Nat felt the weight in the pit of his stomach that had not left him ever since Sue's phone call. 'I've hammered myself over and over again for being so stupid; for not realizing how Myles was using me.'

'Don't be too hard on yourself, Nat. We're obviously up against someone uncannily clever. Imagine what any of Myles's barrister friends would do in open court to the story we've got. Do we have a shred of proof?'

'I suppose that depends on Holt's eyewitness and anything concrete your Birmingham colleagues can turn up.'

He scrutinized the inspector's worried features. 'I get the impression that you think all this is too fanciful.'

'No, Nat, I've always thought there was much more to that business at Coln back in the summer than we had turned up and I'm very grateful to you for doing all this thinking. It's just that when we're dealing with folk like the Myleses we're walking on eggshells. I don't want either of them even to get a whiff of my investigation until I'm sufficiently sure of my ground to question them.'

'I can't imagine anyone at Coln warning them. The entire community would be delighted to see the high and mighty Myleses brought low.'

'Which raises another problem. The Myleses' lawyer could make capital out of the fact that his clients are thoroughly hated and claim that there is a local conspiracy against them. No, we have to play this one very close to our chests.' He stood up and extended his hand. 'Thanks again for this, Nat. I'll go over it carefully and come back to you if I have any more questions. And I'll certainly keep you informed. By the way, how are the plans coming on for your new series?'

Nat picked up his briefcase and headed towards the door. 'Still in what the TV people call the "concept stage" but they're pretty confident of selling the idea. Then, of course, they'll want everything yesterday.'

Nat had plenty to think about as he drove back to Cambridge. After a subdued family supper he went to his study and made a couple of phone calls. When he had read the boys their bedtime story he went downstairs and found Kathryn sitting in the middle of the living-room floor amidst a scattering of highly coloured pictures.

'Cover designs for March,' she explained, looking up with a half-smile. 'Have a look. Tell me what you think.'

Nat squatted beside her. 'I think I'd like us to talk –'

'Oh, Nat, not now. I really do have to sort these out and get them biked back to the office tomorrow. After that I've a bag bulging with –'

'No, darling, not now. Not when we're both up to our necks in the bits and pieces of over-busy lives. I called Sonia Pedersen earlier. She says Strand Cottage is free this weekend and she'd be delighted for us to go there.

155

I explained that we both needed a break and that the boys keep pestering us to go back to the seaside – both of which statements were true.'

Kathryn fixed her eyes on the design in her hands, a montage of a crimson Ferrari and a private jet against a backdrop of Mediterranean beach and sky. 'Oh, I don't think that's such a good –'

'Well, I think it's a great idea and so will the children.' He put his hands gently on her shoulders and turned her to face him. 'About last night – I just want to say I'm sorry. I let other things get in the way of what really matters. I reckon we've both been doing that for a while. We need some time to stand back and have a look at ourselves. Greg was right, we have to talk things over.' What Nat did not say was that he wanted to get the family away to where an angry Jack Holt could not find them.

Kathryn was silent for some moments. Then she said, 'Compromise?'

'I'm listening.'

'I go to the cottage on Saturday. You and the boys join me on Sunday. I need some space. I need to sort myself out first.'

'Fair enough. Let's open our problems up to some of those sea breezes.'

Marriage or Mirage?

Strand Cottage was part of a cluster of houses built for eighteenth-century excisemen and stood a couple of hundred yards back from the clifftop near the Norfolk town of Cromer, protected from the North Sea gales by a brake of wind-flattened holm oak. It belonged to a faculty friend of Gye's who used it whenever she felt an unbearable longing for the raw landscape and iron seas of her native Norway but was otherwise delighted to allow colleagues to use it.

It was in darkness when Nat parked outside in the afterdawn of a November morning. He had made an early start from Great Maddisham, tucking up the still-sleeping Ed and Jerry on the back seat. They were flat out after a very full Saturday. Nat had deliberately kept them away from the house for several hours. An outing to the new swimming pool alongside Parker's Piece had been followed by a McDonald's lunch and a trip to the cinema. Afterwards they had all gone shopping for computer games and Nat had taken the boys to Beaufort and let them use his console to play on while he did some paperwork. Only when their tiredness began to express itself in tears and fights did Nat take them home, and even then he checked the house carefully before bringing the children in from the car.

Now he left them sleeping while he let himself into the cottage. For the next hour or so he busied himself chopping wood in the small back garden, laying and lighting a fire in the open grate and brewing fresh coffee. By then the boys were awake and he got them dressed and washed, using the kitchen sink so that they would not go upstairs and disturb their mother. It was 8.15 when he took coffee to Kathryn and gently woke her.

'Hi,' he said, as she sat up, forcing her eyes open. 'How was yesterday?'

'Peaceful,' she replied with a long sigh. 'Yours?'

'Not peaceful!' Nat laughed. 'But the boys had a great time. I'll let them tell you about it. Breakfast in twenty minutes suit you?'

'Fine.'

The morning passed quickly. They walked along the beach as far as Cromer where they bought ice creams for the boys and a couple of Sunday papers. During the journey back Ed and Jerry managed to get themselves soaked splashing among the rocks and had to be dried out in front of the fire on their return. It was not until mid-afternoon, when the boys had been settled down with a feature-length cartoon film on video, that their parents had some time to themselves. A path behind the cottage led through the copse to a lookout point on the clifftop where a wooden seat stood in the shelter of a stone arbour. Kathryn and Nat sat, hands thrust deep into anorak pockets, and watched a slate sea crumbling in foam on the seaweed-strewn sand below.

'How was your chat with your policeman friend?' Kathryn asked.

'Oh, to hell with that! Let's talk about something that really matters.'

Kathryn seemed to ignore the objection. 'I was thinking a lot about the Myleses yesterday. I never told you about my first meeting with them, did I?'

'No.'

'It was bizarre. I guess I should have realized . . .' The words faded away as she pushed back a wisp of wind-blown hair from her face.

'Realized what?'

'Oh, I don't know. There was a big meeting of CROW, the feminist organization, at a hotel just off Parliament Square and June Myles was down to speak. I thought I'd go along and see whether she might be good for a slot in a series we were running on women in power. Her subject was "Coping with men in the workplace" or some such and she produced all the usual groping and griping horror stories, plus details of the law on harassment, how to get justice through the tribunals and the courts, and so on. She was very feisty and very bitter. Listening to her you felt: she knows what it's like; she's been through it and come out the other side; here's a woman who stands no nonsense from the opposite sex. So, she seemed exactly what I needed for the magazine – a powerful woman. I button-holed her afterwards and fixed a date for an interview. So, a few days later I turned up at her swanky Thameside apartment to do the bizz. Boy, was that an eye opener!'

'In what way?'

As he listened to Kathryn's narrative, Nat also found it a revelation – but not for the same reason as his wife.

A Filipino maid opened the door and ushered Kathryn into a spacious room straight out of the pages of some glossy magazine. Opposite the door a wall of glass afforded a panoramic view of the river and Tower Bridge. Within, the colour scheme was dominated by aggressive white, softened by greys and startled by splashes of crimson in the cushions and drapes. Kathryn was well accustomed to the habitats of the rich and famous and quickly read the messages presented by the decor – the leather upholstery, the wall of books, the geometrically arranged photographs of Shelley with prime ministers, royalty and other celebrities, the state of the art TV/hi-fi system, the scattering of newspapers and magazines (including a prominently displayed copy of the current *Panache*) on the stark glass and chrome coffee table. Impersonal, she thought. Masculine. Designed to impress.

159

'What a wonderful home, Mrs Myles,' she said, advancing to shake Juniper Myles's proffered hand, and thinking to herself that 'home' was the one word that least accurately described this millionaires' pad.

'Thank you.' The hostess accepted the compliment graciously. She was wearing an off-white woollen dress and a scarlet silk scarf arranged with careful nonchalance and caught at the shoulder with a brooch of silver and garnet. 'If one has to live at the centre of things one might as well be comfortable and this is very convenient for all the entertaining we have to do. Oh, and please call me June. It's short for Juniper.' She grimaced. 'I can't imagine what my parents were thinking of but I was in no position to protest.'

The maid set a tray on the table and June poured decaffeinated coffee from an antique silver pot. Kathryn produced her tape recorder and began her questions. First they covered June's upbringing. Had she always wanted to follow in her father's professional footsteps? Yes. Had he encouraged her? Quite the contrary; as a woman she had had to prove herself every inch of the way. It had taken years to earn her father's approval but eventually, she thought, the old man had become proud of her. As a pioneer woman barrister what had been some of the obstacles she had had to overcome? The reluctance of lawyers to believe that she was tough enough to fight hard for their clients. 'They thought I'd burst into tears if the opposition challenged me or that I'd be unable to concentrate on "off" days!' The idea was frequently put forward that she could only be really effective in cases involving women and children. Colleagues had tried hard to persuade her to concentrate on the Families Division or the juvenile courts. It was in reaction to this pressure that she had decided to specialize in commercial law.

Next, Kathryn wanted to turn to some of June's more successful cases but the barrister steered the conversation in the direction of her defence of women's rights as a member of professional tribunals. 'Most abused women (and we are talking abuse here) have to be persuaded in the first place to lodge formal complaints against their bosses if they've been harassed or discriminated against. They're just as worried about winning as losing because, if they win, their names are mud, not only in their own firms, but throughout the old boy net. Nobody wants to employ someone with a reputation as a neurotic trouble-maker. I actually have to advise distressed women who come to me to decide whether they want compensation or a career. They can't have both. It's so unfair!'

They were about twenty minutes into the interview when Sheldon Myles made an entrance. That theatrical terminology was wholly appropriate. The door opened suddenly and June's husband was not only in the room: he was filling it. He stood looking at the two women, obviously surprised to find Kathryn there. She was imme-diately aware that she was being appraised by his search-ing eyes and had to resist a ridiculous urge to look demurely down at the carpet.

'Darling, who is our charming guest?' He advanced to shake Kathryn's hand, lingering momentarily too long over the formality.

Introductions were made. Myles insisted that Kathryn call him Shelley.

He glanced down at the table and pulled a face. 'Coffee? I'm sure Kathryn would like something a bit more interesting.'

'No thank you,' she replied. 'It's a little early for me.'

'You don't mind if I do?' He crossed to the bookcase, pressed a concealed switch, and a false front opened to reveal a drinks cabinet. He helped himself to a large scotch, then came and sat on the sofa next to Kathryn.

She had been watching June, who sat opposite her, stiff and immobile, a statue carved in ice, all emotion frozen.

'So, what are you girls up to?' Sheldon asked boister-ously.

Kathryn explained the article she was preparing. It seemed to amuse him. He smiled condescendingly over the rim of his glass.

'Oh, I'm sure your readers don't want all this feminist stuff.' He picked up the copy of *Panache*. 'Damned good magazine, this. Very entertaining; very irreverent. The style takes me back to the rags we used to churn out in varsity days. Hardly a suitable medium for airing women's rights issues, I'd have thought. Now, as it happens we've got a far more interesting story, haven't we, June? You've told her about Coln Manor, I assume.'

His wife shook her head.

'No? Oh, you must. It's a great story and we've got some excellent pictures you can use. Darling, run and fetch the album, will you?'

Without a word, June went into an adjoining room and returned with a leather-bound volume of photographs. Shelley took it and made the most of his opportunity to open it across his own lap and Kathryn's.

He launched into the Coln Manor story. 'Seven years ago, we came across this Jacobean mansion deep in the Cotswolds. As you can see from this shot, it was in a terrible state, but we fell in love with it, didn't we, darling? We made some enquiries and discovered that the owners couldn't afford to keep the place up. I won't bore you with the business details but eventually we were able to buy it. Best decision we've ever made. June's always been fascinated by history and she absolutely adores the place, don't you, darling.'

'I did,' his wife replied flatly.

Kathryn raised an eyebrow. 'Did?'

Sheldon bulldozed the interruption to his narrative. 'Oh, there were some local legends about the house being haunted and a couple of nasty incidents – which had nothing to do with the supernatural, but you know how superstitious country folk are.' He hurried on with the story of the renovation.

'The trouble was,' Kathryn explained to Nat, 'the odious Shelley was quite right. It *was* a good story. Our meeting ended up with June being instructed to make sure I received an invitation to the housewarming and a promise that I could have an interview on the night. The rest you know.'

Nat stared out at the heaving grey sea. One detail from his wife's account had set lights flashing in his brain. 'Tell me again exactly what he said about *Panache*.'

'Oh, it was just flannel. Part of his come-on to me.'

'Nevertheless, what did he say?'

Kathryn repeated that section of her account.

'And those were his exact words?'

'As near as I remember. Why?'

'Oh, just a passing thought. You said you should have realized something from that first meeting with the Myleses. What was it?'

'How much June hates her husband. All her life she's been dominated by men. First her father, then Shelley.'

Nat nodded. 'Some people seem to need to be controlled or to feel dependent on others. It's a well-known psychological condition. Therapists constantly have to be on the watch for patients who want to set up a master–servant relationship with them.'

'It's not that way with June. She resents it like hell.'

'But does she confront Shelley with her resentment? Do they have blazing rows and get things off their chests? It sounds to me as though June lets herself be a doormat. Then she sublimates her anger by working feverishly to help other women hit back against male abuse.'

'Well, Nat, whatever diagnosis you shrinks offer,' Kathryn grabbed hold of his hand, 'I don't want the same thing to happen to us.'

'Darling, there's a world of difference between you and June Myles.'

'Is there? She's been prevented from fulfilling herself and it's turned her into a bitter neurotic.'

163

'Hardly unfulfilled. She's one of the leading women barristers of her generation.'

'Yeah, and I'm pretty good at what I do but, darling, if I can't grab the opportunities that come along, if I'm prevented from spreading my wings I could end up like her, brooding on what might have been, nursing a corrosive anger. I might even end up hating you. This New York job isn't just about my career; it's about us.'

'That's one thing I'm fully aware of. You don't really see a comparison between me and Myles, do you? I seem to recall that "monster" was your word for him.'

Kathryn half turned to hug him. 'No, of course not. But I just want you to understand that I must give this New York job a try. If it doesn't work out . . .'

Nat brushed a tear from her cheek. 'Wind's getting up,' he said. 'We ought to go in. Don't even think of it not working out. I want you to be a roaring success at everything you turn your hand to.'

At that more tears appeared and Nat held her very close. 'Hey, cheer up,' he said. 'One good thing that's come out of this is that we have friend Greg over a barrel. He's given you virtual carte blanche to demand whatever you want. You make sure you get every cent you're worth.'

Next morning Nat made two telephone calls. The first was to Barny Cox, suggesting a new line of research he might like to follow up. The old lawyer was as eager as ever and agreed to call in at the porter's lodge straight away to pick up a photograph Nat said he would leave there for him. The second call was to Dave Mitchenor. The DCI was busy but rang back just before noon.

'Sorry to bother you,' Nat began, 'but I am rather concerned about the Holts. How did the interview with Jack go?'

'He wasn't best pleased at having to answer questions. Strange how our leading citizens are very keen on the maintenance of law and order until they're called upon to do their little bit towards it. Then, suddenly, the police are guilty of infringing the liberties of respectable law-abiding folk. Still, we're used to it.'

'Is he annoyed with me?'

'He was till I pointed out that you had only done what he should have done weeks ago. I don't think you've got anything to worry about in that quarter but if you get so much as a sniff of one of Jack's vans in your neck of the woods . . .'

'I'll be on to you like a shot. Did you get anything useful out of him?'

'Eventually. He insists that Myles was the only person who went to the area of the upper lake around the time of Mrs Pensham's death.'

'Yes, but what's his proof?'

'Holt says that Myles was seen by Tom Pensham.'

'Tom Pensham? What was he doing there?'

'That's something I hope to find out when I pop over to Coln this afternoon. Not,' he added after a pause, 'that Pensham's evidence will do us much good, however detailed it is.'

'Why do you say that?'

'Because Mr Myles has an alibi that could scarcely be stronger. I've checked his statement and it claims that from about 11.45 to 12.10, when Mrs Pensham's death was reported to him, he was in his private rooms at the manor having a heated discussion about the inadequacies of police protection.'

'Do you believe him?'

'I have no choice. I double checked with the person he claims to have been with.'

'Who was that?'

'The chief constable.'

'Ouch! Where does that leave us?'

'Up a certain creek without a paddle, I'd say. I did manage to get the super's permission to send a couple of officers over to Coln Manor to have a ferret around the lake. There's scarcely a snowball's chance of finding anything significant after all this time, so it's more a knee-jerk reaction than a piece of intelligent detection, but you never know. The trouble is it's going to bring Myles's wrath down about my ears.'

'You mean he'll know that the police are back at Coln Manor?'

'Sure to. The caretaker couple who live there are bound to report back to their boss and there's no way we can stop them. I reckon the chief constable's phone will be white hot before the sun goes down. Then we'll be ordered off the case. I'm certainly not going to flush my promotion prospects down the pan by arguing with him.'

'So, we're getting to the end of the road. Any news from Birmingham?'

'Yes, something very slightly more hopeful. The post-mortem on what was left of Owen revealed a nasty skull fracture and the pathologist says it was definitely inflicted before fire reached the body.'

'So it will have to be treated as a suspicious death.'

'Don't I wish! No, it's not cut and dried. Forensics and the fire brigade are putting their heads together to see if they can come up with anything more definite but at the moment all they can say is that Owen might have been struck by some flying object caused by the explosion.'

'Just as Tracy Pensham *might* have sustained a blow to the head when she fell into the lake! It looks as though our murderer has thought of everything.'

'Either that, Nat, or we're barking up the wrong tree. The one ray of hope at the moment is that I've got the super's backing – and that's only down to politics.'

'How so?'

'This investigation could be an embarrassment to the chief constable, who is on very good terms with Myles. Both Freemasons and you know what that means! Now, the super and the chief are at daggers drawn and that means almost every time one of 'em says yes the other says no. Good job too, as far as I'm concerned. It gives me a few more days before I have to call a halt to this enquiry. So, if you can come up with anything new, I shall be all ears.'

As Nat put the receiver down some of the inspector's words tumbled around in his brain. Somehow he knew that they were important. But why? They were meaningless enough in themselves. He sat back in his desk chair, screwed his eyes shut and forced himself to think.

There was a tap at the door. When he did not answer it the knock was repeated, louder this time, and almost immediately it opened. Barnaby Cox strode in.

'Dear boy, if you're in silent meditation and don't want to be disturbed you really ought to sport your oak.'

Nat waved his friend to a chair. 'The photo's waiting for you at the porter's lodge, Barny. I'm sorry, I thought I'd explained –'

The old man scowled at him. 'Nathaniel, you are not dealing with someone in the last stages of senile dementia. You did explain about the photograph. I did understand your simple instructions. I did collect the aforementioned photograph. And I did carry out the small research commission you entrusted to me.'

Nat laughed. 'I'm sorry, Barny, it's just that I didn't expect to see you back so soon.'

'Well, I must confess to a modicum of good fortune. Before consulting the law faculty archive I popped into Trinity Hall, which, as you know, has always had a strong legal fraternity. I know the college secretary – charming girl, daughter of our own domestic bursar – and she let me have a browse through the photographic record. Here's the result.' He laid a file on the desk with the air of a conjuror producing a rabbit from a hat.

Nat extracted the two items. One was the piece of paper he had supplied to Barny, the 1972 article from the *Northern Courier*, which included the earliest photo Nat had of Myles. The other was a photocopy of another picture, a posed group of college freshmen. Around one of the fifty or so young faces Barny had drawn a neat red circle.

Nat was exultant. 'I knew it!' He slapped a hand down on the tooled leather desktop. 'When Myles came to see me here in Cambridge I got the distinct impression that he was familiar with the town. I told him I wanted to go to the UL and he never asked for directions; just drove me straight there, or rather to the bottom of West Road. Then he took me for a drink at the Granta Inn and knew that it would be a quiet spot to talk. Well, of course, there was nothing odd about that. If I thought about it at all at the time I assumed that he had studied here or perhaps grown up in the area. It was only when I checked later and realized that he took his degree at Durham and, as far as I could tell, had no contact with Cambridge that I was set to wondering. Then, only yesterday, my wife told me of a conversation she had had with Myles in which he referred to his alma mater as "varsity", a term only used by Oxford and Cambridge men. So, I began to suspect that he must have been here as an undergraduate. But why would a person of Myles's massive hubris want to conceal the fact that he had read for his degree at one of the two senior universities?'

'Something to hide,' Barny suggested.

'Indeed.'

'Then you'll be interested to know what else I discovered at Trinity Hall.' The old lawyer leaned forward and prodded a long finger at the group picture, enjoying to the full his moment of revelation. 'My young friend very obligingly looked up the records. That student disappeared from our midst at the end of his first year.'

'Sent down?'

'Just so.'

'Was there a scandal or did he just make a mess of his exams?'

'Ah.' Cox shook his head. 'As to that I can't help you.

168

My informant tells me that if we want personal details of that nature we'll have to go to higher authority.'

'I don't suppose it matters. The important thing is that Myles transferred to Durham where he proceeded to redeem himself.'

'But there is more.' Barny's mischievous smile announced that the conjuror was working up to his best trick. 'That young man,' he announced slowly, 'is not Sheldon Myles.'

'Not . . .' Nat stared at the two faces. Even though the image in the newspaper sported a heavy beard, there could be no mistake. 'But they are . . .'

'Either identical or doppelgangers. The name of this student is Henry Baker. I rather think your Mr Myles is a fraud.'

Scene of Crime

There was a long silence during which Nat scrutinized the two photographs. No doubt about it. Sheldon Myles was Henry Baker or vice versa. He looked at the legend at the bottom of the group picture. 'Hang on, there's something else odd here. The date on this is 1961.' He turned to his computer and brought up the Myles file. 'According to all the records he was at St John's, Durham from 1959 to 1962.' He shook his head. 'What on earth does this mean?'

Barny Cox shrugged. 'I am the mere provider of information, dear boy. I leave the interpretation to my betters. Are you coming in to lunch?'

Nat shook his head absent-mindedly. 'Not today, Barny. There's something else I have to do.'

After his friend had gone, Nat sat for several minutes in thoughtful silence. Then he scribbled a note and pinned it to the outer door of his rooms. It read, 'Dr Gye has been called away on urgent business. Please contact him tomorrow to reschedule supervisions.' He made a quick call to DCI Mitchenor. Fifteen minutes later he was in his car heading westwards out of Cambridge.

As arranged the policeman met him at the main gate of Coln Manor. He got out of his car and walked across to the Mercedes as Nat pulled up. 'You were very mysterious on the phone, Nat. What have you come up with now?'

Nat lowered the side window. 'I'll tell you when we get up to the house, Dave. I need to go over things *in situ* to get them clear in my mind.'

Mitchenor spoke into the intercom and the gates swung open. As soon as they had parked, Nat led the way to the West Lawn. He found the arbour and the stone bench. He sat down and closed his eyes while Mitchenor looked on quizzically.

'What information do you have on Tracy Pensham?' Nat asked, looking up.

'Quite a bit. What is it you want to know?'

'Education? Upbringing? Social habits?'

'She went away to boarding school – Sebton College.'

Nat whistled. 'Expensive.'

'Nothing was too good for Old Man Holt's little girl. The boys could bring in the brass. They didn't need fancy education for that. But Tracy was going to grow up to be a lady: foreign finishing school, university, entrée to the smart set, and, eventually, marriage into a society family. That was the plan.'

'What went wrong?'

'Daddy discovered too late that his would-be debutante had a mind of her own. And a body of her own that she was determined to do what she wanted with.'

'Which is where Tom Pensham comes in?'

'Yes. He must have been a good-looking, muscular brute at one time, though it's hard to believe that, looking at him now. Anyway, he swept young Tracy off her feet. She was seventeen at the time and the inevitable happened. The family wanted her to get rid of the kid. She point blank refused. The upshot was the old-fashioned shotgun wedding. The Holts reckoned that Pensham was only interested in their money but they made the best of a bad job. Tracy's father set Tom up in the garage and made it clear that, from then on, the couple were on their own. As you might suspect, the marriage never really worked out. Tom and Tracy were chalk and cheese. She was bright, cultured, had wide interests. Tom was . . . well, you've seen Tom.'

'Did she sing?'

Mitchenor looked surprised. 'Yes, as a matter of fact she

did. Belonged to a couple of choirs and the local operatic society. What's all this got to do with anything?'

'I'm just putting some bits and pieces together. The first and last time I saw Tracy Pensham she walked off in that direction,' Nat pointed towards the house, 'and she was humming or singing.'

'So?'

'Beyond recognizing the tune as one of Gilbert and Sullivan's, I thought no more about it, but later on something kept nagging me, telling me that it was important to identify that song. But it wasn't until this morning that I nailed it – or, rather, you did.'

'Me?'

'Yes, you were telling me that your superintendent and chief constable were on bad terms. "And a good job too", you said. That was the link. It's a line that appears in the Judge's Song from *Trial by Jury*. Do you know it?'

Mitchenor shook his head. 'I'm not into classical music. More a country and western man.'

'Well, in this song the judge tells everyone how he climbed the professional ladder by ambition, trickery and ruthlessness. The important lines are, if I remember them correctly:

> Now I'm a judge
> And a good judge, too.
> It was managed by a job
> And a good job, too.
> It's patent to the mob
> That my being made a nob
> Was effected by a job
> And a good job, too.'

'Job?' Mitchenor looked puzzled.

'A put-up job, a fix,' Nat explained. 'You see the significance of this?'

The policeman looked at his watch. 'No, you've lost me.

And I really must go and see how my troops are getting on at the lake.'

Nat jumped up. 'Hang on. This isn't just pointless whimsy.'

'OK, tell me as we go.' He set off towards the rear of the house.

Nat caught him up. 'Picture it, Dave. Tracy is excited. She's thinking about the much-loathed Myles and the comeuppance he's about to get. Wherever it is she's going, whatever she's about to do, whoever it is she's going to meet, it's all about exposing Sheldon Myles and his shady past. Do you get the picture?'

'Not really but I'm still listening.' Mitchenor crossed the terrace with long strides and descended the steps leading to the lawn which sloped to the lake.

'Then try this. Sheldon Myles is bogus, a fraud, a counterfeit, a fake, a man who's been living a lie for over thirty years.'

Mitchenor stopped and stared at his companion. 'What on earth . . .'

Nat succinctly explained what Barny Cox had discovered and had the satisfaction of watching Mitchenor's mouth open wide in astonishment.

'Bloody hell!' the policeman exclaimed.

'Wouldn't you say that if Tracy stumbled across that information the blackmail opportunities would be immense and that stopping her using it would be a pretty good motive for murder?'

'Yeah, if what you say is true the man would be finished. His career, his social position, his ambition . . . He'd probably be lucky not to end up in prison.' He ran both hands through his thick, fair hair. 'But are you sure about this? I mean, is it possible for a public figure like that to pull the wool over everyone's eyes, to masquerade year after year and get to the top of his profession?'

'He wouldn't be the first. Think of Anthony Blunt and the Cambridge Five – respected pillars of society. Myles is

173

just another con-man, the only difference being that he's a damned good one.'

'So what do you reckon went on back in the sixties between these two young men, Baker and Myles?'

Nat shrugged. 'Heaven knows. Did they agree to swap identities or was there something more sinister? Presumably you have the resources for checking these things.'

'Oh, yes, I'll get Records on to it first thing tomorrow. And if they come up with the goods on Myles's murky past a whole batallion of chief constables won't save him from investigation. We may not be able to nail him for murder but he'll be called to account for something. Now, let's go and see –'

'Chief inspector!' Mitchenor was interrupted by a black-jacketed figure hurrying across the terrace yet making the movement look dignified.

The DCI groaned. 'Myles's butler and general factotum,' he muttered. 'Good afternoon, Mr Brunnage,' he said, as the sergeant-major-like man approached.

'Chief inspector,' Brunnage said, with an air of authority, 'I have just had Mr Myles on the telephone. He was not at all pleased to hear that you and your men are here. His instructions to me were to see you all off his property immediately.'

'Were they now?' Nat saw Mitchenor bristle. 'Did my sergeant show you the search warrant when he arrived?'

'Yes, but –'

'And did you inform your employer that you had seen this warrant?'

'Of course. However –'

'Then, kindly convey my respects to Mr Myles and tell him that me and my men are investigating a crime scene and that we'll leave when we damn well please.'

The butler opened his mouth to say something but thought better of it and turned abruptly on his heel.

Mitchenor called after him. 'And you might also say that I shall be wanting another interview with him in the next day or two.' He turned to Nat. 'Do you know, I rather enjoyed that.'

Nat pointed towards the retreating figure. 'I wouldn't want to be in his shoes when he reports back to Myles,' he said with a laugh as they continued their stroll towards the lake.

The large watercourse known as the Lower Lake was an uneven oval some hundred yards in length and fifty in width, its banks unadorned by shrubs. At its upper end, to the left, it was crossed by a rustic bridge and here it narrowed to where water tumbled over a series of staged falls from the smaller Upper Lake. This, by contrast, was surrounded by clumps of rhododendron and azalea, which almost completely concealed it from view.

As the two men approached, a uniformed WPC, her legs encased in waders, hurried across the bridge towards them. She was carrying something in a transparent plastic bag and this she held out as she reached them. 'Good afternoon, sir. We've just turned up this. Seemed a bit odd. We thought it might be the murder weapon.'

'Thank you, Mandy,' Mitchenor said. 'Well done for finding it but you'd better leave the speculation to those of us who are paid for it, eh?'

The inspector held the package up to the light, smoothing out the plastic wrinkles to see the contents more clearly. Nat peered over his shoulder. The object was about a foot long and dull brown in colour. It was fashioned to resemble a dog standing on its hind feet or, more probably, in the process of leaping.

'Quite a pretty ornament,' Mitchenor commented.

'More than an ornament,' Nat corrected him. 'It's an animalier bronze and probably worth a great deal of money.'

'You know about these things?' the DCI asked.

'I know that June Myles collects them.'

'And, presumably, doesn't throw them away. Where did you find it?' Mitchenor asked the constable.

175

'In the water, sir. Quite a way from the bank. I marked the spot with a stick.'

'Show us,' Mitchenor said. He held the bronze by the head and felt the weight of its circular marble base against his other hand. 'And Mandy . . .'

'Sir?'

'You're right about it being a possible weapon. Well done.'

'Thank you, sir.' The young woman concealed her smile of pleasure by turning to lead the way to the Upper Lake.

They crossed the bridge and turned left along the far bank. A narrow path opened out into a semicircular alcove formed by the shrubbery within which there was a stone seat similar to the one Nat had briefly shared with Tracy. In the water some seven or eight yards from the edge an unhappy-looking police sergeant was cautiously prodding the bottom with a bamboo cane. Close by a similar stick protruded from the surface. Mandy pointed to it.

Mitchenor called out, 'Come in, Number Seven; your time is up.'

Thankfully the uniformed officer waded ashore. 'Bloody cold in there this afternoon, sir,' he muttered as the constable helped him scramble up the bank.

'OK, Bill, you can call it a day now. With this we've got enough evidence to warrant a full-scale specialist search. How much ground have you covered?'

'We worked our way right down from the top end of the lake on this side. Searched the bushes first, then the water. We couldn't go very far out. The bottom shelves quite steeply after a few yards, specially at this end where it narrows towards the waterfall.'

'And this is your only find?' Mitchenor held up the figurine.

'One or two bits and pieces over there on the bench, but they don't amount to much.'

The inspector went over to peer at the little collection of

muddy objects on the seat – a couple of squashed plastic beakers, a pound coin, a champagne bottle and the sodden remains of what had once been a paperback novel. 'Looks like some of this is party debris. You're probably right, Bill. Still, bag 'em up and let Forensics have a look. They might as well earn their money.'

He turned to Nat. 'Nice secluded spot for an assignation, wouldn't you say?'

'Yes. Where exactly was the body found?'

'Wedged on the first of those little waterfalls. It must have gone in about here. There wouldn't have been time for it to travel farther.'

'Especially as the water level was lower after the long dry spell.'

'Yes. Though it was running surprisingly fast towards the big lake. I reckon our murderer miscalculated there. Probably thought the body would stay pretty much where it was thrown.'

Nat stared around. The arbour was completely hidden from view on all sides. He envisaged Tracy sauntering across the bridge, triumphant, semi-inebriated, eager for her confrontation with Myles. What had she planned to do? Extort money? Sell her information to the highest newspaper bidder? Or simply enjoy wielding power over the owner of Coln Manor? He tried to picture the scene: the barrister cautiously approaching the shrubbery. The audience for the madrigals has dispersed at the end of their performance (Myles's comment about persuading them to go on longer must have been a lie; it was the last thing he would have wanted). He looks about him to make sure he is unobserved and slips quickly around the end of the rhododendrons. Tracy is standing at the edge of the lake. She turns to greet him. From beneath his cloak he produces the figurine which he's brought from the house for the purpose. A single blow and his victim falls backwards into the water. He steps down the bank to hold her head under. He finds it not as easy as he had thought. The

177

current has already caught the body. But Tracy is unconscious and her heavy clothes are pulling her down. There is no time to make absolutely certain that she is dead and in the panic of the moment he has lost track of the bronze. He jumps back, returns the long way round to the house and changes his wet shoes and hose. It all fitted together perfectly.

Except that, according to the chief constable, Myles was nowhere near the lake when Tracy Pensham met her death. The clever bastard had equipped himself with an unassailable alibi. How had he managed it? Or was it, in fact, the Pensham-Holt version of events that was wrong?

'Right, we've just about finished here.' Mitchenor was briskly organizing his little troop. 'Bill, I want this whole area taped off and an officer on duty until the crime scene people get here. I'll organize that by phone and see that you two are relieved. Mandy, put those things in my car when you've finished bagging them up. Usual rules: no one, but no one comes near here without my say-so.'

He led the way over the bridge and Nat followed. They had gone no more than a few paces when a shrill voice stopped them in their tracks.

'You! You there! Stop this instant!'

They turned to see a figure striding towards them down Tripletree Hill, a large cloak billowing out behind her. Morgana in full sail.

Evil Forces

'This man is creating mayhem!' Morgana spoke to Mitchenor but pointed with a theatrical gesture at Gye.

When neither man responded, she continued, 'I warned him that if he carried on meddling he would become a channel for the release of unspeakable evil. Inspector, you must add your entreaties to mine. In his scientific arrogance he dismisses me as a batty old woman.' She folded her arms across her monolithic frontage. 'Perhaps he will listen to you.'

Mitchenor glanced quickly at Nat, raising his eyes heavenward. 'Ms Simpson –'

'Morgana!' the woman corrected abruptly.

'Very well, Morgana, Dr Gye is helping the police with our investigation into suspicious deaths. Now, if you have any –'

'Deaths!' She screeched the word. 'Did you say deaths, plural?' She clasped her hands together and raised them above her head, as though making agonized supplication to the spirits. 'Then it has begun already! Ohhh!' The groan could have been comical but Nat felt the hairs rise at the back of his neck. However often he encountered people who believed themselves to be lightning rods receiving charges of supernatural power, and however sceptical he might be about their claims, he never ceased to be disturbed by them. Before him stood a dowdy, overweight, middle-aged woman. Yet her presence filled the landscape and her tiny audience stood transfixed by her dramatic words and gestures.

But there was another reason for his disquiet. She was right about his 'meddling'. If he had not given Owen's address to Myles the little Welshman would still be alive. But then, if he had kept his suspicions to himself what chance would there be of flushing out a premeditating murderer? Morality was seldom black and white.

In gentle tones he said to Morgana, 'You're right. There is great evil here. You and I might differ about what we mean by that word but can we not work together, with the police, to combat it?'

The eyes that glared at Nat from beneath heavy brows glowed with both indignation and pity. 'Do you really think that throwing someone in prison will put a stop to what has built up here over the centuries? It is poised to consume any who stand in its path. You, yourself, Nathaniel Gye, are in the gravest danger. I have protected you as much as I can – you and your family – but if you persist –'

'What do you mean, "protected"?' Nat demanded.

'Tripletree has reached out through its agents to your very doorstep. Night after night they approached but I warded them off.'

'You've been to my house?' Nat stared hard at the woman and recalled a half-seen cloaked figure floating across the lamplit green at Great Maddisham.

Morgana waved a hand impatiently. 'Not in the physical body,' she said sharply. 'I projected my astral being for your protection.'

Mitchenor interrupted. 'Look, Morgana, we have work to do. And, strictly speaking, you're trespassing. But since you're here you won't mind answering a few questions, will you?'

He received a non-committal shrug by way of answer.

'Good. Were you here at the Myleses' big party in August?'

180

'Certainly not.'

'Not even for a short time during the evening? It's not difficult to get on to the estate and you must have been curious to see what was going on.'

'I didn't need to be at Tripletree to know the evil mischief that was afoot.'

'You mean all the things that went wrong with the arrangements?' Nat asked.

Again Morgana shrugged. 'Mr Myles defied the spirits. He'd had plenty of warning.'

'You warned him?'

Her cackling laugh set rooks fluttering out of the shrubbery. 'Do you really imagine that stupid, proud man would listen to me? He spurned our protection so, of course, the spirits of the place became stronger. Ever since the Myleses came here they have learned nothing about the forces that hold life together in Coln St Ippolyts, holding past and present in harmony.'

'Unlike the Johnsons?' Nat suggested quietly.

'The Johnsons accepted and because they accepted they understood.' Morgana smiled at the reminiscence. 'The manifestations began very soon after the Myleses arrived.'

'Would that have been about the time Mr Myles put a stop to your rites?' Nat asked.

The woman nodded. 'He took no heed. He destroyed the balance of nature. So, of course, things slipped out of control.'

'The hauntings became more frequent?'

'Hauntings!' Again the cracked laugh. 'It was obvious things would come to a head when they filled Tripletree with all their London friends.'

Mitchenor tried to earth the conversation. 'How well did you know Mrs Pensham?'

'Coln St Ippolyts is a small village.'

'It's big enough for not everyone to be on speaking terms.'

181

'Oh, we're united well enough here, inspector,' Morgana replied with a smile and there was something about her answer that Nat found strangely disturbing.

'So, you knew Mrs Pensham well,' Mitchenor persisted. 'Why didn't you say so? Can you remember when you last saw her? I'd like to get some idea of how she appeared to others in her last few days. Was she happy, elated, depressed, worried?'

'You'd really need to ask her husband about that sort of thing, inspector.'

'Oh, I intend to.'

Morgana swept her cloak about her in a wide circular gesture. 'It seems my journey here was wasted.' She was about to turn and make a dignified exit but, at the last moment, changed her mind. 'Dr Gye, there are none so blind as those who will not see. Tonight we hold a purifying rite. Here, at the main gate to Tripletree. Eleven o'clock. If you care to join us and leave your cynical modern mind behind you might find your eyes opened.' With that curtain line the witch did leave, striding with remarkable speed across the grass.

Mitchenor tapped his forehead. 'Calling her as nutty as a fruitcake would be an insult to fruitcake. Time I was off.' He turned towards the house. 'I have to have that chat with Pensham. Do you want to come? As far as we know, at the moment, you were the last person, apart from the murderer, to speak with his wife. He might relate to you.'

'I doubt that. He didn't strike me as exactly the grief-stricken widower. But, yes, I'll tag along if you think I can be of any use.'

Tom Pensham was not in the garage. The mechanic called Steve said casually that the boss was probably 'next door'. This vague direction led the callers to a large bungalow with an overgrown front garden. When the door was opened by a teenage girl in a school shirt and tie their ears were assailed by the insistent beat of a pop song thudding through the house at full volume. Mitchenor announced that they had come to see Mr Pensham and the girl shouted 'Dad' at the top of her voice above the din. She then promptly disappeared.

Pensham came to the door in his shirtsleeves. In one hand he held a tumbler containing a generous measure of whisky and he surveyed them warily. He was not, Nat immediately noticed, the boisterous garage owner he had met three and a half weeks before. He waved the visitors through a door to the right of the small hall and they found themselves in a room which, though quite expensively furnished, was almost as untidy as Pensham's office. Papers, articles of clothing and the remains of at least one meal littered a scattering of coffee tables and spilled over on to floor and chairs. Pensham's living quarters decidedly lacked the feminine touch.

They sat in deep armchairs and Mitchenor said, raising his voice, 'Sorry to trouble you, Tom. I wonder if you'd mind answering a few . . .' He gave up the unequal struggle and held his hands over his ears.

Without moving from his seat, Pensham bellowed, 'Kylie! Shut the row!'

He was answered by a distant wail of protest but the decibel count did drop to a level which made conversation possible.

'What's all this, then?' Pensham demanded. 'I answered all your questions weeks ago. Can't you leave us in peace? And what's he doing here?' He nodded towards Nat. 'He came prying round the place a while back. If he wants to make trouble –'

'Dr Gye is helping us clear up a few loose ends. One concerns the statement you gave us at the time of your wife's sad death. You told us then that you spent your evening at home and knew nothing about Tracy's death till two of our officers called here at about three in the morning.'

Pensham took a gulp of spirit but remained impassive.

Mitchenor continued. 'Now, I had a word with Jack Holt last Friday. Perhaps he's been in touch with you over the weekend?' The big man's eyes flickered almost imperceptibly. 'Good, so you'll know that he gave us a different version of events. Now, Tom, I appreciate that it was all very distressing for you at the time but withholding evidence relating to a criminal offence could put you in serious trouble.'

'I was in shock,' Pensham muttered.

'Of course you were, Tom. Of course you were. So now let's get the record straight, shall we? Were you in the grounds of the manor on the evening of the party?'

Pensham's head was slumped forward and he spoke almost into his glass. 'Only for a little while. Went to see what was going on.'

'Very natural, Tom. Big dos like that are pretty rare, aren't they? So what time would it be that you slipped in through an unguarded gate or a gap in the hedge?'

'About half eleven.'

'And did you go looking for your wife?'

Pensham suddenly glared at the policeman. 'What are you trying to say? You'd better watch your mouth!'

The inspector continued calmly. 'I'm just suggesting that it would be perfectly natural for you to seek out your wife. Find out how she was getting on.'

'How could I? The whole place was swarming with people and it was dark.'

'So you didn't see her, then?'

'I didn't say that!'

Mitchenor sighed, his patience beginning to ebb. 'Suppose you tell us in your own words just what you did do and what you did see.'

The big man drained his glass and, reaching out a hand to a bottle on the table beside him, poured another generous measure. 'I did see Trace – but not to talk to. She crossed the bridge over the lake. There was a lot of light there.'

184

'And exactly where were you?'

'On the hillside opposite. I saw her cross from the other side and then go behind the hedge by the little lake.'

'And all this would be about, what, twenty to twelve?'

'Bit later.' Pensham hesitated, took another large mouthful of whisky, then rushed on. 'I was going to follow her but then I saw bloody Myles go in after her. I turned round and came back here. Went to bed. Next I knew your blokes were trying to bang the door down.'

Mitchenor ran a hand through his hair. 'Let me get this straight, Tom. You saw your wife and Mr Myles go into that secluded spot and you didn't follow them? You weren't curious to know what they were up to?'

Pensham shrugged. 'None of my business.'

Nat could not restrain himself. 'None of your business! By God, if I saw my wife going off for a secret get-together with another man I'd make it my business!'

Pensham smirked. 'Well, that just goes to show, doesn't it? There are marriages and marriages.'

'You're sure it was Mr Myles?' Nat asked.

'Course I am. He was wearing that long cloak with a big white star on the shoulder.'

Nat pounced on the flaw in Pensham's account. 'How did you know? You'd only just arrived.'

Pensham sneered again. 'Because, Sherlock, I'd already had a run-in with him.' He looked from one to the other of his interrogators. 'Oh, you might as well know it all. I got on to the estate from the village side of Tripletree Hill. I'd just reached the trees at the top when bloody Myles jumped out of the shadows and grabbed me, shouting about gatecrashers. Well, I wasn't standing for that. We scuffled a bit then he backed off – realized what would happen if he made a real fight of it. He shouted at me to clear off. Told me I hadn't heard the last of it. Then he went back towards the house.'

Into Nat's mind flashed a picture of Myles striding angrily down the hillside.

Mitchenor took up the questioning again. 'You see, Tom, what I'm having trouble getting my head round is why you didn't tell us all this at the time. If you'd given us this evidence we'd have treated Tracy's death as suspicious. We'd have pulled Myles in for questioning and found out what really did happen to your wife. You want that, don't you?'

The big man was now sweating profusely. Nat guessed that he was in the grip of something other than alcohol. Pensham stood up, a menacing figure in the small room. 'You got no right to come pestering me and my family. I don't need to tell you nothing. Now bugger off!'

Mitchenor got to his feet in a leisurely fashion. 'This isn't helping, Tom. You know that. If you refuse to volunteer the information I want I'll have you pulled in for questioning. Perhaps when you're sober you'll stop playing silly buggers with me.'

As the two men retreated down the cracked concrete of the garden path with the crash of the slammed door still reverberating in their ears, Mitchenor said cheerfully, 'At last we're getting somewhere.'

'You found that helpful?' Nat sounded puzzled.

'Oh, yes. It was a half-confession. I'll give him twenty-four hours to stew, then bring him in and charge him.'

'You really think Tom Pensham murdered his wife?'

'Sticks out a mile, doesn't it? You saw how worried he was. I always knew this was a straightforward domestic – well, perhaps not straightforward, but strip away all the bizarre elements and what you've got left is a bog standard scenario: angry husband with a strong tendency to violence and an errant wife who commits one infidelity too many. The only thing that surprises me is the clever way he planned to do it. I wouldn't have credited him with the brains.'

'What's your reconstruction, then?'

'I think, like he said, he went on to the estate when the party was in full swing looking for his wife.'

'Hmm!' Nat sounded doubtful. 'He couldn't risk being seen.'

'Probably had a bit of luck. Spotted her down by the lake and grabbed his chance.'

'And all that story about seeing Myles going to the murder location?'

'Oh, that's easy. He's just told us. He bumped into the Squire of Tripletree as soon as he got near the house. So, Myles knew he was there. If that came out Tom would be the number one suspect. All he could think of in his muddled way was to accuse Myles.'

'So he spun that yarn to brother-in-law Jack about a secret assignation between Myles and Tracy.'

They reached the cars and the policeman activated the lock of his Ford but did not open the door. 'I reckon so. And they decided between them that they'd never get anything to stick against the clever barrister and his friends, so they'd say nothing and find their own way of dealing with him.'

'That's a bit thin, isn't it, Dave?'

'Not really. Jack Holt had already fought a long and costly legal battle with Myles over the sale of some building land. Once bitten, twice shy.'

Nat considered the interpretation. 'So Tom invented the story for Jack Holt's benefit and now he's stuck with it.'

'That's right, and once I get him down the station without benefit of scotch his story will fall apart.' The inspector spoke with relish. 'I'll crack him.'

'What about the bronze figurine?'

'Totally irrelevant, in my opinion.'

Nat shook his head. 'Well, I'm sorry, Dave. It seems I've led you up the garden path.'

'Not at all, Nat. Not at all. If it hadn't been for you I wouldn't have been able to get the case reopened. And your theory about Myles was a good one. The man certainly had something to hide and poor Tracy may well have stumbled upon it. Perhaps she *did* try her hand at blackmail. In a way it's a pity that Myles has a first class alibi. There's a whole new story there but, fortunately, it's outside my province. I'll pass on your information to the Met. I'm sure they'll want to unmask the great barrister and find out what he's succesfully hidden all these years.'

Nat felt deflated but, at the same time, unconvinced. 'Secrets,' he muttered.

'Come again.'

Nat stared mournfully along the darkening village street. '"A riddle wrapped in a mystery inside an enigma", as a friend of mine quoted to me recently. I think he might have said the same thing about Coln St Ippolyts. It's almost as though this place has got a life of its own and it's determined to keep us at arm's length. It's saying, "We'll sort out our own problems in our own way."'

Mitchenor shrugged. 'I'm just a plain copper. That sort of fancy thinking is more in your line than mine.'

'I don't mean to be obscure. It's just a feeling I have that we're nowhere near getting to the bottom of this business.' He shuddered. 'This is a horribly introverted little community with deep roots in the past and a passionate sense of identity. Old legends and superstitions are as vital to the the folk here as modern sanitation and parking facilities.'

'Come off it, Nat. This is the end of the twentieth century.'

'Oh, don't let's fool ourselves, Dave. We may like to think we're a sophisticated, rational, high-tech society but just under the surface we're like our medieval forebears – huddled together for security in an alien and incomprehensible universe. That's why people like Morgana and her followers still hold so much sway in places like Coln. I shall be fascinated by her "purifying rite" tonight.'

Mitchenor stared at him. 'You're not going to that ridiculous shindig!'

Nat smiled. 'Call it professional curiosity.' He looked at his watch. 'But first there's something I must do in Oxford. Goodbye, Dave, and good luck with your interrogation of Tom Pensham. I'm glad all this has got you out of having to interview the chief constable.'

'Me, too, Nat. Thanks again for all your help. Keep in touch. Bye!'

The premises of the *Oxfordshire Post and Gazette* were all but devoid of life when Nat arrived. The only person in the front office was a studious-looking young man hunched over a computer console. In answer to Gye's request he shook his head. 'Archive's only open in office hours. Gwen – that's our archivist – went home twenty minutes ago. You'll have to come back and see her in the morning.'

'Oh dear.' Nat looked crestfallen. 'I have to get back to Cambridge tonight.' He produced a visiting card from his wallet. 'I urgently need to check some information for a television programme and I was hoping . . . Is there anyone more senior here I can talk to?'

The trainee puzzled over the card through his glasses. 'Gye. Gye. I've heard of you, haven't I?'

Nat assumed the mantle of reluctant celebrity. 'Well, you may have seen –'

'Got it!' The young man clicked his fingers. 'Programmes on the supernatural. I haven't seen them but my mum's a great fan. That sort of thing goes down a treat with old folk, I suppose.'

Nat smiled, graciously accepting the accolade of being recognized as the darling of the over-fifties. 'So I believe.'

'I'm more of a hard news man, myself,' the young journalist confided. 'I'm aiming to get into TV news. This is only the bottom rung of the ladder for me. I'm definitely a visual person.'

'It's the best way to start. Most of the people I know in the news and documentary departments cut their teeth on local newspapers or radio channels. From there it's a matter of determination and making the right contacts.' Nat tried his most disarming smile. 'I don't suppose you could let me have a very quick look at some past articles? But no, it's wrong of me to ask. You don't have the authority . . . If there's no one *older* here I'd better –'

The barb struck home. 'What exactly was it you wanted, Dr Gye?'

'Do you keep a calendar, a list of all published editorial material?'

'Of course. It's on computer for the last seven years. Anything earlier is in the archive office.'

'Seven years should be enough for my purposes. I'm interested in anything you have on Coln St Ippolyts Manor.'

The young man turned back to his console. 'Well, let's see what we can find.' His fingers rattled over the keyboard. 'There we are,' he announced with a proprietorial air. 'Twelve items – nine reports and three features. I'll do a print-off for you.'

Moments later Nat was looking at a list of dates and titles. The entries were fairly well spread over the years 1992–1998. 'I don't suppose any of these are on the computer?'

'Ooh no! Our hard drive capacity is huge but that would clutter it up something chronic. All this stuff is in our copy library. We're gradually getting it on microfilm for the county record office but we haven't got as far as 1992 yet.'

'So these will all be here, in this building, as hard copies. Look. I don't want to get you into trouble but it would be a great help if I could have photocopies of some of these. It wouldn't take long and it would mean we could get the

190

programme scripted on schedule. You must be only too familiar with the sort of deadlines we media people have to work to.' He watched the young man wavering.

'Come on, then,' he said at last. He led the way along a corridor, stopped before the last door and opened the lock with a key code. Racks ran along two walls containing the newspapers bound up into tall, leather-covered volumes. 'They're in date order, starting on the left,' the guide announced. 'Photocopier in the corner.'

It took Nat about half an hour to find and copy the items he wanted. The young guardian looked up from his screen as Nat emerged. 'OK?' he asked.

'Fine. Thank you very much. I really appreciate your help. Good luck with the career. You have my card. Let me know if I can repay the favour sometime.'

'I might just do that. Cheers!'

Nat walked to the Randolph Hotel and settled himself in a quiet corner of one of the lounges with a brandy and ginger to read the pieces from the *Post and Gazette*.

Coln Manor was obviously a godsend to the editor of a local paper. Dramatic events whose reporting added spice to the catalogue of summer fayres, road bypass protests and amateur theatricals were common. Several of them concerned supposedly supernatural happenings. In fact, in June 1992 the house had merited a whole feature-length article as part of a series on 'Haunted Oxfordshire'. Entitled 'Tripletree and its ghosts', the piece was written by the then chatelaine, Amanda Johnson. Nat read it with close interest.

Mrs Johnson began with a potted history of Tripletree House, dwelling in sombre detail on the events of 1643 which had culminated in the violent death of Simon Bygot and several of his household. She went on:

It is tempting to assume that the manifestations we and others have experienced stem from the horrors of the Civil War. Some connections can certainly be made. We once had a French au pair here who knew nothing about Coln's history. One afternoon she heard a crowd of people outside the front of the house. They were shouting angrily and, she thought, throwing stones at the windows. When she went to look out, there was no sign of anyone except the gardener, who was clearing leaves on the drive and had neither heard nor seen anything. The tall figure which we and many visitors have seen standing on top of Tripletree Hill may be the unquiet spirit of the Bad Lord Bygot. When Sir Bernard Sumption had the cedars planted there his workmen came across the skeleton of a man around six foot in height, which seemed to confirm the local story that Bygot's body had received peremptory, unceremonious burial at the foot of the gallows. For my part, I hope the ghost is Simon's; from all I've heard about him he does not deserve to rest in peace.

Other sightings are less easy to explain. Several people claim to have observed a 'fuzzy' white shape in a corner of the courtyard close to where there was once a well, long since filled in. Conversation and laughter have sometimes been heard coming from the hall and I have twice caught snatches of music there. It seems that all Tripletree's 'memories' are not unhappy ones.

The writer went on to describe the stock in trade of haunted house stories: ghostly footsteps, cold spots, lights flashing on and off and doors that slammed themselves.

Nat leafed through the papers and found three reports of strange, unexplained events. One was the accident to the plasterer who had been working for the Myleses in the Great Hall. Interviewed in his hospital bed, the workman was insistent that on three occasions he had been conscious that someone else was on the scaffolding with him. The last time, this 'presence' had exerted steady pressure, forcing him over the edge. Back in November 1993, a group of psychic researchers had carried out a series of experiments and had allowed a reporter to be present. His highly coloured account – 'A night with the Tripletree ghosts' – could not disguise the fact that all the readings and measurements taken by the experts were as inconclusive as such investigations usually were.

The third article, a one-column feature which appeared in November 1997, was more interesting. 'New light on Coln ghosts' was written by Paul Greer. 'Coln St Ippolyts Manor, popularly known as Tripletree House, has gained something of a local reputation for being haunted,' it began. The writer went on to itemize the common stories of strange sights and sounds that had been reported over the years. It continued,

Recent research in the county record office and the private archive of Mr and Mrs Sheldon Myles, the owners of the manor house, indicate that its spooky reputation is by no means new. Residents and guests as far back as the mid-eighteenth century have left on record accounts of bizarre happenings at the house. No less a person than Jane Austen stayed there in the summer of 1790, while she and her mother were visiting one of her brothers at the university. In a letter to a friend she graphically described how workmen repairing an old well had come across some skeletal remains and promptly downed tools. Could this explain the shadowy figure some have claimed to see in the courtyard, close to the site of the old well?

Fifty years later, the diocesan bishop passed an extremely unpleasant night in what is now the Green Sollar and his experiences are recorded in a diary kept by his wife: 'The Prince of Darkness appeared to him in vivid form within the confines of the bed, but the good man, calling upon the hosts of heaven for his protection, tumbled through the curtains, took up his pectoral cross, lying upon a nearby table, and, holding it aloft, defied the hell fiend, which departed from him with a hideous screech.' Could it have been, I wonder, that his lordship had partaken rather too freely of Sir Bernard Sumption's legendary table hospitality?

Greer's entertaining piece included more references, ancient and modern, to weird goings-on at Tripletree and ended with some lines that Nat found curious.

Stories grow in the telling and once a house has gained a reputation it undoubtedly plays on the imagination of people who regard themselves as 'receptive' to psychic influences. However, several of the incidents recorded at Coln Manor cannot be attributed to impressionable or sensation-seeking witnesses. Even sceptical observers, like myself, have experienced 'manifestations' for which there appear to be no rational explanation.

From 1993 there was a brief account of the midsummer dawn ritual on Tripletree Hill, which was too short on specifics to be very informative. It was, however, accompanied by a photograph showing a group of robed figures, among which Nat recognized not only Morgana but Tracy Pensham and, possibly, her brother Harry. All the other items were concerned with the estate's change of ownership. A March 1994 headline confidently asserted, 'Haunted manor to be conference centre' but four months later the newspaper was revealing, 'Hitch in plans for Coln Manor' and by the end of the year readers were being informed, 'Coln Manor to remain family home'. As a corollary came the story of Roger Johnson's presumed suicide, which merited sensational front-page treatment: 'Mystery disappearance of ex-landowner'.

The story Nat was able to piece together from these scraps made it abundantly clear that the Myleses had inherited a wealth of bad feeling from the moment they set foot in Coln. On establishing the consortium which wanted to develop the estate, 'local millionaire businessman', Jack Holt had resigned from the chairmanship of the local council and all other positions which might be seen as enabling him to influence the decisions of the planning authorities. The elaborate project (plans of which covered a two-page spread of the newspaper) was ambitious and included, as well as the provision of luxury facilities in the house, a leisure club and golf course (which would be available to other users when not required by residents) and, on the village side of Tripletree Hill, a development of affordable homes for local people. After a great deal of toing and froing, the scheme had commended itself to the Heritage Department in London and to local planners as the best way of preserving Coln Manor. It was also welcomed by the village because the popular Johnsons would remain at the house, several jobs would be created and Coln St Ippolyts would be put firmly on the map.

Clearly, the last-minute collapse of negotiations, when all had seemed signed and settled, had come as a real shock to the community. Petitions had been presented to the authorities but now it seemed that the Heritage Department wanted the house to remain a private residence and a new mystery bidder had appeared. The consortium were given no time to reorganize and their concept collapsed in clouds of bitter recrimination. Coln St Ippolyts had only been able to express its feelings by giving the Johnsons – Roger, Amanda, twins Sam and Ralph, and Frank (a mentally handicapped boy who had spent some years in a special school at nearby Lechford) – a lavish send-off. Subsequent news of Roger's suicide had come as a great shock to all who had known the family. The last news about the Johnsons was that they had moved abroad to some, unspecified, location, 'to put their tragic past behind them'.

Nat had a leisurely dinner in the hotel and lingered for

an hour or more over coffee thinking through all the day's developments. Some things were now much clearer in his mind but others seemed more obscure than ever. However on one point he had no doubt whatsoever: Tom Pensham had not murdered his wife.

Ill Met by Moonlight

Soon after nine o'clock Nat made a telephone call.

'Hello.' A young woman's voice answered.

'Good evening. Is it possible to speak with Dr Greer?'

'Sure. I'll fetch him. Who's calling?'

'Dr Nathaniel Gye.'

After a pause Nat heard the historian's acerbic tones. 'Dr Gye, my spies told me you had returned to our little backwater.'

Nat laughed. 'One can't keep any secrets in a village.'

'Absolutely not. What people don't know they find out and what they can't find out they make up. Actually, my informant was Tony Brunnage at the manor. I happened to call earlier and he mentioned that you had been there with the police. I must confess that raised my curiosity. Are you in a position to satisfy it?'

Nat replied with caution. 'Some fresh evidence has come to light and they wanted me to help in checking it out.'

'Oho! May we expect dramatic developments?'

'I think an arrest may be imminent but beyond that I can't really say . . .'

'No, no, of course; I quite realize. The local plod work in mysterious ways and don't always perform wonders.'

'Well, I hope they get it right. It's time the tragic events at Coln were laid to rest. But that wasn't why I phoned. You've awakened my professional interest in Tripletree, and earlier today I was reading some accounts of the hauntings in the local rag. I came across an article you wrote a couple of years ago.'

'"New light on Coln ghosts"? Yes, it is "an ill-favoured thing but mine own".'

'On the contrary, I found it very entertaining. There was one comment that puzzled me though. When we met briefly in London I got the impression that you dismissed all accounts of supernatural phenomena as superstitious nonsense but your article suggests that there have been certain manifestations at Coln which you are inclined to take seriously.'

'Really? I don't recall –'

'I have a copy here. The concluding words are, "Even sceptical observers, like myself, have experienced 'manifestations' for which there appear to be no rational explanation."'

There was a grunt at the other end of the line. Then, after a pause, Greer said, 'Now I remember. That was the work of the editor. He slipped in that little phrase "like myself" in order to water down the tone of light-hearted cynicism. He said he was concerned that if I was too dismissive the paper would be inundated with letters from publicity-seeking readers eager to see their own ghost stories in print. I was very annoyed at the time. I don't appreciate having my copy messed about.'

'So you remain convinced that there are no unquiet spirits mooning about the chambers of Coln St Ippolyts Manor?'

'Absolutely. May I ask the reason for your continued interest?'

'You have a right to know why I'm asking all these questions.' Nat chose his words carefully. 'But what I'm going to tell you is in the strictest confidence.'

'Of course.' Nat could hear the eagerness in the man's voice.

'Mr and Mrs Myles are concerned about the frequent, supposedly supernatural events that have been taking

198

place ever since they came to Coln and they've asked me to do some discreet investigation.'

'I must confess to having suspected something of the sort.'

'I hope I wasn't too obvious. You see, as a parapsychologist, one of my areas of study is fraud – fake mediums and that sort of thing. It occurred to me to wonder whether something of the sort has been happening at Coln. You don't have to be psychic to realize just how unpopular the new owners are. Now, if someone wanted to make life unpleasant for the Myleses, or even to force them out, it wouldn't be very difficult to manufacture spooky sounds and sights. It's certainly been done before. Have you ever had any supicion of anything of that sort?'

'Noo . . .' Greer appeared to give the suggestion careful thought. 'That kind of thing has never occurred to me.'

'You see, what makes me suspicious,' Nat continued, 'is that some of the events the Myleses have told me about are repetitions of things that have occurred before – the invisible crowd at the front of the house; the haunted well. Anyone could have read these up with a view to faking them.'

'I suppose so. I know how distressing Mrs Myles found some of the things that have happened and I've done my best to reassure her. I've certainly got to the bottom of one or two supposedly inexplicable events. You may have heard of the workman who claimed to have been pushed off his scaffolding by invisible hands.'

'Yes.'

'Well, I've discovered only recently that he had a medical condition and was prone to sudden blackouts. That's why he fell and injured himself. Now, he didn't want his employer to know about his problem, because he was afraid of getting the sack, so he thought it would be a good idea to blame the "Tripletree ghost". Apparently, his gullible boss believed him. You see what happens when you give a house a bad name!'

'That was a good piece of detective work. So you've no reason to suspect organized skulduggery?'

'As I say, I've given the matter no thought but I certainly will do so now. Have you any suspects in mind?'

'Well, that's the problem. There are so many people who have a grudge against the Myleses: Jack Holt had his very lucrative building plans scuppered; the Penshams also hoped to profit from the development of Coln Manor; the witch woman, Morgana, might not content herself with sticking pins into effigies of the Myleses; the Johnsons were swindled out of house and home –'

'Oh, I think we can discount them,' Greer interposed perhaps a fraction too hurriedly.

'Really? What became of them, by the way?'

'Moved to South Africa. Amanda's sister lives there. I do hope they manage to rebuild their lives and I wouldn't want to think that they would be troubled by any fresh investigations into events at Coln. They need to put all their past tragedies behind them.'

'There's a mentally disturbed boy, isn't there?'

'Poor Frank, yes.'

'What exactly is his problem?'

Nat could tell from the long pause that his question was an unwelcome one. At last Greer said, 'Frank suffers from what the experts call diminished social and sensory ability.'

'Autism?'

'Something akin to that, I believe. But you'd be quite wrong to think him capable of carrying out a campaign of vengeance against those responsible for his father's death and, anyway, as I said, the family is now in Cape Town.'

'Yes, of course. Well, thank you, Dr Greer. I hope you don't mind me pestering you like this but I feel strongly about twisted people who deliberately set out to frighten others. If something like that is going on at Coln I think we should all try to put a stop to it. Do let me know if anything relevant occurs to you.'

200

'I certainly will, Dr Gye, but I must say that I'm sure your fears are unfounded.'

Nat returned to his quiet corner of the hotel lounge musing on the historian's closed mind. It was something which, as a parapsychologist, he was very familiar with. The world of supposedly 'rational' science was very uncomfortable with his chosen discipline. Apparitions, near-death experiences, poltergeist activity, extra-sensory perception, psychokinesis, spiritualism and everything involved in what is known collectively as 'psi' were sources of embarrassment to scholars who believed that human knowledge of the universe could only be extended by controlled experiments and ever closer observation of objects upon which microscopes or telescopes could be trained. Nat had frequently suffered the jibes of those who refused to regard his field of study as 'proper' science. His standard retort was that there was no philosophical difference between the physicist, the astronomer and the parapsychologist. All were engaged in exploring the unexplored, seeking to explain the apparently inexplicable. One could not call oneself a scholar and refuse to countenance inconvenient facts which lay beyond the scope of laboratory investigation. Furthermore any 'scientist' who claimed to be guided by pure rationality, unalloyed with guesswork and intuition, was a self-deluding fraud.

It was intuition that now persuaded Nat that something complex and profoundly evil was going on at Coln St Ippolyts. Not the kind of intuition that may be described as a vague hunch. The fear and hatred in this drab village and its ancient manor house had coalesced into a force which was almost tangible and had the potential to be vastly destructive. The Myleses, the Penshams, the Holts, the Johnsons, the members of Morgana's cult, perhaps even the aloof sceptic, Dr Greer, were caught up in something beyond their comprehension and beyond their power to control. Nat had meant what he said to Morgana about the evil which pervaded these few acres of rural

England. She might try to confront it with her spells and incantations, just as Dave Mitchenor might employ the prosaic methods of criminal investigation, but neither would be able to stop it. Nat sensed with a growing conviction not entirely centred in the cerebral cortex that he was misreading the situation at Coln. There was a beast eluding him in the labyrinth of conflicting evidence and engaged passions and if he could not locate it among the twisting, interconnecting pathways it would wreak havoc on a scale as yet unseen.

Nat opened his laptop. He must think, think, think! Use the computer as an alter ego with whom to argue his way through to the truth. He reopened the Juniper Myles file and recorded the date.

Monday 6 November

DCI Mitchenor seems to be on the point of charging Tom Pensham with the wilful murder of his wife. This is wrong, I know it.

Need to think things through from scratch.

Sheldon Myles has a murky (criminal?) past.

Revelation would destroy him.

Tracy Pensham had almost certainly discovered this (blackmail?).

More than adequate motive for murder.

Yes, but Myles has an apparently unassailable alibi.

But Tom says he saw him following Tracy to the murder site immediately before she was killed.

Possible solutions to this paradox:

a) Tom is lying. Mitchenor thinks he has made up a wild story to cover his own guilt. Tom has changed his original account (that he was home all evening), so it looks bad for him. He was certainly in the grounds. He had an argument with Myles. That can be verified.

MOTIVE? Angry, cuckolded husband? Unlikely; not that kind of a marriage. If Tracy was on the lucrative blackmail trail Tom would not kill the goose about to provide an endless supply of golden eggs.

MEANS? How could he get hold of the bronze, and why? Other weapons lay to hand.

OPPORTUNITY? Just about the worst possible. Why risk going to the party where he might be (and was) seen? He could bump his wife off anytime, anywhere.

OK, then why was he there?

Hypothesis: He was there to sabotage the party. He could have set off the fireworks. If so, he would take care not to be seen. It was bad luck running into Myles on Tripletree Hill.

He told Jack Holt what he had seen. Why did he not tell the police?

The Holts were also involved in messing up the party and had almost certainly been faking the supernatural events at the manor. Perhaps they were in on the blackmail. This would explain their attempt to warn me off. Jack must have told Tom to keep his mouth shut for fear that a murder enquiry would uncover all these nefarious activities.

Therefore,

b) Tom is telling the truth.

But how could he see a man who was not there? He must have been mistaken.

THAT'S IT! He thought he saw Myles because he saw someone wearing the same costume. From the hillside he would only have recognized the cloak with the very distinctive Garter insignia on the shoulder and the steeple hat. Any man could have been wearing it.

Or woman.

Absolutely! How hideously brilliant! If anyone sees the murderer they will identify him or her with the only person at the party allowed to wear a Charles I outfit.

So we are dealing with someone capable of conceiving and carrying out an extremely elaborate plan.

Everything was perfectly calculated – the weapon, the

disguise, the timing (even though the cancelling of the firework display nearly threw a spanner in the works). Any suggestions?

One name occurs to me but I hesitate to mention it.

It would have to be someone who hated both Myles and Tracy; someone who would take a delight in seeing Myles arrested at the very moment of his social triumph; someone very clever who knew the evening's programme well in advance; someone who could lure the victim to her death because Tracy would never suspect.

Only one person completely fits that description.

Nat stared at the screen. Could it really be true? Had he got everything so hopelessly wrong all these weeks? And, if he was now right, would there be the remotest chance of proving it? He switched off the computer and ordered more coffee.

Later that night Nat passed the Coln St Ippolyts village sign board, swung round the final bend and was sucked into something brittle, black and sinister. The empty, moonlit street was like the stage set of a western ghost town. Harsh, angular shadows stencilled the tarmac. House fronts with unlit windows reared up on either side and could have been freestanding clapboard façades. Nat shivered despite the cocooning warmth of the car's interior. He felt as though some magnetic force was pulling him through the village; that if he took his foot off the accelerator it would make no difference.

The Mercedes passed Pensham's darkened garage, began the slow ascent towards the manor and encountered another disturbing image. Nat slowed to drive carefully past a long column of people. They shuffled up the hill – men, women and children straggled into groups, walking with steady, solemn purpose. Some carried lanterns or flashlamps. They were herded by white-robed figures bearing flaming torches which garishly illuminated the procession. Nat guessed that there must be more than a hundred people on the march and wondered whether anyone was left behind in the village. The word 'exodus' came most readily to mind.

He passed the foremost walkers and, after another hundred yards, pulled into a lay-by. He parked the car, donned a warm overcoat and strode the short distance to the main entrance of the manor. A field gate opposite was open and on its far side a wide circle of fire was marked out by more torches. At its centre stood a makeshift altar of hay bales over which a white cloth had been thrown bearing runic symbols in red. Morgana and a pair of acolytes were already in position and arranging various objects on the altar. Nat found a vantage point close to the hedge and positioned himself there as the witch's congregation began filing into the field.

'Congregation' was an apt description, for what struck Nat most strongly was their silence. Everyone moved with quiet reverence to the places allotted to them within the circle by the robed marshals, as though they were in church. There was a hush of expectancy. Nat glanced at the illuminated dial of his watch. It wanted six minutes to eleven o'clock.

An attendant approached and whispered in his ear. 'Come inside the circle, friend.'

'I'm fine where I am, thank you,' Nat replied in a suitably subdued tone.

The man laid a hand on his arm. 'You must be inside the circle. 'Tisn't safe beyond.'

Nat resisted the gentle pressure. 'No, really I'd rather –'

The marshal's grip tightened. 'I must insist, friend. Everyone has to be in place. The circle can't be breached. The protection won't work else.'

Reluctantly, Nat allowed himself to be led to the outer fringe of the crowd.

He was placed at the edge of one of several 'aisles' that radiated like spokes from the centre and had an excellent view of the proceedings. He saw that Morgana had moved to a position before the altar and now stood, arms raised in silent supplication towards the full moon. Nothing else seemed to be happening but, then, beginning almost imperceptibly, a wave of sound engulfed the assembled company. A low, melodious moaning seemed to well up from the very earth. Nat looked around him. Men, women and children were following the witch's lead. Hands aloft, eyes closed, they swayed to the sinuous rhythm of the wordless chant. The music sent a shiver down Nat's spine. It was, he now realized, the humming of a hundred throats. Led by the robed figures, who now formed a two-part choir arranged on either side of the altar, the people were joining in a primal, mesmeric pagan 'psalm'; a non-rational fusing of worshippers with the spirits of nature; an ecstatic utterance steadily growing in intensity and drawing Nat into the ritual. He had to force himself not to add his voice to those of the ardent devotees around him.

Tenaciously he held on to his role as observer. Twice before – once in Nigeria and once on an Indian reservation in Montana – he had experienced rituals which were, in essence, the same as the one he was now witnessing. But to come across something so primitive and frighteningly compelling in the heart of 'sophisticated', 'materialistic', 'agnostic' England was fascinating. It confirmed his conviction that the removal of a generally accepted religion from the life of a people left a vacuum into which any and every superstition from earth magic to UFOs, from Free-masonry to veneration of pop idols, was readily sucked.

The chant went on and on until Morgana was presumably satisfied that it had achieved its desired effect. Then, in a strident voice, she addressed the elemental forces. Purification and protection seemed to be linked in her pantheistic supplication. She called on earth, air, fire and water to shield the people from evil, and there could be no doubt about where she and her followers located the heart of that evil. A high point of the ceremony arrived when Morgana's sub-priests brought from the altar silver bowls, some containing earth and others water. They advanced down the aisles sprinkling the worshippers with the contents of their sacred vessels.

A white-robed figure came towards Nat, broadcasting droplets of water to right and left. As he drew level the official let out a gasp. Nat peered at him and recognized Harry Holt. For several seconds the businessman stood transfixed. Then he leaned forward urgently and whispered, 'We must talk. As soon as the ritual's over.'

There was not much more to it. After another communal chant Morgana dismissed her followers and they began drifting back towards the gate. Immediately Harry Holt returned. 'Come along,' he said and then, when Nat hesitated, added in a tone of urgent pleading, 'Please!'

'What's all this about?' Nat demanded as Holt hurried him from the field.

'It's about Tom – among other things. Have you got a vehicle here?'

'My car's just down the road.'

'Good. We can go to my place. It's only a mile away.'

'I'm not sure I want to subject myself to another Holt interrogation. The last one is still a vivid and unpleasant memory.'

'Nothing like that,' Harry muttered. 'Things are getting out of hand. We need help.'

Holt's house was a substantial modern building standing in its own grounds. He led the way to a room which was part study and part sitting area. 'Drink,' he muttered, unzipping his white habit and flinging it into a chair.

Nat asked for a brandy and, while Harry was busying himself with glasses and a showy array of decanters set out on a brass-bound trolley, he asked, 'How long have you been mixed up with all that nonsense?'

'Morgana's a remarkable woman,' Holt replied. 'If you'd

seen her do some of the things that I've seen you wouldn't be so sceptical.'

'Such as?'

'Curing a child of leukaemia by holistic magic – a combination of herbs and charms. Most sick folk in Coln will consult Morgana before they go anywhere near a GP.' He handed Nat a generous measure of spirit in a cut glass goblet. They sat either side of a stone fireplace in which gas flames flickered through a pile of imitation logs. Holt paused to light a cigarette. 'Five years ago my business very nearly went down the tubes. I had some sessions with Morgana and, well, as you can see,' he waved a hand around the opulent furnishings, 'I more than survived.'

'What exactly did she contribute to your recovery? I don't imagine she put up capital.'

'You can mock all you like, Mr Gye. But I know that she helped me get my thinking straight and called on supernatural forces to intervene on my behalf – and it worked. But we're not here to talk about me. Tom Pensham's in a panic. He says the police have got the crazy idea in their heads that he murdered Tracy. Is that true?'

Nat could see no reason to deny it. 'I believe that's one line of enquiry DCI Mitchenor is following up.'

'That's ridiculous! Tom hasn't got many brains and he certainly has a violent streak in him but he'd never have done . . . that . . . to Tracy. He might be a scumbag but he did genuinely care about her. You seem to be in thick with Dave Mitchenor.' Holt rattled the cubes of ice in his tumbler of whisky. 'What's he think he's got on Tom?'

Nat shrugged. 'He sees Tracy's death as a *crime passionnel*, a variation on the eternal triangle theme. She was having an affair with Sheldon Myles, so he killed her and tried to put the blame on her lover.'

'Bloody fool!' Holt snorted. 'If he thinks Tom Pensham is capable of thinking out something as clever as that he ought to go back to police college!'

'Tom didn't do himself any favours by changing his

story. First of all he denied being anywhere near the manor when his wife died. Now he not only admits that he was there, but says he virtually saw the crime carried out.'

Holt stared mournfully into the fire. 'Things look pretty black for him, then?'

Nat said quietly, 'For what it's worth, I don't think Dave can make his case stick.'

Holt looked up sharply. 'What's your take on all this, then?'

'I believe that there are several people who know a great deal about what was going on at the party that night.' He stared directly into Harry's eyes. 'I also believe that until those people come forward to tell their stories there will be a lot more suffering and the murderer will probably get away scot-free.'

Holt shook his head. 'Oh, no,' he said bitterly, 'that's one thing you can be sure of. Myles is going to pay for my sister's death.'

Nat replied quietly, 'Sheldon Myles did not kill your sister.'

Harry glared back. 'Don't be bloody ridiculous!'

'No, Mr Holt, however much you may want to believe it – and I have a certain amount of sympathy with you on that score – it was quite impossible for Myles to be involved in Tracy's death. He was nowhere near the lake and he has the most impeccable of witnesses who will testify to that fact.'

'But he was seen –'

'No he wasn't. Look, Mr Holt, I'll make a deal with you: an exchange of information. I'll tell you what I know if you'll be completely open with me. That may be embarrassing for you but I can see no other way of getting at the truth.'

Holt stood up to refill his glass. 'I don't think you know what you're asking. Jack –'

'If brother Jack was here I'd be saying exactly the same

to him. Of course, if you'd prefer to have the truth dragged out of you by the police . . .'

Holt lit another cigarette and returned to his chair. He inhaled deeply and stared at Nat through a swirl of tobacco smoke.

'Look,' Nat offered, 'I'll make it easy for you. I'll tell you what I think has been going on at the manor and you tell me if I've got anything wrong.'

Harry nodded and Nat outlined the recent history of Coln St Ippolyts Manor as he had pieced it together in his mind. 'A few years ago, when Roger and Amanda Johnson were struggling to keep the estate going, a group of people came up with a bold business plan that would save the mansion and turn a tidy profit. You and your brothers were involved. So were the Penshams, along with a number of major commercial concerns. A lot of effort went into developing the scheme and a lot of capital.'

'Two point three million,' Holt muttered blankly.

Nat whistled. 'That much?' He continued, 'At the eleventh hour it all went pear-shaped thanks to the single-handed intervention of a certain Sheldon Myles. Now more money had to be poured in to finance a legal challenge. That all went down the pan, too.'

Harry nodded. 'Bastard lawyers cost us another million plus.'

'Was that when you had your own commercial crisis?'

'Yes. I came within an ace of being wiped out totally. You can see, now, how much I owe to Morgana.'

Nat smiled. 'Oh, I suspect your own ability and the support of your family would have pulled you through without the aid of elemental spirits. However, Myles moved into Coln and set about playing the local squire in no uncertain terms. It must have seemed that he was rubbing your noses in your defeat. Except that I believe you had already decided that you weren't defeated. You were going to do everything possible to drive the Myleses out just as they had ruthlessly driven out your

210

friends, the Johnsons. Whose idea was it to stage the fake hauntings?'

'Fake hauntings? What do you mean? Everyone knows Tripletree has ghosts. If they were more active after the Myleses came it was because they were pulling the place about – and preventing Morgana from protecting the house against evil spirits.'

Nat looked sceptical. 'You're seriously telling me that you weren't involved in a plan to give the resident spooks a little human assistance?'

'No need for it.'

'Hmm, well, be that as it may, you're not going to deny that you made full use of your sister as a Trojan horse, are you? She had worked for the Johnsons as a chatelaine-cum-PA and she carried on in much the same capacity for the new owners, except that before long she was serving Sheldon Myles in other ways.'

'The man was a predator!' Holt burst out. 'No woman was safe when he was around.'

Nat thought but did not say that when it came to beasts of prey in the sexual jungle there was probably little to choose between Shelley and Tracy. 'It was very useful, though, wasn't it, to have someone inside Coln Manor who enjoyed Mr Myles's confidence? What was the thinking – that there must be a chink in his armour somewhere and that, given long enough, Tracy could find it?'

'Can I get you another cognac?' Holt asked and when Nat shook his head, he continued reflectively. 'Tracy said the atmosphere in that place was poisonous. The Myleses were at each other's throats much of the time and Mrs Myles's health was suffering. She was fed up with her husband's womanizing and annoyed at the way he was alienating all the local people. Tracy felt sorry for her, though the feeling was, understandably I suppose, not reciprocated. From certain things that the couple said or shouted to each other Tracy knew that there were some unsavoury past incidents that they wouldn't want publicized. So she hung on and put up with Myles's obscene gropings in the hope of learning something really useful.'

'But it wasn't until last summer that she was successful,' Nat suggested.

Holt stared at him open-mouthed. 'How the hell did you know that?'

Nat met question with question. 'What did Tracy discover?'

The other man gazed mournfully into his glass. 'I haven't the remotest idea.'

'What? Are you trying to tell me that, after years of searching for something that would give you all leverage –'

But Holt's patience was at an end. 'Mr Gye, before we go any further, I want some straight answers to some simple questions.'

'If I can.'

'Are the police going to charge Tom with Tracy's murder?'

'It's possible. But I don't think so.'

'Are they convinced that Myles is in the clear?'

'Very.'

'Do they have any other suspects?'

'To the best of my knowledge, no.'

'Are they planning to bring any other charges against Tom?'

'Such as?'

Holt looked uncomfortable. He lit another cigarette before replying. 'My family doesn't have much time for Tom Pensham.'

'I'd rather gathered that.'

'We're respectable business people. Tom mixes with some very shady characters and gets involved in deals that we know nothing about. But he is sort of family and we owe it to Tracy's memory to try to keep him out of trouble.'

'I can understand that,' Nat responded, 'but I don't quite see what it is you're trying to say.'

'Well, let me spell it out very simply. We will stand by him in the business of Tracy's murder because we don't believe he's guilty and we want to see whoever is brought to book. But if the police investigation leads to him being charged with any other crime he's on his own. We are in no way involved. If you're in a position to make that clear to Dave Mitchenor please do so.'

Nat nodded, at the same time recalling what Mitchenor had said about the Holts' connections on the wrong side of the tracks. 'And you honestly have no idea what unsavoury facts Tracy had unearthed about Myles?'

Holt shook his head. 'Look,' he said, 'we had one aim and one only: to get those bloody people out of Tripletree.'

'By hook or by crook?'

'By any legal means.'

'Making a mess of their party wasn't exactly the behaviour of law-abiding citizens. Who masterminded all that sabotage?'

'It was too good an opportunity to miss – embarrassing him in front of all his smart friends.'

'But by then you knew that Tracy was on to something that was potentially much more damaging to your enemy.'

'Yes, but we didn't know what. She wouldn't tell us. Only Tom was in on the secret and he decided to play a lone hand.'

'Financial blackmail.'

'Yes, the bloody fool could never see further than the end of his nose. We would never have got mixed up in anything like that and we only found out about it today. Tom phoned Jack in a blue funk and told him the whole story and Jack went ballistic. He came over here and put me in the picture (Quentin's on a business trip to Brussels). He left just before me and the wife set off for the ritual. When I saw you there . . . well, I just thought you might be able to help keep the police off our backs.'

213

For several moments both men stared into the fire. At last Nat said, 'For what it's worth I don't believe Tracy's death has anything to do with her attempts to blackmail Sheldon Myles. I'm convinced that she was murdered by someone masquerading as him, for totally different reasons. Whether I can persuade Mitchenor to follow another line of enquiry I don't know, but I'll certainly give it my best shot.'

Holt looked up eagerly. 'So who –'

'No,' Nat said, holding up a hand, 'that is for Dave Mitchenor's ears only.'

As Nat made the two-hour drive back to Great Maddisham he kept his tired mind alert by going over the events of the day, particularly the implications of Harry Holt's last passionate apologia. Had he been right, he wondered, to give Tracy's brothers cause to hope that her murderer would be brought to book? There were still gaps in the chronicle of events that had resulted in two violent deaths but of one thing he was now increasingly convinced. The person responsible for them, the only person who linked them together, was Juniper Myles.

Ends – Loose and Dead

Tuesday 7 November was not a good day. Nat woke reluctantly after less than four hours' sleep to find Kathryn rushing from the house to attend an early meeting and leaving him to get the boys organized and off to school. He was painfully aware that his morning lecture was turgid and that his usually attentive audience were restless. Instead of an eager bunch of students clustering around him with question and argument at the end, they all scurried out on the dot of twelve. After lunch he attended a dreary committee meeting on the subject of university policy towards narcotic abuse, which fell prey to the impotence induced by clashes between the liberals who wanted to legalize possession of soft drugs and trust to the undergraduates' common sense and hard-liners for whom any relaxation of the rules implied getting into bed with the devil. When he at last regained the sanctuary of his college rooms it was only to have it invaded by a hysterical female tutee who had just discovered that she was pregnant and wanted Dr Gye to intercede for her with her parents.

The truth was that Nat's concentration was on none of these activities and about that he felt guilty. He was supposed to be professionally dedicated to stimulating the minds of young people and offering some degree of guidance to help them along the path to becoming fulfilled and valuable members of society. Yet his mind kept returning to the fact that an innocent man was possibly about to be charged with murdering his wife and that a scheming woman responsible for two brutal killings would continue to enjoy wealth and liberty unless he could find some way of assisting the course of natural justice. In the few intervals of his busy day Nat tried to reach Mitchenor by phone but the inspector's mobile was always either busy or switched off and a call to the Oxford police HQ produced the information that he was out on a case and no one knew when he would be back.

When, soon after four o'clock, Nat did succeed in making contact he could tell from Mitchenor's manner that he was under pressure.

'Nat, hello. What can I do for you?' The words were clipped, the tone abrupt.

Nat decided on an emollient approach. 'Sorry if this is a bad time. I tried earlier but you were obviously tied up. I guess this is a busy day.'

'You can say that again. I've had a team out around the seamier parts of the city trying to round up members of a ram-raiding gang.'

'Any luck?'

'Shan't know till later. We've got a couple of them cooling their heels in the cells. Whether they'll give us anything when we interview them is anybody's guess. We could be in for a long night.'

'Well, look, I don't want to hold you up. It's just that I've been doing some thinking about the Pensham business.'

'Still worried I've got it wrong about a straightforward domestic killing?'

'No, I'm sure you're right about that. Tracy's death was inspired by jealousy and revenge. I just don't see Tom Pensham . . . I suppose what I'm saying is please don't close your mind to other possible lines of enquiry.'

'Such as?'

'Well, I reckon the state of the Myleses' marriage would bear examination.'

There was a long-suffering sigh at the other end of the

216

line. Then Mitchenor said, 'If you're still thinking about that bronze ornament, I can put you straight. It had nothing to do with the murder – that's official.'

'But that's ridiculous! What was it doing –'

'It's scientific fact!' Mitchenor snapped the words. 'I got back here half an hour ago and found the forensic report on my desk. It tells me there's no correlation between the statuette and the injuries sustained by Tracy Pensham. Furthermore, our experts reckon the ornament hadn't been in the lake very long – perhaps no more than a couple of weeks.'

'I see.' Nat felt thoroughly deflated.

'I'm sorry, Nat.' The policeman's tone softened. 'As I said yesterday, I'm very grateful to you for your help. If it hadn't been for you I wouldn't be on the verge of making an arrest. But, well, we *are* the professionals. We have the technology and the experience. When we bring Pensham in here tomorrow we'll get at the truth.'

Nat watched his certainties crumbling. 'I'm sorry if I've complicated your enquiry, Dave. It's just that Mrs Myles was the only link I could see between the deaths in Coln and Birmingham.'

'There doesn't have to be a link – though, if it's any consolation to you, you were right about Owen. He was murdered. The post-mortem indicated that he died from a savage blow to the back of the head which was inflicted some time before the fire reached him. The internal organs were reasonably intact and showed no signs of smoke inhalation. Fortunately, that case is up to the boys in the big city to sort out. Now, if you'll excuse me, I've got a couple of young thugs to see to. Goodbye, Nat.' He hung up.

Which puts you in your place, Dr Gye, Nat thought as he returned the receiver to its rest. But it was not the wrist slapping that bothered him, as he explained to Kathryn when they were relaxing that night with a bottle of wine after the boys were asleep.

'I just know that Mitchenor's got it wrong. Barny was on the right track when he tried to make me see that having Tracy prancing round dressed up as Nell Gwyn was like a red rag to a bull.' Nat stretched out his long legs and closed his eyes, imagining the two women confronting each other at the party. 'Suppose she came upon them in some quiet corner. Tracy told me she was off to a meeting with someone.'

'Yeah, but not for a smooching session. Didn't she make it pretty clear that Shelley Myles was going to get what was coming to him?' Kathryn, legs tucked up beneath her on the sofa, laid aside the book she was reading.

'That's no problem. All June had to do was see Shelley and Tracy together having an urgent conversation and something snapped, as Barny suggested. She's patiently put up with years of humiliation from her husband. She's found herself in an alien environment at Coln just because Shelley wants to own a big, impressive house as part of projecting his own inflated self-image. On the evening everything's going wrong. The party's falling apart and people are laughing at her – or she thinks they are. And what's Shelley up to while she's trying to keep all the guests happy? Amorous dalliance with his latest conquest. She doesn't bother to eavesdrop on their conversation. Her anger overwhelms her. She follows Tracy, waiting for her moment, and does the deed. Only her conscious mind refuses to acknowledge what she's done and she genuinely suffers from stress amnesia.'

Kathryn shook her head. 'Sorry, darling, but if it's a choice between your version and Mitchenor's, my money's on the cop. There's no way June Myles is guilty of double murder.'

'But there's no other connecting link between the deaths of Tracy Pensham and Caradoc Owen. I told Myles where to find Owen and if he didn't kill the man the only person who could have got the address from Shelley was June.'

'Hold it right there!' Kathryn's dark eyes stared unblinkingly into Nat's. 'That's what's really bugging you, isn't it? You're still blaming yourself for Owen's death and that's blinding you to the obvious.'

'What obvious?'

'Well, aside from the fact that June Myles isn't the type to go racing round the country on a homicidal spree, your reconstruction of events at the party doesn't hold water. For instance, what about the cloak and dagger?'

'Cloak and dagger?'

Kathryn frowned impatiently. 'Well, OK, cloak and bronze, if you're being pernickety.'

'Go on.'

'According to your scenario, June suddenly goes berserk, grabs up a weapon, stalks Tracy and then Bop! Well, we now know that the weapon wasn't a bronze – unless you want to challenge the technical expertise of Mitchenor's boys. Then there's the disguise. Does she go up to her husband and say, "Excuse me, Shelley dear, I'm just off to murder your mistress and I need to borrow your hat and cloak so that, if anyone sees me, they'll think it's you"?'

Nat scowled. 'Sarcasm does not become you. So you go along with your good-looking policeman, do you? You point the finger at Tom Pensham.'

Kathryn laughed. 'Hey, lighten up! I don't know who killed who but I hate to see you getting stressed out by it.' She came over to kneel by Nat's chair and put an arm round him.

He sighed. 'I guess you're right. I shouldn't let it get to me, especially when we've got this business with Greg hanging over us. Have you thought any more about it?'

'I've thought about little else.'

'And?'

'I wish you wouldn't see it as a choice between marriage and career. It's really just moving to a new phase of our lives.'

'The Gyes go international?'

'Something like that. Oh, Nat, it could be fantastic!'

'I suppose I have difficulty seeing myself as a member of the jet set – lunch in LA, dinner in NY, breakfast in Paris, that sort of thing. Some men are driven by ambition. Sheldon Myles, for example. They want it all – whatever "all" may be. Others of us are content with what we've got – and scared as hell at the possibility of losing it.' He held Kathryn close and for a long time neither of them spoke.

At last Kathryn said, 'I wonder if it was ever like this for the Myleses.'

'What, being really close, you mean?'

'Mmm!'

'Difficult to imagine. I reckon June was just a rung in Shelley's ladder to the stars.'

'But she must have loved him once – probably as fiercely as she now hates him.'

'I expect he swept her off her feet. He was one of the up and coming stars of the bar, brilliant, confident, audacious, a young man everyone was talking about, destined for a bright future. Only it was all an act, a masquerade.'

'What do you suppose actually happened between him and the real Sheldon Myles?'

'Who knows? Probably only Shelley and June and they're not going to tell anyone.'

'Hmm, I wonder.' Kathryn's words were half murmur, half whisper.

'What does that mean?'

'Oh, nothing. I hope the London police do follow up on your leads and expose the odious Myles for what he is.'

'Me, too. Somehow I feel we owe that much to Tracy. Unfortunately, his type have an instinct for survival. He could still come out of all this smelling of roses.'

'My God, that's a depressing thought.' Kathryn moved on to his lap. 'I'm beginning to see why this wretched business has gotten to you. Sheldon has hurt and damaged so many people but what he has systematically done to his wife over the years – that's unforgivable.'

Around two o'clock the next morning, after a couple of sleepless hours, Nat slipped gently from the bed and went along the landing to his study. He switched on the computer and opened the Myles file.

Wednesday 8 November

I was convinced that June Myles had murdered both Tracy and Owen, because she was the only link between them, and also what the police call the MO was similar in both cases – a blow to the head and then things arranged to look like an accident. But I see now that the hypothesis doesn't work.
Find another connection then.
How did June get to hear of Owen? Who introduced them?
Obviously the person who wanted to prey on June's fears and anxieties. Someone who knew how close to the edge she was.
That information could have come from Tracy. She had told Tom and her brothers how bad things were between the Myleses. Tom wouldn't have had the brains. No reason to believe either he or the Holts had any connection with Owen. Who, then?

A sudden picture flashed into Nat's mind. A fleeting memory. A figure in a long black cloak hurrying away from the garage on the occasion of his own first visit to the village.

Morgana! In thick with Tom and with Harry Holt. Would she have had any connection with a disgraced stage hypnotist?
No, but she could have had contact with the Unicorn Bookshop. Mitchenor had described her as a producer of magic books. As a self-publisher she would have visited all the shops in a wide area likely to deal in her brand of arcane merchandise. There can't be all that many. Not

difficult for her, then, to have met Owen or to have learned about his earlier brush with Sheldon Myles. They would have discovered that they had a common enemy. It might have seemed the most natural thing in the world to plan a common revenge.

So, where does that take us? Think! Think! Think!

My visit to the little Welshman puts the wind up him. What does he do? Gets straight on the phone to his accomplice. What does he say? 'That meddling Gye fellow is on to us.' Next day someone bashes his skull in.

Morgana? Surely not.

Don't jump to conclusions. What do we know about her?

She was the one person who seemed really worried when I turned up in Coln. She tried to warn me off in no uncertain terms. Then she went straight to Tom Pensham and told him to have nothing to do with me. Within minutes my ailing car made a miraculous – and cheap – recovery. Morgana knew Tom couldn't be trusted not to let something slip.

Morgana and Tom, then, deliberately turning Tracy's death to advantage. Probably the Holts were in on it, too. Was that what they meant by dealing with things their own way? Was that why they, too, tried to scare me off?

So who disposed of Caradoc Owen?

The conspirators couldn't risk having his connection with them brought to light. He had become a liability. So they acted and acted quickly.

A fine theory but you've no evidence.

True. Hang on a bit, though. What happened yesterday? As soon as Morgana realized the police were back at Tripletree she came there hot foot.

Why?

To find out what they were doing and what they knew. What happened next? Remember! In detail!

222

Mitchenor told her they were investigating suspicious deaths and she set up a horrible wailing. Then she went on about protecting me from evil.

But there was something before that; something I'm missing. She screamed the word 'deaths' as though she were surprised and horrified that more people had come to an unnatural end. Anyone else would have been equally appalled. But, surely, anyone else would have gone on to ask 'What other deaths are you investigating? Who has died apart from Mrs Pensham?'

So, you reckon she didn't ask because she already knew the answer?

Let's explore that hypothesis. Morgana or one of her cronies put paid to Owen. They made it look like an accident and, anyway, they were safe as long as no one found a connection between Owen and Tracy. But Morgana knew that I could make that connection. So, when I turned up in Coln again with the police she had to find out what I knew.

Bit flimsy, isn't it?

No! No! No! It fits! What happened next was that she did some quick thinking. She invited me to the ritual. Probably she hoped that I wouldn't be able to resist the chance to witness one of her rites at first hand. Then she told Harry Holt to watch out for me and, if I showed up, try to question me in detail. And what was it Harry wanted to know above all else?

Nat stared at the screen and smiled. Of course, that had to be it! He closed down the Journal file, logged on to the Internet and fired off a brief email to Mitchenor. Then he went back to bed. And slept.

Comings and Goings

It was the following afternoon when DCI Mitchenor responded. He phoned at Beaufort while Nat was conducting a supervision group.

'I just thought you'd like to know that you were right,' the policeman said briskly. 'Thanks for the tip-off.'

'He confessed?'

'I should be so lucky. No, he stared goggle-eyed, turned all the colours of the rainbow and started screaming for a lawyer. It's a pretty good sign of guilt when a suspect wants a legal prop. Anyway, we had enough to interest Birmingham CID, so friend Pensham is, at this very moment, on his way to the big city to be interrogated by the lads there. That means he's out of my hair. So, many thanks.'

'Your colleagues will probably want to talk to Morgana, too. In my opinion, she's the real villain of the piece. She has an amazing hold over the minds of lots of people in Coln.'

'I'm a step ahead of you there. I alerted the local station at lunchtime and a couple of uniformed men went to collect her. Unfortunately, she was too quick for us. They missed her by about an hour. Our men got very little out of the neighbours but it seems she did create a bit of a stir by driving herself out of the village.'

'What was unusual about that?'

'She had no car and folk in Coln didn't know that she could drive. However, she picked up a vehicle from

Pensham's place and set off like a bat out of the proverbial. Still, I don't think she'll get far. We've put out a call for her and she's hardly the sort of woman who could easily lose herself in a crowd.'

'Thanks for letting me know, Dave.'

'My pleasure. Cheers!' He rang off and Nat returned thoughtfully to his students.

When they had gone Nat decided to try another call to Dr Greer. It occurred to him that Tripletree's historian might have picked up some scraps of information about Sheldon Myles's past. With his intense dislike of the barrister and his love of gossip he just might be able to throw some light on Myles's deeply shaded past.

'Hello.' Once again the phone was answered by a young woman.

'Good afternoon. Is Dr Greer there, please?'

'No. I'm afraid he's in London for the day. Can I help?'

'I don't think so, thank you. That's his daughter speaking, is it?'

There was a pleasant laugh at the other end of the line. 'No, Uncle Paul doesn't have any daughters. He's the biggest misogynist in the county. My name's Sam, Sam Johnson.'

'Oh!' Nat was taken aback. 'That's Sam as in Samantha, is it?'

'That's right.' Again the light, soprano laugh. 'Have we met?'

'No . . . no . . . but I've heard about you. Sorry, this must sound rather rude. It's just that you took me a bit by surprise. I thought you lived in South Africa.'

'Only in the vacations. My brother and I are at Oxford, except for the occasions when we come to stay with Uncle Paul for a few days. When he gets in I'll tell him you called. What's the name?'

'Please don't bother. I'll try again tomorrow.'

'OK, but you'll have to call early. I think he's planning to spend the day in the next village, Coln St Ippolyts.'

Scarcely had Nat replaced the receiver when the phone buzzed again. 'Bramley here, Dr Gye. There's a Mr Jack Holt here at the lodge asking for you. Shall I send him up?'

'Er, yes, yes, by all means, Mr Bramley.'

The wiry, well-dressed businessman who entered a couple of minutes later showed no trace of the aggression he had displayed on their last meeting. He advanced with a smile and an extended hand as though the incident at the Travellers' Oasis had never happened. 'Sorry to come without an appointment, Dr Gye' (Nat noticed that now he even managed to get the title right) 'but events have taken a few unpleasant twists and turns since last we met and I hoped you wouldn't mind if I came to see you as a matter of some urgency.'

Nat offered a chair, which the visitor accepted, and tea, which he declined.

'I'm sure you know why I'm here,' Holt said.

'I imagine I know what prompted you to come but I don't know what you think I can do.'

Jack Holt seemed to sag and Nat realized that inside the shell of success and affluence and tough commercialism was a very weary man. 'Presumably you despise people like me.'

'Why should you think that?'

'Because I've met lots of clever, arty and scientific types over the years and seen them look down their noses at mere self-made men, who lack the advantages of book learning and can't discuss abstract ideas or appreciate what they call the "finer things of life".'

'Well, I certainly like to think that I'm not an intellectual snob. You have your own specialist knowledge which is well beyond me. I wouldn't know where to start on building a house.'

Holt was not really listening to Nat's response. 'I'm

proud of what I do,' he said, 'and of what I've created. The same goes for my brothers. Harry's not all that bright; that's why he's got mixed up with that mad cow who calls herself Morgana. And Quentin has more testosterone than is good for him. But they've both worked hard to get where they are.'

'I'm sure the Holt empire is a great achievement,' Nat agreed.

'Yes, it is.' Holt nodded emphatically. 'And we've got more sense than to risk it by being mixed up in serious crime.'

Nat stood up to draw the curtains and to switch on a couple more lamps. 'Look, Mr Holt,' he said, 'can we stop circling round the central issue? Your brother-in-law has been arrested on suspicion of murdering a man called Owen in Birmingham.'

'I know. My lawyer called to tell me on my way over here. Stupid shit!' Holt snorted.

'Who, Tom or Owen?' Nat returned to the chair facing Holt's on the other side of the empty hearth.

'Both of 'em! The whole bloody business was crazy – the idea of that crackpot woman.'

'Just how much have you and your brothers been involved in the scheme to implicate Mrs Myles in Tracy's murder?'

'Are you going to go running to your police friends with whatever I tell you?'

Nat shrugged. 'Whatever passes between us here you can deny later and it'll be your word against mine.'

Something of the old truculence came back into Holt's manner. 'You told Harry that Mitchenor only wanted to talk to Tom about Tracy's murder. Now, he's being carted off to Birmingham in connection with Owen's death. Was it you who put the police on to that?'

'Did Tom bludgeon Caradoc Owen and then create a fire in the hope of destroying the evidence?'

'Have the police got any hard evidence against him?'

Nat leaned forward. He said quietly, 'Mr Holt, if we're going to swap question for question this will be a very dull and pointless conversation.'

The other man nodded. 'Tom will have my lawyer beside him in the interview room. He's the best. And if the case comes to court he'll be supported by the finest defence counsel money can buy. I'll do that for him for Tracy's sake. And it's the last thing I'll do for the stupid, ungrateful little toerag.'

'Are you sure this magnanimity is all in your sister's memory? Isn't it really about making sure the Holt family doesn't get involved in criminal proceedings?'

'We aren't involved!' Holt shouted. 'We've done nothing wrong!'

'Most people would say blackmail is a particularly nasty crime.'

'We have *not* been involved in blackmail! Look, Myles swindled us out of what was rightfully ours. And when I say "ours" I don't just mean the Holts. When that bloody man used his influence in high places to get his hands on Coln Manor he stole what belonged to the Johnsons, to the village and to all of us who were trying to preserve the place for the local community. Well, we weren't about to let him get away with it. We couldn't fight him through the courts; he'd proved that to us very convincingly. So we had to use other weapons. We knew Myles had a chequered past and we all agreed that the best thing to do was probe that past till we found something we could use to lever him out of the manor. It would take time but we were absolutely determined.'

'We?'

'Just about everyone who had anything to do with the place – me and my brothers, Tom, Tracy, the staff Myles employed locally to work in the house and grounds, Paul Greer, the historian, the Johnsons –'

'I thought they went off to live in South Africa.'

'Distance didn't make any difference to Amanda. She

had the best reason of all for wanting to be revenged on the Myleses. They had driven her husband to suicide. And the twins felt the same way. That's why they came back here to Oxford University. They were determined to play their part.'

'It sounds like a formidable army. It must have taken some organizing.'

'That gives the wrong impression.' The worried head of the Holt clan was visibly relaxing as he developed his story, externalizing calmly and clearly, perhaps for the first time, thoughts and emotions long locked inside. 'Perhaps I will have that tea after all – unless you've got something stronger.'

Nat went across to a corner cupboard and busied himself with glasses and a bottle of scotch while his guest enlarged on the nature of the anti-Myles campaign.

'You've been down there. You must have sensed the feeling there is against the interlopers at the manor.'

'That's for sure.'

'There's never been an organization – unless you count Morgana's jiggery-pokery sect. No one set up a "Get the Myleses" committee. There was no need for it. We were all like-minded. If someone came up with an idea to make the Myleses feel uncomfortable he could count on complete support. Harry tells me that the vicar once preached a sermon on loving our enemies and cited the Myleses as an example. Next week hardly anyone turned up at church and he never got all his congregation back.'

Nat handed Holt a generous measure of spirit. 'What was your part in this uncoordinated campaign?'

'Thanks. Well, as I said, we gathered material about Myles's past. I had a private investigator on the trail. My idea was to come up with something he wouldn't want revealed to the Bar Council. Then I could give him the option of quietly selling up or facing exposure.'

'But you had no luck until Tracy discovered something

discreditable about Myles? What was it that she found out?'

'I wish to hell I knew! All she told me was that it was dynamite. That it would finish Shelley-Welly, as she called him, for good and all.'

'And you've no hint?' Nat probed. 'Was it, perhaps, something to do with his early life?'

Holt shook his head. 'All Tracy told me was that Mrs Myles had let something slip in an unguarded moment and, as a result, she'd done some thorough research and come up with proof. Anyway, she wasn't going to open up to big brother because Tom had persuaded her to play a different game.'

'Financial blackmail.'

Holt nodded. 'Tom reckoned all his money problems were solved for ever and a day. He'd lost everything over a scheme he'd come up with for the development of the Tripletree estate.'

'Yes, I've heard about that.'

'It was actually a very good proposal. I was amazed that my low IQ brother-in-law had thought of it all by his little self. Of course, it needed a lot of detailed work and considerable capital injection and there was no way he could ever have handled it.'

'So you masterminded it.'

'That's right.'

'And lost a packet when Myles single-handedly blew the plan out of the water.'

'Yes, Harry explained all that. So, you can see, now, why any suggestion that Tom would have murdered his wife is absolutely crazy.'

'And he had also observed Myles, as he thought, going for a secret assignation with Tracy about the time she was killed.'

'Now you know why we were all convinced that Myles murdered Tracy.'

'Yes, and why you couldn't go to the police with your

story. It would be Tom's word against Myles's and any attempt to prove it would have brought the blackmail business into the open. Chances are Tom and perhaps you would have ended up in prison instead of Myles.'

'Yes, the bastard was laughing at us again.'

'So, what did you decide to do about it? Plan an assassination?'

Holt thoughtfully swilled the whisky round in his tumbler. 'Let's just say that an eminent barrister might have had a tragic accident once the interest in Tracy's death had died down. That was the point at which you came blundering on to the scene. You seemed determined to reopen the whole can of worms and suddenly we had police swarming all over Coln again. Can you wonder that we were desperate to find out just what your game was? Well, we still don't know. Dr Gye, what's in it for you? A sordid story for your next TV series?'

'Mr Holt,' Nat spoke earnestly, 'all I was interested in was who was using Caradoc Owen to persecute Mrs Myles and why. If you'd levelled with me then Owen would still be alive and Tom wouldn't be in police custody for a murder which he really did commit.'

Holt looked at him sharply. 'You sound very sure of yourself.'

'But I'm right, aren't I? That's why Harry wanted to talk to me on Monday night. He wanted to make it clear that if Tom went down for Owen's murder, the Holts were in no way involved.'

For several seconds Jack made no reply. Then he said, 'The police will have a hell of a job to make anything stick.'

'I wouldn't bank on it. They'll give Tom a hard time. They may find witnesses that place him at the scene of the crime. They'll almost certainly be able to connect Morgana with the occult bookshop which shared Owen's premises – she's scarcely inconspicuous. And, by the way, she's done a disappearing act.'

'What!'

'Took one of Tom's cars this morning and headed out of Coln without leaving a forwarding address. Scarcely the behaviour of an innocent woman.'

Holt jumped to his feet. 'May I?' He indicated his empty glass.

'Be my guest.'

Holt went across to the cupboard to refill his tumbler. His movements were agitated. Suddenly he let his feelings go. 'Bloody, bloody, bloody, bloody woman!' he shouted.

'You knew about her plan to get at Myles through his wife?'

'Only when Tom came running to me for help after everything had gone pear-shaped. I had nothing to do with it, nor did my brothers, and if I had known about it I'd have warned Tom off in no uncertain terms.'

Nat tried to calm his visitor. 'I can see why Morgana's idea appealed to him, though. It must have seemed like the only way of getting back at the Myleses for Tracy's death and cheating him out of a steady unearned income. He couldn't take his story to the police and he couldn't screw money out of the Myleses without Tracy's evidence. He must have felt impotent, frustrated. At least by backing Morgana's plan he could make the Myleses' lives as miserable as possible. Perhaps he even persuaded himself that he could get Mrs Myles into court for Tracy's murder.' Nat drained his glass. 'So, just for the record, am I right in assuming that Morgana and Tom between them schooled Owen for his role by giving him enough background information about the house and Tracy and the Myleses to create a fake past life experience?'

Holt nodded, staring mournfully into his tumbler.

'Then, when Owen panicked after my visit, he phoned Morgana and she told Tom to go to Birmingham and silence him.'

'The way he tells it, Morgana fixed up the meet and Tom drove her to Owen's place. They quarrelled. Owen said you'd threatened to put him out of business and have him sent back to prison. He demanded money to get away and start up where no one knew him. When they told him they didn't have that sort of cash he warned them that if the police came round he'd tell them everything.' Holt paused. He seemed to be weighing up whether to go on with his story. Then, with an air of weary resignation, he continued. 'Tom swears what happened next was an accident. But . . .' He shrugged. 'Anyway, it was Morgana who, cool as a cucumber, organized the gas explosion. Tom certainly couldn't have thought of it. Apparently there was a very old water heater in the room below. Faulty. Tom says it was a tragedy waiting to happen. It was easy for him to rig it so that it leaked.'

Nat sat back in his chair with a grim smile. 'Morgana, of course. I should have realized that Tom could never have carried it off all by himself.'

'Batty old cow! Who'd have thought . . .'

'I should have, for one. She's almost a classic case of Adler's inferiority complex. The unattractive, overweight woman adopting a lifestyle which enables her to exercise power over the very people who would otherwise humiliate her. She becomes the local wise woman, witch doctor, shaman, priestess – it doesn't matter what you call it; it's the sort of control figure that appears in every kind of enclosed community, primitive or otherwise – and she dominates the village. Whatever they might think about her in private, everyone is a bit frightened of her and no one dares to stand up to her. Until Sheldon Myles appears. He puts a stop to her rituals and drives her off his land. She's furious. It's a personal affront, a challenge to her authority. All she can see is that Myles is threatening to undermine her position. He must be stopped – at any cost.'

'And now she's absconded, leaving Tom to face the music by himself.'

'Oh, I don't imagine she'll get far.'

'And then it'll all come out?'

'I imagine so.'

'None of us are going to end up smelling of roses, are we?'

'I expect your expensive lawyer will be able to keep the Holts clear of any criminal proceedings.'

Holt frowned. 'OK, Dr Gye, I suppose I deserved that after what happened at our last meeting. If you still believe that I'm only interested in preserving the family honour at all costs I can't really blame you. But you don't know how we've carried Tom all these years. That bloody man's been a liability ever since he trapped Tracy into marrying him. Even now that she's gone . . .' He rubbed a hand wearily over his eyes. 'I wish to God I knew who killed her. Are you sure it wasn't Myles? We were absolutely convinced.'

'We were all meant to be convinced. Whoever it was went to a great deal of trouble to create that illusion.'

'And the police have no idea?'

Nat shook his head. Then, he said tentatively, 'Tell me about Roger Johnson's suicide. Was any doubt ever cast on it?'

'You mean whether he staged his disappearance because he couldn't face up to his problems any longer?'

'It happens.'

'Not to someone like Roger, it doesn't. He was as straight as a die. His death made things very much worse for Amanda and the kids. If some of us hadn't helped out . . . But, no, it would have been out of the question for him to fake his suicide in cold blood. He was just at the end of his tether and something snapped, poor sod. And now there's Myles sitting there smugly in Roger's house, laughing at us all. By God, he's got a lot to answer for – Roger, Tracy, Tom, Owen, Morgana! I'll tell you this, Dr Gye, I'd cheerfully put a bullet in the bastard – and hang the consequences!'

There was a long silence before Holt recovered his composure and added calmly, 'You can forget Roger Johnson. Anyway, he had no reason to kill Tracy. He was very fond of her. Everyone was.' Holt pulled out a handkerchief and quickly rubbed it over his eyes. 'Sorry, getting maudlin. Must be the whisky.' He stood up. 'Time I was going. Thank you for seeing me, Dr Gye.' He held out his hand.

As Nat shook it the older man stared him straight in the eye. 'Find out who killed my sister, Dr Gye.'

'The police –'

'Have got no more clue than I have. Give it your best shot. Please! If you need money, just ask.' Holt turned abruptly and strode to the door.

Nat was left standing in the middle of the room. His head buzzed with new questions. Yet something told him that the answers were there, too, if he could only locate them.

The Mists of Time

The dank haze of an autumn morning hung like a gauze curtain through which the south bank of the river could be glimpsed only vaguely by people walking along Tower Wharf. Much closer the twin bastions of Tower Bridge reared up into the prevailing grey. Few people occupied the broad walkway in front of London's ancient fortress and those who did hurried along with coat collars turned up against the all-pervading damp. Except two.

'Melancholy.' Juniper Myles savoured the word. 'It's the only way to describe this place. So many people brutally done to death here or confined or tortured within its slimy walls.' She thrust her hands deeper into the pockets of her camel hair coat and nestled her chin into the fur collar.

Strolling beside her, Kathryn Gye recited pensively,

> 'Hail thou goddess sage and holy,
> Hail divinest Melancholy,
> Whose saintly visage is too bright
> To hit the sense of human sight,
> And therefore to our weaker view
> O'erlaid with black, staid Wisdom's hue.'

'Milton?' June asked.

'Yes, I majored in the seventeenth-century poets at Princeton.'

'Was that where you met Nathaniel?'

'Yes, he came there to lecture when I was in my final year.'

'You're lucky.' June's sigh seemed to well up from the very depth of her being.

'Why so?'

'You knew what you were getting – a solid, straightforward Englishman.'

Kathryn laughed. 'I'm not sure Nat would appreciate that description.'

June remained serious. 'Love is such a confidence trickster, don't you think? He lures us into long-term relationships without letting us read the small print.'

Kathryn surveyed her companion who was gazing out over the shrouded Thames and thought she had seldom seen a woman so miserable. She wondered whether she should proceed with the questions she had come to ask.

When Kathryn had phoned June asking for another interview, the barrister had agreed without demanding to know the purpose of the proposed meeting. And when she had arrived at the Myleses' apartment June had suggested a walk with the enigmatic explanation, 'I have to get out of this place.' They had crossed the bridge, talking in generalities, but Kathryn sensed that her companion was desperate to unburden herself. 'You heard about Caradoc Owen?' she asked after a long silence.

'Yes, I'm sorry. It was my fault.'

Kathryn's response was automatic. 'That's nonsense! You can't blame yourself for the death of a man you hardly knew.'

June shook her head agitatedly. 'No, you don't understand! I shouldn't have . . . Look, let's sit down for a moment.'

They went to a nearby bench and June continued, all the time looking straight before her. 'I knew what Owen was, of course I did, and being recommended by that ridiculous Morgana woman, well, it was hardly the most satisfactory introduction.'

'Then why –'

'Because I was desperate. Things had been building up to a crisis for years but after what happened that night –'

'The night of the party?'

'Yes.'

'How much do you remember about it?'

'Everything.'

'Everything? But I thought –'

'Oh, there was a long time – several weeks – when I simply didn't know what had happened. There was a big gap. Not a complete blank. More a hazy, jumbled dream . . . Oh, it's so difficult to explain . . .That's why I grabbed at the funny little Welshman's offer to help me recover my memory.'

'He only made things worse.'

'Yes, I see that now. Anyway, I didn't need hypnosis. Things gradually came back to me.'

'So, what –'

But Juniper Myles needed no further prompting. Her story poured out in a torrent. 'It was about eleven. I'd just finished a conducted tour of the house when that Pensham woman came up and said she had to talk to me. She'd been drinking and I wasn't pleased at the prospect of listening to her inebriated ramblings. My God, how wrong can you be! I seriously underestimated that young lady. We found a quiet spot and she said she had two things she felt I should know. The first was that she had no sexual interest in my husband. I told her I found that difficult to believe and we had quite a heated exchange on the subject. Then she explained that she had only got close to Shelley to find out about his past and that she had succeeded and that she intended to make him pay for his crimes. She wanted to warn me so that I could distance myself from Shelley.' June closed her eyes. 'You can't imagine what a shock that was. It was the one thing I'd feared for years and years. Shelley was always so sure of himself but I knew that one day the truth would come out. I had black visions of my husband in the dock and me being mobbed by paparazzi outside the court and being shunned by all my friends and. . . . Oh just the utter humiliation of it all.'

'What was it that Tracy had dis–'

But June was telling her story in her way. 'After that I seemed to go into a daze. I couldn't think about anything else but what Tracy had said. I found myself following her, not paying any attention to the guests or the programme, just keeping an eye on the creature in that absurd, revealing, yellow dress. Heaven knows why. I watched her go across the lake and into the arbour. I was just about to cross the bridge when I saw Myles go in after her. I couldn't bring myself to eavesdrop so I waited. Myles came away again almost immediately and I went into the arbour. That was when I saw . . .' She shuddered. 'All I could think was, My God, he's done it again.'

'Again?' Kathryn was aghast. 'Do you mean that Shelley had murdered someone else?'

June stood abruptly and began walking slowly back towards the bridge. Kathryn assumed the confessional was at an end. She was wrong.

'It all happened a long time ago. Shelley had dropped out of college – sent down I suspect, though he denies it. He must have been bone idle as a student. He's always believed he had a right to fame and fortune; that they'd drop into his lap with the minimum of effort on his part. Anyway he wasn't very popular at home, as you can imagine. His parents were quite ordinary people, terribly proud of having a son at Cambridge and terribly cut up when he made a mess of it. So he decided to travel. India was the beckoning golden land for young people in the sixties, a land flowing with drugs and mysticism. Shelley (only that wasn't his real name; he was born Henry Baker) set off with a backpack and precious little else. Somewhere along the trail he teamed up with another young man, the real Sheldon Myles. He was, apparently, a pretty dull companion but he had two things that Henry lacked: a first class brain and a good law degree. They got as far as eastern Turkey and there they ran into an earthquake. It wasn't a major disaster as these things go but several hundred people were killed and the two English boys had a narrow escape. And that gave young Henry his idea. He and Sheldon were helping the locals to clear rubble and recover bodies.' June paused.

Kathryn said, 'Look, if this is too painful you don't need to spell it out, I think I can guess what's coming next. Sheldon was discovered dead in the ruins. Only the body was identified as Henry Baker because Shelley had changed identities with him.'

'That's right, except that there was no question of the other lad having come by death accidentally. Shelley quite deliberately bludgeoned him.'

'And Shelley told you all this?'

'Only after we'd been married a few years. And then without the slightest hint of remorse. He's actually quite proud of his sordid little crime. He says he led Fate by the nose ring and that, anyway, he's a better barrister than the real Sheldon would ever have been. My dear husband is, I'm afraid, utterly amoral.'

'How on earth did he get away with it?'

They had now reached the pedestrian walkway of the bridge and a thickening mist was swirling around them. June allowed herself a cynical little laugh. 'Luck of the devil. The body was buried locally and amidst all the confusion no one knew exactly where it was. The two young men were of similar build and appearance and, armed with various "proofs", it wasn't difficult for Shelley to get a new passport to replace the one supposedly lost in the devastation.'

Kathryn watched a river bus as it passed beneath them and headed upstream. She tried to get her head around the enormity of Shelley's crime. 'So he not only calmly butchered a man who had done him no harm whatsoever, he also allowed his own parents and family to go through years of grief believing that he was dead just so that he could cheat his way into the legal profession.'

'Cheat is Shelley's middle name. He's cheated on me most of our married life. He's cheated and blustered his way through scores of trials. He cheated the former owners out of Coln Manor. When Sheldon Myles wants something that's sufficient justification for him to get it, using whatever means are available.'

Kathryn wanted to ask, 'How on earth could you go on living with such a monster?' but she already sensed the answer. Juniper Myles was terrified of her husband. He had made her a party to his guilty secret. That should have given her a hold over him but, in fact, the reverse was true. As soon as June realized the extent of Shelley's ruthlessness she understood well what might happen to her if she ever told what she knew or hinted at divorce or failed to play her part in the charade of a wealthy, successful, high profile couple. What Kathryn did ask was, 'Why are you telling me this now?'

'Because we must prevent another death.' June spoke the words in a flat, matter-of-fact voice.

Kathryn stopped in her tracks. 'What in heaven's name do you mean?'

June turned to face her. 'Yesterday we had a visit from a Metropolitan Police officer. He was asking Shelley what he could remember about the disappearance of a man called Baker in 1963. Shelley was shaken but he handled it very well. Then, this morning, I overheard him take a phone call from someone who asked him to come to a meeting to discuss Tracy Pensham's death. Shelley agreed to be at Coln Manor at two o'clock. So, you see, it's all unravelling – at long last.'

'But Shelley had nothing to do with Tracy's death. He has an alibi . . .'

June laughed. 'Toby Meadows, our revered chief constable? Let me tell you two things about him. Number one:

he and Shelley are bosom pals. Number two: on the night of the party he was well awash with our champagne. I doubt if he knew what day it was, let alone what time. Of course, he would never admit that. If Shelley says that they had a little chat about security around midnight, then Toby will go along with it.'

'And this person who called – was it a man or a woman?'

'I don't know. Shelley had the speaker on at first but he switched it off after the first few words.'

'And did they say they had evidence to link Shelley to the murder?'

'They said something like, "I know what Tracy knew, so we need to talk". Shelley slammed the phone down, muttered something about "settling someone's hash once and for all". Then he set off for Coln straight away and he took with him an automatic pistol – a souvenir of one of his cases that he picked up some years ago.'

Kathryn stared in horrified disbelief. 'But surely he wouldn't . . . He couldn't think he could get away with . . .'

Again the brittle laugh. 'My dear, the man's a complete egomaniac. He believes he can walk on water. What's one murder, more or less? You may be sure that, even as we speak, he's working out a scheme to silence this would-be informant, walk away scot-free and laugh up his sleeve at the rest of us mere plodding mortals who don't realize just how clever he is.'

'You've told the police all this, I presume.'

'No, I was still wondering what I should do when you arrived. Then, I realized I could unburden myself much more easily to you than to some unimaginative policeman. So, now that you have the whole picture, what . . .'

But Kathryn had already yanked her mobile out of her handbag and was punching in Nat's direct line number at Beaufort.

'Hello.'

'Darling, listen. I'm with June Myles.'

'With June . . . What –'

'Just listen. Shelley is on his way to Coln. *With a gun!*'

'With a what? What are you talking –'

'Someone phoned him to fix a meeting. They know about Tracy's murder. They know Shelley did it.'

'But he didn't. He couldn't have.'

'Oh, *do* stop interrupting. Shelley *did* do it. His alibi is worthless. Someone knows about it and is threatening him and Shelley is determined to silence whoever it is. It seems he's a dab hand at murder. Look I can't explain everything over the phone. You must contact Mitchenor and get him out there to stop another violent death.'

'OK, OK, calm down. Before I go shouting for the seventh cavalry let's just think for a moment. Are you sure June isn't being hysterical or maybe even manipulating? You know how unstable she is.'

'I'd say she's the very opposite of hysterical. Icy calm isn't in it. And I believe her version of events. She's told me the whole story and it all hangs together. Now Shelley's off to Tripletree for a showdown with . . . whoever. It's fixed for two o'clock. Right now, it's,' she checked her watch, 'twenty five after eleven. That should be plenty of time for Mitchenor to get there first with enough armed men to stop Shelley adding to his total of unlawful killings.'

Nat took a deep breath. 'Right. I'll call him now and get back to you later for a clearer explanation. Bye.'

'Bye, darling.' Then she added, 'One more thing.'

'Yes?'

'Don't do anything foolish.'

Nat opened his mouth to reply but the line went dead.

Nat turned from the phone and was aware of three pairs of eyes staring at him in amazement. 'Sorry about this,' he said to his students. 'I've just got to make another quick call. Talk among yourselves about Joanna's critique of

Braud's bio-PK theory. She's raised a couple of important points,' he added as a distraction.

He found Mitchenor's card and called his office number. The phone was answered by an underling who explained that the DCI was out at an area conference and not expected back before lunch. Nat said he would try the inspector's mobile. He did so and listened to a recorded message. He left an urgent appeal for Mitchenor to call him then went back to the Oxford office and asked the same wearily respectful policeman if he could speak to someone in CID of equivalent rank.

The voice was apologetic. 'I'm afraid all the senior officers are at the conference, sir. It's a strategy meeting called by the chief constable.'

'There must be someone responsible there. Or do criminals take a morning off whenever there's a top level police pow-wow?' Nat was getting impatient – and worried.

'The chief superintendent is here, sir, but I can't trouble –'

'Put me through to him!' Nat demanded.

'I'm afraid he's tied up at the moment, sir. Now, if you'd like to tell me what it is –'

'What it is,' Nat exploded, 'is a matter of life and death!' He realized immediately that the cliché was a mistake. The silence at the other end of the line indicated that the officer assumed he was dealing with yet another hoax caller.

Eventually the voice said, 'Right, sir, now you give me your name and number and someone will get back to you.'

Nat restrained the expletive that sprang to mind, announced his name and mobile number and rang off.

The room behind him was silent, the students much more interested in their supervisor's emergency than in the possibility of body changes achieved by the application of mental energy.

'I'm sorry,' Nat announced, 'we'll have to take it on from here next week. Something's cropped up.'

Five minutes later he was making his way towards the fellows' car park when his mobile rang. He held it to his ear as he strode across the small area of tarmac.

Kathryn's worried voice came on the line. 'Darling, did you get hold of Mitchenor?'

'No, he's out of the office and not answering his mobile. I'm afraid I ran into a bureaucratic stone wall.'

'So what's happening?'

'I'm setting off for Coln now. Could you try to raise Mitchenor and put him in the picture?'

'Nat, you can't walk into Tripletree by yourself. Shelley is absolutely ruthless. He's already killed twice and he won't hesitate to do it again.'

'Don't worry, darling. I'm not a hero. What's all this about Shelley being a double murderer?'

'He killed the real Sheldon Myles years ago and he killed Tracy when she found out about it.'

'Did June say he killed Tracy?'

Kathryn hesitated. 'Well, good as. She said the chief constable isn't reliable as an alibi.'

'And she has no idea who Shelley is going to meet?'

'No, but it's obviously someone Tracy shared her information with.'

Nat reached the Mercedes and unlocked it by remote control. 'Possibly,' he said.

'Possibly? What does that mean?'

'Just thinking.'

'It worries me when you think. Look, promise me you won't go blundering in on a murderer.'

'Don't worry, darling. If you get hold of Mitchenor, he'll be there long before me.'

'Then why –'

'Can't stop now, Kate. Let me know when you've alerted the police.' He clicked the machine off and slipped into the driving seat.

Nat drove through alternating sunshine and showers, thinking hard. Mitchenor had said the simplest answers were usually the right ones. But he had identified a jealous husband as Tracy's killer and he had been wrong. Yet that was only because Myles had an apparently impeccable alibi. There was no way the inspector could question the word of his chief. But without that support? Why, then nothing stood in the way of the simplest of all solutions. Forget mysterious malefactors masquerading as the host of the party. Tom claimed to have seen Myles go into the arbour to meet Tracy and that was exactly what he had seen. What could be more straightforward? Myles had motive and means and there was a witness to put him at the scene of the crime.

So, Nat asked himself, as he peered through the windscreen wipers' arc, why don't I buy it? Is it just because nothing in god-forsaken Coln St Ippolyts is what it seems; because the whole community clings so tenaciously to its secrets and ring-fences them with subterfuge? Someone, it now seemed, had been in league with Tracy all along, or, at least had been the recipient of her confidences.

Who was now threatening Myles? Who was in possession of the same incriminating evidence against him that Tracy had found? Not Tom. He was languishing in a Birmingham police cell. Who else could she possibly have told? Was it really credible that her own brothers were not in on the Penshams' blackmail bid? Who else could have been her confidant? Morgana? She had certainly had enough influence over the Penshams and she could well be in urgent need of funds to effect her escape from justice. One of the Johnson clan? What more natural than that Tracy should have shared her knowledge with those old friends who had been most shabbily treated by Myles? Had there, perhaps, been some other grouping at work – Penshams, Johnsons and Greer – whose activities Nat had only obscurely glimpsed? Or did Tracy have some other, completely unknown collaborator?

There was so much deliberate obfuscation. Fake hauntings. A bronze thrown into the lake. Everyone insisting

246

that the Johnsons were in distant South Africa when at least two of them were frequent visitors to the neighbourhood. And what of Roger Johnson's suicide – was that the biggest deceit of all? Nat found himself again concurring with Morgana's analysis: there was a great, hydra-headed evil presiding at Tripletree. But there was nothing supernatural about it. It was the creation of a whole population projecting their hatred on to the owners of the house. Almost he felt sorry for Sheldon Myles, speeding now towards Coln St Ippolyts and a showdown with the agent of the community's vengeance.

But who was it? Nat had the deep conviction that he knew the answer. From all the fragments of truth, half-truth and lies he had picked up over the last couple of months he ought to be able to work out the identity of Sheldon Myles's nemesis – and the facts about Tracy's death – if only he could get a clear view through the mists of rumour, corporate emotion and rural myth. For the rest of the journey Nat forced his brain to recall, sift and evaluate.

By the time he had reached Burford and begun to negotiate the minor roads which wriggled their way into the Cotswolds he knew who if not what was awaiting him at Tripletree.

By keeping his foot hard down on the accelerator Nat reached the gates of Coln Manor at twelve minutes to two. Since the last thing he wanted to do was blazon his arrival, he drove on until he reached the lay-by he had used on the night of the ritual. Walking back along the boundary wall, he found a place where a rhododendron had taken root close by the stonework. Its twisted stems served as a crude climbing frame and he clambered and slithered over damp foliage and lichen-spread limestone. He dropped into long, wet grass and glanced ruefully down at his scuffed and stained suit. Nat suddenly remembered why he was more formally dressed than usual, and grinned. He was supposed to be lunching at the master's lodge. What would his colleagues – jealous guardians of academic respectability – say if they could see him now?

Nat picked his way carefully through a narrow fringe of trees until he had a clear view of the house. It stood, permanent and self-assured in its hollow, its symmetry reflected in the lake, the slope of Tripletree Hill rising beside it. Did it, as Kathryn insisted, have a malevolent aura? Seeing it crouch there, grey amidst the autumn drizzle, one could easily imagine that it was watching warily for intruders. Nat edged along the fringe of copse until he could see the front of the manor. There was Myles's blue convertible alongside the steps but of a police presence or any other visitor there was no sign. Nat used his mobile to call Mitchenor's office. The officer who answered said that the inspector had come in but had hurried out again. No, he did not know where the inspector had gone. And, no, having only just come on duty, he did not know whether the inspector had picked up Dr Gye's earlier message. Next, Nat tried Mitchenor's mobile, only to be greeted once more by the bland, metallic recorded message. Nat cursed machines that posed as miraculous aids to communication while, in effect, setting up new barriers between people.

Having come all this way with no plan of action in his head, what was he to do? 'Don't go blundering in on a murderer,' Kathryn had implored but now, if his calculations were right . . . well, it was good that she did not know. But what else could he do? Skulk here in the undergrowth getting wetter by the minute? Return to the car, drive to the nearest town and try to galvanize the police into urgent action? By then whatever tragedy was destined to take place would already have happened.

Any further debate was cut short by the rain, which now redoubled its efforts. Nat turned up his jacket collar and, under cover of the trees, ran around the house to a point where shrubs and hedges enabled him to get close to the building. For a full minute he stared up at the rows of windows. Satisfied at last that there was no movement behind the diamond panes, he crossed quickly to the foot of the wall. The ground floor here consisted largely of domestic offices and all doors and windows were securely locked. Then, Nat discovered a broad flight of steps leading down to a basement. They were of much later construction than the house and were, he guessed, installed to facilitate the delivery of fuel for the boilers when central heating was first introduced. Gingerly he descended the treacherously smooth and wet stone treads. The solid door at the bottom did not yield to pressure but the window beside it had a missing pane and Nat was able to reach in and release the catch.

His theory had been correct. The gloomy cellar he now entered was dominated by a huge cast iron boiler that looked as though it could well have seen service on the *Queen Mary* and certainly dated from the same era as the mighty Cunard liner. There was an almost choking aroma of fuel oil, presumably associated with a more modern heating system located nearby. An interior door gave on to a large cellar and, as Nat's eyes became accustomed to the murk, he noticed that one end was filled with well-stocked wine racks.

Only after several moments of cautious fumbling did he locate a wooden staircase leading to the ground floor. He made his way up this, still conscious of the pungent fumes, and gently tried the door at the top. It opened inward on well-oiled hinges and Nat peered cautiously out into what seemed to be an old, unused pantry. He crossed the flagstones and, passing through yet another door, found himself walking on polished boards. Still there was no sign of life and Nat withdrew into a corner of what he realized was a panelled inner hall to calm his thudding heartbeat. He tried to remember the layout of Coln Manor's ground floor in order to get his bearings. At the far end of the corridor there were two doors. The one straight ahead should lead, he deduced, to the screens passage and the Great Hall. If he was correct, then the other door, to the right, must give access to the west staircase and the Myleses' living quarters.

It was to this door that Nat moved as soon as he had collected himself. It was ajar. He sidled through and stared up the square well, his ears straining to detect any sound. And at last there was something to hear. As he climbed to the first floor, the house's oppressive silence yielded to the distant murmur of voices. Nat crept to the landing and across to the library door. He stood close to it, listening.

The occupants were exchanging angry words but Nat could only distinguish isolated phrases.

'. . . choice is yours . . . or jail and disgrace . . .'

'. . . threatened by a mere nobody . . . You're not leaving here . . .'

'. . . you wouldn't dare shoot me . . .'

'That's where you're mistaken.' The other voice, recognizable now as Myles's, was louder, closer to the door. 'Since you love this place so much you can die here. Goodbye, you interfering, insignificant . . .'

Nat waited to hear no more. He turned the handle and half ran, half fell into the room. He collided with the figure standing just inside and sent him sprawling. At the same moment there was an explosion and a cry.

Blazing Hatred

Nat was the first to recover. He sprang to his feet, saw Myles reach out an arm for the gun which had fallen beneath the library table, and clamped a foot firmly on the barrister's wrist. While Shelley yelped with pain, Nat reached down and grabbed the weapon. He returned to the door, closed it and rested his back against it, breathing heavily. Only then was he able to take in the scene before him.

Myles was staggering to his feet in the centre of the room and glaring at him with mingled rage and disbelief. Beyond him, close to the rain-splashed window Paul Greer was holding a hand to his left shoulder and staring with incredulity at a red stain which was seeping through a jagged hole in the cloth of his jacket.

Nat, who had never in his life wielded a firearm, waved the pistol in a gesture unconsciously copied from heroes and villains of the big and little screens. It was remarkably gratifying to see how the two men before him backed away a pace or two. Nat made the most of his advantage.

'Sit down, both of you,' he ordered.

Myles glared back but, eyes fixed on the gun barrel, sank on to an upright chair.

Greer made no move. 'I've been shot!' he whimpered. 'I'm bleeding!'

'Stop whining!' Nat snapped, surprised at his own tone of command. 'Take your jacket off and let's have a look at the problem.'

While the historian was, gingerly and awkwardly, slipping the coat off his damaged shoulder, Nat improvised. 'The police will be here in a few minutes. We're going to sit here quietly and pass the time getting to the hideous bottom of all that's been going on here these last few months.'

'You needn't think I've got anything to say to you, you bloody little turncoat. I thought you were on my side,' Myles spluttered.

Greer said, 'That bastard shot me. The bullet went right through here.' He tore the top of his shirt sleeve to reveal the wound.

'Can you move your arm?' Nat demanded.

Wincing, Greer raised the damaged limb.

'Is the blood spurting out or just dribbling?'

'It's sort of oozing. I don't think the artery's been severed – no thanks to him!'

'Then you'll live. Grab one of those cushions and press it to the wound. That's all we can do for now. And sit down!'

Shaking, Greer eased himself into a chair.

'That's better,' Nat said, trying to regulate his breathing. 'Now we can all pretend to be calm, civilized human beings.' He was struck by a sudden thought. 'Is there anyone else in the house?'

'He's sent the Brunnages away,' Greer explained, glaring at his would-be assassin.

Nat smiled with relief. 'Just the three of us then. We can have a cosy chat while we wait.' He moved to the centre of the room and perched against one of the massive library tables.

'I've got nothing to say!' Myles was truculent but wary.

'What a refreshing change,' Nat observed. 'The eloquent Sheldon Myles QC, alias Henry Baker, is not usually at a loss for words. In that case you can sit and listen to me. I have plenty to say.'

'Interfering bastard,' Myles snarled. 'Who told you to go poking your nose in –'

'Why you did, Shelley, or had you conveniently forgotten your offer to pay me whatever fee I asked to discover the truth about Tracy Pensham's death?'

'I hired you to straighten out my wife's jumbled thinking after that charlatan Owen got at her.'

'Ah yes, the late Dr Caradoc Owen, just one of the ghosts from your past come back to haunt you. This whole sorry business has been about revenants, but not Civil War spirits or Morgana's vague evil forces. The manifestations at Tripletree were flesh and blood characters from the colourful personal history of Sheldon Myles QC.'

'I don't know what you're talking about,' the barrister blustered.

'No, you don't, do you? I see that now, but for a long time I didn't. I couldn't conceive that you were so self-absorbed as to be wholly indifferent to the feelings of other people. It simply never occurred to you, did it, that those who were trampled underfoot by the relentless march of your ambition might resent it; might harbour thoughts of revenge and so be a real threat.'

Myles shrugged. 'All criminal judges and barristers make enemies. It goes with the territory.'

'But most of them sleep easily in their beds because their consciences are clear. They haven't knowingly sent men and women to prison for crimes they never committed or blackened reputations just so that the Iago of the Old Bailey could continue his meteoric career. I don't suppose Sheldon Myles's slumbers are disturbed by bad dreams either but that's because he really doesn't give a damn. For a long time I failed to grasp that fact. That's why I was convinced that you murdered George Williams.'

'Who?'

'Exactly! You really don't know that Caradoc Owen was the alter ego of George Williams, a stage hypnotist you got put away to salve your own injured pride. But I couldn't

253

accept that you were ignorant of the fact. So, when Owen grabbed the opportunity to get back at you via your wife, I assumed that you had discovered his real identity, that you were using me to locate him and that you then went to Birmingham to get even with him. How wrong I was! The wretched little man was completely beneath your notice.'

Myles shifted on his chair. 'All I wanted was to stop Owen – or Williams or whatever his name was – from pestering June.'

Nat nodded. 'Oh, I believe that now, but, because your reputation goes before you, I started out by crediting you with every kind of Machiavellian scheme. So did all the folk round here. You were the evil lord of the manor, a reincarnation of the Bad Lord Bygot. Naturally, everyone was convinced that you had murdered Tracy Pensham and frustrated because they couldn't prove it.'

Myles snorted. 'Don't be ridiculous! Why should I want to kill the brazen little slut?'

'Oh, I can think of a couple of motives – a lovers' tiff, or, perhaps, putting a stop to blackmail. It seemed logical at the time that you engaged me to stop your wife confessing to Tracy's murder because, as the real killer, the last thing you wanted was to have the police re-open the case. But, anyway, that's all academic: you had a first class alibi. Yet even today, when someone cast doubt on that alibi, I was ready to revisit old suspicions.'

Greer intervened. 'Dr Gye, I must go and get this wound dressed.' He struggled awkwardly out of his chair. 'I'm really beginning to feel a little faint.'

Nat waved the pistol at him. 'Please stay where you are. The police will take care of you as soon as they get here.'

Greer stared back defiantly. 'Dr Gye, I'm grateful to you for stopping this man shooting me down in cold blood but you can't keep me here against my will.'

Nat held up the gun. 'This little implement says that

I can do exactly that. The police will most certainly want to speak with you.'

'Oh, for pity's sake,' Myles intervened, 'let the little twerp go.'

Nat frowned. 'What a remarkable change of heart! A few minutes ago you were set on ending Dr Greer's life and now you are concerned to let him have a flesh wound dressed without further delay. Could this have anything to do with not wanting the police to discover what he knows about your sordid past?'

Both now looked at him sharply.

'Yes, Shelley, or let's be accurate and call you Henry, I'm afraid the cat's out of the bag. We know all about what happened some thirty-five years ago and no doubt soon the whole world will know.' Nat watched the reaction of his audience, hoping that he would not have to substantiate his claims, since, as yet, he had no details about the ancient murder. He need not have worried; both men seemed to deflate. Myles's head drooped and Greer crumpled back into his chair.

Nat made the most of the emotional advantage. 'Do you know what the most tragic aspect of this whole sordid business is? Poor Tracy need not have died. The secrets she was guarding and hoped to profit from will be banner headlines in the tabloid press a few days from now. If her ghost still hovers round this place I only hope that seeing you sent to prison will give it some peace.'

Myles looked up, attempting a smile. 'Surely, Nat, it need not come to that.'

Nat eased away from the table and began to pace the room, covering his own anxiety. How long could he keep up this bluff? Where the hell was Mitchenor? Had he received the messages with which both he and Kathryn had been bombarding him? He said, 'Ah, Henry, you're trying to buy me off, are you? What's become of the scourge of the criminal classes; the staunch upholder of justice? The pose of the outraged public conscience is one that can be dropped when the prosecutor himself is involved, eh?'

The barrister straightened up, the supreme actor putting on a mask of confidence. 'This alleged crime which I'm alleged to have committed took place a long time ago in a foreign country. Nothing could ever be proved now.'

'Oh yes it could!' Greer blurted out, then snapped his mouth shut as Myles glared at him.

'You'd be advised to hold your tongue!' Myles shouted.

Nat looked at his two captives with growing contempt. Myles (he still could not think of the QC as 'Baker') sat stiffly in his immaculate suit, determined to brazen it out until the last moment. He would play his role, as so often in the past, right up to the final curtain or to the moment when the jury were sent out to consider their verdict. Greer lolled in his dingy cord trousers and bloodstained shirt hugging a satin cushion to the wound and clearly on the verge of going completely to pieces. 'Oh, the time for silence is well past,' he said. 'No evasion, or lies or deliberate smokescreens can save either of you now. You're both going to face murder charges.'

There was a stunned silence.

Greer opened and closed his mouth wordlessly.

Myles looked puzzled. 'But . . . I don't understand,' he stuttered.

'No, neither did I, not for a long time. Not until I realized that it was Dr Greer and only Dr Greer who had thrown me off the scent over and over again. Have you ever played Murder in the Dark? It used to be a favourite Christmas game of ours when I was young. Everyone takes a playing card, looks at it and returns it. The person who draws an ace is the murderer and the one with the king is the detective. The lights go out, the crime is committed, after a count of twenty the lights go on again and the detective begins questioning everyone.'

Myles groaned. 'I hope your police friends arrive soon.

256

I'd rather be sitting in a cell than listening to your child-hood reminiscences.'

'The point of the story is this,' Nat continued. 'Everyone has to answer the detective's questions truthfully, except the murderer. He's allowed to lie through his teeth. What I realized – rather belatedly – is that all the people I've talked to about the events in and around this house have told me the truth, or what they believed to be the truth, except our scholarly friend here. Who was it tried to convince me that there was no question of supernatural activity – and therefore nothing to interest me – at Tripletree, when there have been scores of supposed sightings, including some by his friends the Johnsons? Dr Greer. Who was it who tried to impress upon me that the Johnsons were all thousands of miles away in Cape Town, when at least two of them were frequent guests at his house? Dr Greer. Who was it who threw a bronze statuette in the lake, hoping that it would connect you, Henry, with Tracy's death? It had to be Dr Greer, because he was the only other person with unquestioned access to the house. And who was it who was careful to tell me how fond he was of Tracy Pensham, when, in reality, he dislikes all women and had, in fact, murdered Tracy?'

Myles gasped. 'Is this true, Greer? Did you . . .

'Oh yes,' Nat said, 'and it was all planned with the care and precision you would expect of a scholar. He set up a secret rendezvous with Tracy by the lake and he arranged for it to take place at midnight, when everyone would be watching the fireworks. However, being a belt and braces man, he was careful to put on a Charles I cloak and hat, so that, if anyone did see him go to the meet, he would think it was you.'

'You little bastard!' Myles exploded.

Nat turned to him. 'You can save the righteous indignation, Henry. You were the cause of it all. Greer wielded the blunt instrument – what was it, doctor; a champagne bottle? – but it was the hatred you had inspired which

257

drove him to it. You've made many enemies in this little corner of Oxfordshire but none more dangerous than our quiet, unassuming historian.' He turned to Greer. 'Is there any word strong enough to describe your loathing and contempt for the master of Tripletree?'

'I doubt it,' Greer muttered. 'He's a vulgar little man and a double murderer –'

'How dare you!' Myles jumped to his feet and would have crossed the room if Nat had not interposed. With a scowl, he retreated to the fireplace and leaned against it.

'Double murderer, I say.' Greer was unabashed. 'You drove poor Roger to his death by swindling him out of his home and fortune. Just so that you could lord it here. Well, for all your money and your fame, you can't hold a candle to Roger Johnson. Or to any of the others who have been lords of Coln. You're no gentleman!'

Nat smiled grimly. 'I get the feeling that that's what sticks in your throat most of all. Sheldon Myles – or Henry Baker – is not worthy of Tripletree.'

Greer glowered. 'Well, it's true. This place is a part of our heritage. What it is and what it stands for should be preserved. Far too many of our old estates have been broken up and the great mansions torn down.'

'But the Myleses have saved the house,' Nat suggested.

The historian sneered. 'I wouldn't expect a philistine like you to understand. You scientists are all the same; you can only grasp cold facts and test tube proofs. What you're dealing with here is a community, its social fabric, its roots in the past, its continuity for the future. That was what this . . . this uncouth barbarian was poisoning.'

'So he had to be got rid of, forced out at all costs. First of all you brought pressure on his wife. You and the Johnson twins literally tried to frighten her off. Was that their idea, I wonder? The campaign of fake hauntings has the air of a student prank and could be easily carried out by energetic youngsters with an intimate knowledge of the house and grounds and armed with tape recorders and hidden microphones – especially if they could count on the support of old friends working on the estate.' Nat looked at Greer for collaboration but he stared blankly, defiantly back.

Nat continued. 'When that plan failed you had to resort to something more elaborate. By that time, as you must have known, Tracy was worming her way into the Myleses' confidence in the hope of learning something discreditable that could be used against them.'

'Slut!' Myles muttered.

'It would make sense for you to work together, wouldn't it?'

'If it amuses you to think so,' Greer mumbled sullenly.

'I must admit the possibility didn't occur to me till yesterday. I was talking with Tracy's brother Jack and he referred to her doing some research on Mr Myles's past. It struck me then that word "research" was an odd one to use in connection with Tracy. Hardly the studious type, by all accounts. But, of course, for you burrowing around in archives is life and breath. What were you beavering away at on some of those trips to London? What was it that set you searching diligently in press archives, census returns, records of births and deaths?'

Greer remained silent.

'Still nothing to say?' Nat asked. 'Then you'll have to listen to a bit of my inspired guesswork. I think Tracy was around on several occasions when Mr and Mrs Myles quarrelled. Insults were shouted, accusations made, threats uttered and from them the eavesdropper picked up more than a hint that the great Sheldon Myles QC was not all that he seemed. Did she even overhear some reference to the murder of a fellow student years ago?'

From the slightest flicker on Greer's face Nat guessed he was on the right track. He continued. 'But Tracy could never get at the truth by herself. That required an expert. So she confided in you. And I must take my hat off to you, doctor. You were brilliant.'

Greer smirked. 'Yes, I didn't have much to go on. The best piece of oral evidence was an outburst of Mrs Myles, poor woman. Tracy heard her say "I wish *you'd* died in that earthquake as well as your victim."'

'And from that you began to dismantle the elaborate false identity Henry Baker had built up over three decades. Quite magnificent, the work of a truly dedicated scholar. So, what went wrong? Why did you and Tracy part company?'

Greer sneered at him. 'You tell me. This is your story.'

Nat sauntered across to one of the windows. He glanced momentarily across the sodden parkland and the half-naked trees dripping their moisture. There was no view of the drive from this point but he had vaguely hoped to see some evidence of a police presence. He turned back into the room. 'My guess is that you fell out over money. The Penshams had an old-fashioned, simplistic view about blackmail. The information against Myles could provide an unending stream. Their financial worries were over for all time. That wasn't your idea at all. Your price for silence was the Myleses' departure from Coln. What was supposed to happen to the manor then? Acquired by a consortium? A trust? Secured for the next generation of Johnsons?'

He saw Greer's eyelids flicker. 'That's it, isn't it? The house, now completely restored at vast expense, would be repossessed by the family who'd been cheated out of it in the first place.'

'It's called justice,' Greer mumbled.

Nat threw back his head and laughed. 'I don't know about justice but there's certainly a rough logic about it.'

The next moment Greer uttered a sharp cry. 'Look out!'

Nat turned in time to see Myles rush to the door. He ran after him but only reached the entrance as the heavy timber crashed into place. He heard the key turn in the lock. Automatically, he grabbed the handle. It turned but the door did not budge.

Greer was on his feet, shouting. 'You fool! Now we're done for!'

Nat shrugged. 'It's OK, he won't get far. The police will track him down.'

'You don't understand! He's going to burn the house down!'

'What?'

'That was his plan all along. He told me just before you arrived. He said he was damned if he was going down but if he did he'd take me and what he called "this accursed place" with him. He's quite mad. He was going to shoot me, then set fire to the house to destroy the evidence. Crazy!'

Suddenly Nat remembered the strong smell of fuel oil in the basement. If Myles had soaked that area one match would be enough to have it a blazing inferno within minutes.

'What are we going to do?' Greer was stumbling about the room in a panic. 'The house! We must save the house!'

'Sod the house,' Nat responded. 'How can we get out of here?' He ran to the window overlooking the park. He opened it and looked down. Some twenty feet below were the steps he had descended to get into the cellar. Jumping down there could be fatal.

He crossed to the opposite window.

'That overlooks the courtyard,' Greer wailed. 'There's no way down there!'

Nat leaned across the sill and verified the statement. There was a sheer drop to the cobbles below. There was no ledge under the window and no convenient drainpipe within reach. He caught the first whiff of smoke. 'It's this way or nothing,' he said. 'Is there anything we can use as a rope?'

A quick search of the library revealed that the only

material which might serve was the heavy velvet of the curtains. He pulled a side table across, stood on it and reached up to fumble with the fastenings. 'Give me a hand!' he yelled. 'We haven't much time!'

'I can't!' Greer cried, nursing his damaged shoulder.

'Then do something useful. Phone for the fire brigade. And when you've done that find something to wedge along the bottom of the door. There's smoke coming in already!'

Nat wrestled furiously with the heavy drapes. It seemed to take forever to wrench them from their rails. Once they were down they proved heavy and unwieldy. By the time he had knotted two together and heaved them on to the sill the courtyard was thick with smoke. He leaned over to peer down the wall. Gouts of flame leaped out from the window immediately below.

'Quick,' he yelled, 'help me fix this!'

There was no response and, looking round, Nat saw Greer's prone figure close to the door. 'Oh, God, don't faint on me now,' he muttered.

He ran across to the sprawled man and shook him. Apart from a moan there was no response. He dragged Greer to the centre of the room, clear of the fumes seeping in around the door. Then he ran back to the window.

He could push the makeshift rope out but how was he to fasten it at the top? Glancing desperately round the room, his eye fell on a pair of crossed cavalry sabres on the wall beside the chimney. He wrenched them free. He folded one end of the curtain round the centre strut between the two window openings. He skewered the two sections together with both swords. Looking out again he saw that the flames below were stronger. Out of the question to lower the curtain until they were ready to use it.

Now he ran back to the recumbent Greer and tried feverishly to revive him.

'Come *on*! Come *on*! Wake up!' he yelled, slapping the man's face and shaking him.

Greer's eyes opened but failed to focus. 'Must save the house,' he muttered.

Nat dragged him to his knees, then, half carrying him, drew him to the window. Greer slumped across the sill. 'Wake *up*!' he yelled. 'You've got to do things for yourself!'

He wanted to let the injured man go first but that was clearly out of the question. Half comatose and with only one good arm, he would never be able to grip the curtain.

'Listen!' he shouted in Greer's ear above the crashing of glass and the roaring of the fire that was now almost deafening. 'Can you hear me?'

Greer nodded.

'I'll go first and hold the curtain for you. Then you've got to get on to it and slide down. It'll be like the escape chute on an aeroplane. Do you understand?'

Again the half-somnolent nod.

A spear of flame appeared above the level of the sill. There wasn't a second to lose. Nat threw the curtain out, clambered through the window frame and grabbed the slippery velvet. He could smell singeing cloth as he half climbed, half slid down to the cobbles below.

He fell awkwardly but jumped up quickly as a gust of heat from the lower storey hit him with almost physical force. The curtain was already smouldering as he grabbed the bottom and pulled it towards him.

'Now, Greer! Now!' he shouted.

Staring up through the swirling smoke and flame, he saw Greer's face at the window. The man waved his good arm and seemed to call something. But the sound was lost in the roar of the fire. Then the face above disappeared.

Several times Nat called Greer's name but there was no further sign of him. By now the curtain was in flames. Driven back by the heat, he retreated across the courtyard.

Then he heard the sound of an approaching siren.

263

Tripletree Vengeance

'Doesn't look as though there'll be much left.' DCI Mitchenor strolled back to his car, parked on the grass verge half-way along the drive, and spoke to Nathaniel Gye who was sitting in the passenger seat, and wrapped in a blanket, with the door open. 'The fire chief says he thinks they can save the eastern half of the building but it's touch and go. Bloody shame! Places like this are part of our heritage.'

Ahead of them was all the lurid apparent confusion of a fire-fighting scene. The damp sky seemed filled with black smoke, pierced intermittently by shafts of flame. Before the ruin that had been Coln Manor stood three scarlet fire appliances while helmeted men moved ant-like around the blaze directing water from snaking hoses.

'That's what he said – Greer, I mean. Those were his last words, "We must save the house."' Though Nat was huddled in his blanket, he was aware that he was shivering with delayed shock.

'You OK now?' The inspector frowned his concern. 'I can get an officer to take your statement if you're up to it but if you prefer you can write it at the station.'

'Give me a minute or two. Any sign of Myles?'

'No. Well, we haven't actually started looking yet. First things first. My men have towed his smart BMW away to a safe distance. He's not going to get far on foot.'

Suddenly there were confused noises from behind them – a blaring car horn and angry shouting.

Mitchenor stared back along the drive to where two uniformed policemen were trying to stop a small car advancing along the gravel. 'Damned reporters!' he muttered. 'Load of ghouls. As soon as there's a tragedy there they are. The place will be swarming with TV vans within the hour.'

Nat leaned out to follow his gaze. He recognized instantly the vehicle determined to break through the police barrier. 'It's not the press, Dave. It's Kathryn, my wife.'

'Oh well, in that case . . .' Mitchenor waved to his men, who stood aside to let the Mini through.

Nat clambered out on to the drive as Kathryn roared the car the short distance, then braked hard, spraying small stones.

Kathryn was immediately out of the Mini and running forward to throw her arms round him in a vice-like hug. 'Don't you ever do that to me again,' she muttered, her words half muffled by the blanket. 'I saw the smoke from a couple of miles away. God, I've never been so scared.' She drew back to look at him. 'Are you hurt? You look dreadful!'

Nat's face was smeared with soot and there was congealed blood on his forehead from a scratch gained in the scuffle with Myles. He grinned. 'I think I'll live.'

'You don't seem to have been trying very hard.' Kathryn's eyes glared but they also glistened with tears. 'I distinctly said, "Don't do anything stupid. Leave it to the police." My God, you don't know how angry I am . . . No I'm not . . . I'm . . . Ooh, you fool!' She hugged him again as though she never meant to let go.

Mitchenor laughed. 'I reckon you were better off with the fire!'

Nat said, 'Darling, you remember Inspector Mitchenor, don't you?'

'Do I not!' Kathryn directed her emotional energy on the policeman. 'What the hell took you so long? I called you a dozen times . . . Oh what a dreadful sight!' She seemed for the first time to be aware of the blazing building. 'Oh, that's so awful. All that beauty. All that history!'

The three of them were still gazing at the scene of desolation when a constable ran up to report to Mitchenor. 'Sir, they've found a body. Do you want to come and see?'

Mitchenor nodded with a sigh and followed the man back to the house.

Nat shook his head. 'Poor Greer!'

Kathryn looked puzzled. 'Greer? The historian guy? What's he got to do with it?'

'Just about everything. He was the man Myles came here to meet. It was he who murdered Tracy.'

'But that's crazy!' Kathryn protested. 'I thought Shelley –'

'No. It's a complicated story. I'll explain it later and you can fill me in on what happened to the real Sheldon Myles back in the sixties. As for *our* Shelley Myles, well, I hope he gets hauled into court and suffers some of the humiliation he's dished out to others over the years. He may not actually have killed Tracy but he's certainly responsible for her death. And Greer's.'

'What happened to Greer?'

Nat explained how the historian had been wounded and because of combined shock and loss of blood had not been able to make his escape from the burning building. There was a sickening roar as part of the front wall of the stricken house caved in. The Gyes stared at the melancholy sight. 'Poor Greer,' Nat said again. 'He just loved the place too much. Still, I suppose there was nowhere else he would rather have died.' He grabbed his wife's hand and together they were silently engulfed in the tragedy that was Tripletree.

Mitchenor came striding back. 'Well, we've found him,' he said.

'Greer?' Nat enquired.

266

'No, Myles. He was in a ground floor room at the back. The flames hadn't reached it before the brigade arrived but the smoke had.'

Nat looked puzzled. 'But he had plenty of time to get away.'

The inspector shrugged. 'We'll have to wait for the post-mortem to shed some light on that.'

'Ironic, isn't it? At the end of the day Myles actually wins.' Nat stared at the road ahead lit up by the beam of the Mercedes' headlights.

It was early evening and he and Kathryn were on their way home. Nat had dictated his statement to an efficient WPC but had deliberately underplayed the violent confrontation between the fire's two victims. Then they had left the Mini with the police at Chipping Norton and arranged to pick it up in a day or two. Nat had recovered from his ordeal and felt better after they had found a hotel where he could freshen up and where he and Kathryn could enjoy a light supper while comparing notes on what they had discovered about Myles and Greer. However, Nat did not want to drive back to Cambridge and Kathryn was, therefore, at the wheel. They had been travelling for some time without conversation and listening to the sadly beautiful strains of Schubert's 'Death and the Maiden' quartet on the car radio before Nat made his observation.

'What do you mean?' Kathryn asked. 'The man's dead and most people would say good riddance.'

'Yes, but the truth is never going to come out. The headlines in tomorrow's papers will be "Prominent barrister killed in country house blaze." The obituaries will feature his outstanding career at the bar and bewail the curtailed promise of his mature years.'

'But surely the police will publish the facts.'

'Why should they? Everything's ended very neatly for

Mitchenor and Co. They've got Tom Pensham for Owen's murder and it's only a matter of time before they pick up his accomplice. Tracy's killer is dead so the inspector can stamp "case closed" on that one. As for the murder Myles really did commit thirty-odd years ago, what point can there possibly be in opening that up now?'

'Odd about Shelley's death, isn't it? As you said to Mitchenor, he had plenty of time to get out of the building. Do you think he was careless enough to let himself get overtaken by smoke?'

Nat shrugged. 'Could have been a heart attack. He might even have committed suicide. He knew his past had finally caught up with him and that he faced disgrace, disbarment and prison. Still, however he died, there's no doubt how the locals will remember it. The Vengeance of Tripletree!'

'Poor old house,' Kathryn murmured. 'It had a long and unhappy life. And,' she added sharply, 'don't you dare lecture me about being fanciful. I know that place had a bad feel about it.'

'No, I think you're right. The manor became the battle-ground of two powerful forces, Shelley's arrogant ambition and proud local identity rooted in the past. I guess it was doomed. *Requiescat in pace*, Tripletree!'

'Amen!'

They drove for some miles in wordless silence while Schubert's andante reached its stately conclusion.

As the final chord of the movement hovered in the air Kathryn switched the radio off. Glaring fixedly ahead through the windscreen, she said, 'Before I left the office I emailed Greg.'

Nat felt a heavy weight in the pit of his stomach. 'And?'

'I turned him down.'

Nat made no response while the car negotiated a double bend. Then he said. 'Am I allowed to ask why?'

'No, I don't want you to gloat!'

'I wouldn't dream of it. I'm just very, very thankful.'

After a long pause, Kathryn added, 'It's obvious from today that you can't be trusted on your own.'

Nat laughed. 'I don't intend to make a habit of getting trapped in burning houses.'

'Good.' She added reflectively, 'I can't really explain. It had something to do with Myles and his relentless pursuit of success. And seeing June so miserable and so bitter. And, I suppose, balancing what I might have with what I've already got.'

They were driving along a straight stretch of country road. Suddenly, Nat said, 'Slow down.' Then, as she did so, 'Pull on to that track there by those trees.'

Kathryn stared at him quizzically but turned the steering wheel. 'What's this – delayed shock?'

'Now stop!'

'Darling, what are you up to?'

'I'm about to make love to you in the back of the car.'

'Don't be silly. We're too old for that sort of thing.'

Nat opened the passenger door. 'Says who?'